Selena

Selena

Gordon Randolph Willey

Walker and Company
New York

Copyright © 1993 by Gordon Randolph Willey

First published in the United States of America in 1993 by Walker Publishing Company, Inc.

Published simultaneously in Canada by Thomas Allen & Son Canada, Limited, Markham, Ontario

Library of Congress Cataloging-in-Publication Data
Willey, Gordon Randolph, 1913–
Selena / by Gordon Randolph Willey.
p.   cm.
ISBN 0-8027-3227-5
I. Title.
PS3573.I44723S4   1993
813'.54—dc20   92-44855
CIP

Printed in the United States of America
2 4 6 8 10 9 7 5 3 1

$\bigtriangledown$

1

Sᴛ. Cʜʀɪsᴛᴏᴘʜᴇʀ's. Tʜᴇ ʟᴏᴡ-ʟʏɪɴɢ ᴛᴏᴡɴ by the sea at
the river's delta. Coming up on it rather suddenly, as I drove
across the highway bridge last summer, I found it almost
too familiar, too real, but with the surrealism of a dream.
It was pleasantly exciting to be back after so long a time—
and oddly disturbing, too. St. Christopher's! A place of
memories and of mixed emotions. It was also, as it turned
out to be last summer, a place of sadness, of dark things, of
hidden things.

My name is Colin Edwards, Colin R. Edwards. The R stands
for Randall, not that I ever use that middle name, but it is a
part of the story, a Randall story, and I am a part of them. I
should explain that I am old now. I feel all right. I am in good
health for a man of my age; but I feel beyond emotions, certainly emotions of the kind that I have just experienced. "Sentimental journeys" are something to be approached with
caution. Not that I am not cautious, but, at the same time,
I suppose I've always had a penchant for nostalgia, a sentimental streak. And some might say that sentimentality is
separated from masochism by only a fine line.

I am back in Boston now, Boston, where I have lived most
of my adult life and where I hope to continue with the rest
of it, safe and secure from old dreams. I was born, though,
in St. Christopher's, that small town on the Florida Gulf in
what was, at least in those far-off days of my youth, a slightly
rustic and unfashionable part of that state. I was the only
child of Robert and Genevieve Edwards. The Edwardses were

one of St. Christopher's "old families." The Edwardses, the Randalls, the Bulls, the Crawfords—we were the town's aristocracy, as frayed and precarious as our condition may have been from time to time. Our beginnings there went back to the 1830s, when this part of Florida was first settled, at least first settled by white—and black—settlers.

As my name might suggest, my mother, Genevieve, was a Randall. I should explain that the Randalls and the Bulls were always considerably richer than the Edwardses, or the Crawfords, and they certainly were so when I came along. Perhaps this fact, as well as his intelligence and drive, led my father to move, with my mother and me, to Boston, when I was fourteen. He had been a struggling lawyer back in St. Christopher's, but his part in a long and expensive railroad case had brought him to the attention of a prominent Boston law firm, where he also had friends from his Harvard Law School days, and the firm hired him and eventually made him a partner.

I was sent to a New England preparatory school and, eventually, to Harvard. I grew up to become pretty much of a Yankee—or at least I am considered one now by those who remember me in St. Christopher's. I didn't follow my father into law but became a college professor—a professor of archaeology. I can't think of any very definite reason why I should have been drawn to archaeology, except that it appealed to me from a very early age, which, perhaps, is the best kind of reason. However, I might confess that there is a certain remoteness about the ancient past which I find comfortable and emotionally reassuring.

I retired two years ago. My dear wife, Helen, to whom I was married for more than forty years, and who was a New Englander, had died shortly before this. We had three daughters, who are now married and living nearby, the respective parents of my nine grandchildren, all of whom I see frequently. This résumé sounds contented and prosaic, as indeed it and I were. I hope now only to return to such a condition.

When I drove into St. Christopher's that afternoon last June, the clouds over the delta were dark and threatening, and at the same time comfortingly familiar, just as I had remembered them from those many other summer afternoons of years before. They were both a foreboding and a promise of a rain squall, which might or might not come but which, if it did, would bring relief from the heat. I could hear the cries of the gulls and the lonely bell-gong of a buoy somewhere out in the bay. They sounded much as they used to when I was a child. St. James's Island was as I remembered— a low, green-blackish line out there in the gulf, close and yet remote. St. James's Island. Did the name still give me a slight visceral tug of excitement after all these years?

I turned from the highway onto the old river road, where the red-brick warehouses along the river's edge looked sleepy and peaceful and familiar. From the river road I took one of the streets that led into the main part of town. The buildings along the principal business thoroughfare were one- and two-storied affairs of years ago. Some of them had been gussied up with black glass facades or false mansard roof fronts, but in spite of these "improvements," or perhaps because of them, they looked a bit more run-down and dingier than I had remembered. The courthouse, with its Confederate soldier on a pillar in the lawn before it, was unchanged, the soldier maintaining his military watch in silent dignity. Why, I asked myself, had I made this trip, this excursion into the past?

Before going to the hotel, I took a leisurely drive through some of the residential streets. They were quiet, just as they always were on summer afternoons. Charles was on my mind—my cousin Charles Randall. It was on his insistence that I was here. So I drove by the old Randall house. I wasn't going to stop now. I'd see Charles later. But I was attracted by the house, as I'd always been. After all, the place had had a magic about it when I was a boy. It had been the "enchanted castle" where a "princess" lived. The Randall mansion it had been called then. It looked a little run-down now;

it needed a coat of paint, and the grass hadn't been cut. Was Cousin Charles running out of money or just inattentive to such details? Well, with Selena back here now, perhaps the place would be looked after better. Even in its present condition, the house was a handsome old Victorian structure. It dated from sometime in the 1880s, when the Randall fortunes had risen after the Reconstruction years.

Our old house—the Edwards house—where I was born and had lived for the first fourteen years of my life, was on the opposite side of the street, a few doors down. It looked like I remembered it—respectable, comfortable, and not very special. It had been freshly painted, though, and the lawn was well manicured. I wondered who lived there now. Probably somebody I didn't know, or had never heard of.

Why had Charles been so insistent that I come down to St. Christopher's for this late visit in my life? I thought I knew. He hadn't said so in his letter to me. He'd simply said that there was something important he needed my help in and that it could be explained better "here"—meaning St. Christopher's—than in a letter. It was another cousin, Webbie—Webster Bull—who had given me a clue to what was on Charles's mind. He had done this in a conversation we had had when Webbie was in Boston some six weeks before.

I was thinking about what Webbie had told me as I turned a corner and passed by the Bulls'. This had been St. Christopher's other impressive residence in the old days. Now, in contrast to the Randalls', it appeared well painted and well kept. I caught a glimpse of a corpulent figure in the driveway, just coming around the corner of the house. Was it the lord of the manor? Yes—think of the devil—it was Cousin Webbie. Had he seen me? In the rearview mirror I watched him peering after the car. I'd rented it in Tallahassee, so with Florida plates it shouldn't have attracted his attention all that much, and I doubted if he'd had a good look at me as I went by. If he did, I thought, we'll have to go into why I hadn't stopped. Sometime during my visit I would have to see him and talk about what he had told me in Boston, but right now the simple shock of returning to St. Christopher's—a world of the past, or at least the shell of that world—had been sufficient unto the day, without confronting Webbie, at least until I had had a chance to get my bearings.

I should explain I had seen Webster Bull several times in recent years, in fact, more often than I had seen Charles. Webbie came up to Boston on business on frequent occasions, and when he did, he never missed the opportunity to look me up and I'd usually take him to lunch at my club. Webbie was a conversational assailant, someone who beat you aggressively with accounts of his doings—the important business connections in Boston and New York that demanded his attention. There were other things, too, he would confide, that needed a hands-on touch. For the most part, these seemed to be other people's lives.

On that last visit, Webbie had given me to understand that the Randalls were now demanding his particular attention. I could imagine how thrilled Charles must have been by that. Charles had spent a lifetime avoiding Webbie. Not physically avoiding him—I don't suppose that would have been possible in a place as small as St. Christopher's—but with a special withdrawn quality of which Charles had always been a master. "Poor old Charles," Webbie had told me—moving in close with that slightly cross-eyed, watery, and morose expression that I remembered from boyhood— "poor old Charles" was "having his troubles." He was behaving very strangely. He was becoming paranoid. He thought people were persecuting him, trying to drive him crazy, or even murder him. Worse yet, because of his paranoia, Charles was becoming downright dangerous—"criminally dangerous" were Webbie's exact words. I must have looked shocked, and I told him I couldn't believe it. But Webbie shook his head and said what it amounted to was that Charles urgently needed psychiatric care, perhaps even institutionalization. As things stood now, he wasn't responsible for his own behavior.

I asked Webbie to be more specific about it all. What had

happened? What had Charles done? Webbie enjoyed keeping me in suspense, inwardly savoring this ominous gossip with solemn shakes of the head and pursed mouth. I said that whatever it was, I didn't think things could be as bad as he was portraying them. On Charles's last trip north, two years ago, he'd certainly seemed his old usual self. Secretly, I wondered what Charles had been doing to Webbie to upset him like this. Charles had never liked Webbie and in our youth often took a certain malicious and sadistic delight in teasing him. Was Charles up to something like that now?

As if in answer, Webbie looked at me very solemnly and said, "Colin, I think Charles tried to kill me just last week."

"Rubbish!" was my retort.

But Webbie shook his head. "No, it's true," he said. Then he leaned forward over the lunch table and informed me in a conspiratorial whisper, "Colin, Charles shot at me with intent to kill, I'm sure!"

"But how?" I wanted to know. "What in God's name happened to make you think a thing like that?"

I thought Webbie looked both a little self-satisfied and martyred as he leaned back and began his story. "Colin," he said, "Charles began behaving strangely sometime in early April. Do you remember that old Indian mound over there on St. James's Island? The one you dug into a long time ago? Well, Charles has suddenly decided he wants to dig there, too. We've tried to talk him out of it, to put some sense into his head, but, instead, we've put him in a rage."

I said I remembered the Indian mound all right. I also reflected that Webbie giving Charles advice about anything would be the quickest way to get the latter's back up. I went on to ask, "What would make Charles want to dig into an Indian mound? I can't recall that he has ever shown any interest in the local archaeology."

"Well, he hasn't," Webbie replied. "Not archaeology like you do anyway. No, it's just that somehow he's suddenly got a bee in his bonnet about there being a family treasure buried over there."

"This family treasure on St. James's Island is a new one on me, Webbie, but why not let him exercise his folly?"

"The trouble is, Colin, the family trust that owns the island had agreed, earlier in the year, to sell the island to the state. They've offered us a very good price for it, and the four of us in the Island Trust—Charles, Selena, me, and Lydia— were all delighted. Everything seemed to be going along on track, with the papers to be passed at the beginning of the fiscal year, this coming July, but then Charles came up with this nutty scheme. He'll get us into trouble." Webbie paused and looked at me a little suspiciously. "Has he written you about this? Asked your help?"

I smiled. "You mean because I'm an archaeologist? No," I said, "I've heard nothing about it. I'm not really a treasure hunter, you know, Webbie. Anyhow, I haven't had a letter from Charles for some time, only a card last Christmas, and he didn't mention anything like that on the card." When I told Webbie this, I had not yet received my recent letters from Charles asking me to come down to St. Christopher's.

"The difficulty," Webbie resumed, "is that I'm sure the state Park Service, who will be taking over the island, will be concerned about this digging plan of Charles's. They're aw- fully fussy about things like that now—digging into Indian mounds, 'cultural resources' they call them. If Charles digs there, it might jeopardize the sale or at least mean negotiat- ing again about the sale price, to our disadvantage."

Webbie took a sip of wine and shifted that intent, slightly cross-eyed stare he had been fixing on me to look out the window. "Selena and I are both very much opposed to it," he said, then added, "Selena, who came back at Christmas to stay with Charles in St. Christopher's, is very worried about this and Charles's behavior in general."

That surprised me—that Selena had returned to live in St. Christopher's. From something Charles had told me on one of his visits some time back, it had been my un- derstanding that she had chosen long ago to make her life in New Orleans, or anywhere other than in her old hometown, and that he rarely heard from her. But now it would appear she had returned to stay with Charles on a permanent basis.

I got back to Webbie's story of Charles's attempt on his life. I asked him, "What about this business of Charles trying to shoot you? What actually happened?"

"He did, all right. I'd been over to see him, to try to talk him out of this mound-digging scheme. It was one evening after dinner. Selena had asked me to do it. But I couldn't budge him on it. He just kept telling me that there was something in the mound over there that belonged to the Randalls and that it was his right to get it. I told him he'd only cause a lot of trouble now by doing what he wanted to do." Webbie paused, then went on. "It would be illegal, wouldn't it?" he asked me.

"I don't know for sure, Webbie," I told him. "But I agree it doesn't sound like a very good idea in view of the upcoming sale."

"Well, Colin, that's when he said he was going to get in touch with you, that you could make it legal, that you were an archaeologist, an 'Indian mound expert,' and nobody could object if you said it was all right."

"No, Webbie, I can't make anything like that 'legal.' But, as I've told you, Charles has never communicated with me about any of this."

Webbie continued, almost menacingly, as if he didn't believe me. "Colin, I made it clear to Charles at that time that I would not put up with anything like this, and that if he tried to dig over there on the island that I would notify the state about it immediately and have him arrested!"

I wondered about the specific grounds for arrest in this instance. I also couldn't help smiling at it all—although I had some trepidations, too, about being sucked into such a peculiar family quarrel.

"We had some very bitter words that night, Colin. Before I left, Charles told me that if I tried to block what he wanted to do over there on St. James's, it would be the last thing I'd ever do! I didn't know quite what to think of that then, but now I know it was a threat to kill me!"

"Webbie, he was mad at you. Charles can get pretty mad on occasion. You should know that. He said something in anger. You can't take that seriously as a threat to murder you."

Webbie shook his head. "No, Colin, he meant it. He was mad, all right—or he is crazy mad is more like it. That night I went on home after our quarrel. I read for a while. Later, I went upstairs to bed. I was standing at a window of my bedroom, a room that looks out over the backyard of our house. I'd just turned away from the window. Maybe this saved me. I heard a shot. A bullet was fired from the yard down below, going through the window and striking the ceiling. It just missed me. Well, I was pretty shaken up, but I turned out the light and looked out the window. I couldn't see anybody—but I know—I know damn well it was Charles! He'd tried to kill me!"

"Nonsense." I didn't know what else to say except to tell Webbie that he hadn't actually seen Charles and that I couldn't imagine Charles doing such a thing.

Webbie went on to relate that he'd had the police in, that they'd taken a bullet out of the ceiling, and that they were investigating.

I asked Webbie if he had said anything to the police about his suspicions that it was Charles who had shot through the window, but he shook his head with a scowl and said no. While he didn't actually say so, it was almost as if he felt this were a family matter—one that couldn't really be revealed to the plebeian ears and eyes of the police. I was glad to hear that he hadn't made a direct accusation. It would have made them both look like fools. On that note, we finished our lunch. Webbie had departed for the South the next day, and I had not heard from him since.

I mused over all this driving toward the hotel on the afternoon of my arrival in St. Christopher's. I supposed some of the outward events as these had been related to me must have had some reality. Webbie didn't have the kind of imag-

ination to conjure up such a story. But I still couldn't believe
that Charles had actually shot at him. That must have been
somebody else, some kind of an accident.

I wondered, too, if Charles was really planning an excavation over on St. James's Island. It didn't sound like him, or
I didn't think it did. Could Charles really be becoming a little
off, a little crazy, as Webbie had said? He had certainly
seemed all right the last time I saw him. Still, things can
come along rapidly at his age—or our age, I reflected. Charles
and I had been born in the same year. Charles had always
been a bit strange, even when we were boys. Usually we got
along well enough, but there had been times—I could recall
them now—when he had had peculiar moody spells or what
I thought were unreasonable flare-ups of temper.

But there had been nothing in Charles's recent letter to
me to indicate that he didn't have all his wits about him,
nor did he say anything about being unwell. I was, I admit,
a little surprised by the tone of the letter. It was more intense
than usual. Actually, we had never corresponded much, especially in later years. There'd be a letter now and then, or
a Christmas card; sometimes he'd clip a piece out of a Florida
newspaper and send it to me, usually to indicate some local
political foolishness. On those occasions when we met, he'd
just show up in Boston, or sometimes he'd call ahead, from
Philadelphia or New York, and let me know he was coming.

In the past, he often suggested that I come down and visit
him and, as he put it, rather ironically, "renew your ac-
quaintance with St. Christopher's." I never knew just how
serious these invitations were. I think they were often given
half-jokingly, as if he knew I was unlikely to take him up.
But this invitation of two weeks ago sounded different. He
said he really needed to see me. In light of what Webbie had
told me a month or so before, I suspected that it might have
something to do with his mound-digging idea, but he didn't
say so in the letter. He said he knew I didn't like to travel
much anymore, but wouldn't I make an exception? It
sounded like a serious plea for my presence. It would be nice,

he said, if I could plan on staying for several weeks—sometime this late spring or early summer. He added that Selena was there with him and that she would very much like to see me after all these years.

I was not entranced by the idea of such a trip and extended visit, nor did I relish being brought in on some half-baked search for treasure. I wrote back trying to find out more, but all he told me in a second letter was that he would explain it when I got there. Although I had cut all my real ties with St. Christopher's so very long ago, I did feel some sense of loyalty to Charles. He was much more than a second cousin once removed. He had been my oldest and best friend in boyhood, and it would be unfeeling to refuse his request, whatever it was he wanted to see me about, and in spite of Webbie's stories, which I couldn't really believe.

After saying this to myself, I thought of his twin sister, Selena. So she was back home now, after all these years. Does one want to see an adolescent flame after almost sixty years? I suppose it's the kind of sentimental idea that is usually regarded with humor, but instead I found it a little unsettling. And then I asked myself why I found it unsettling. What difference did it make after all this time?

It must have been about four o'clock when I reached the hotel that Saturday afternoon, the first of June. Charles had asked me to stay with them, but I was reluctant to do so. While I had feelings of loyalty toward him, I didn't think I'd be very comfortable moving in with him for two or three weeks, especially with Selena there. I wanted to approach the past more cautiously. So when I wrote last to Charles, saying that I was coming down, I gave the excuse that the time of my arrival was still uncertain, owing to a press of business (nonexistent) in Boston and Cambridge, and that it might be better and less disturbing for them if, coming at the last minute, I put up at the St. Christopher House. I mailed the letter just before my departure so that it wouldn't be received until after I had left Boston, and they wouldn't have the opportunity to write or call and insist that I be a houseguest.

I didn't think that Charles would do any insisting, but Selena might. Or did she really want to see me? What was she like now? She had liked to run things as a child.

The St. Christopher House fronted on the highway, facing the sea. An old, white wooden structure with big screened porches, it had a simple charm. My earliest memories of it went back to Sunday dinners there when I was a boy. The hotel had been going in 1940, when I came back and spent that summer in St. Christopher's. I had stayed there then. It had been owned and operated, for as far back as I could remember, by a Miss Connie—Miss Constance Larrabee, who had inherited it from her father. Miss Connie was gone now. A Yankee entrepreneur had taken over the hotel sometime after the Second World War, and the interior had been extensively renovated and refurbished. A pleasant but impersonal young white man was behind the desk when I came in. I checked in, took my key and my luggage, and went up to the second floor. I found Room 22. I had asked for it when I made my reservation by telephone from Boston. It was the one I'd had in 1940, and I had remembered it for its fine view of the gulf. It had now been remodeled to include a private bath in one corner, but otherwise it appeared the same.

I took off my shoes, jacket, and tie and stretched out on the comfortable bed. I was tired, physically and emotionally. The early flight down to Tallahassee from Boston in the morning, the renting of the car at the Tallahassee airport, the drive over, the stop for lunch at some little roadside restaurant on the way, and then St. Christopher's, coming up at me out of the past. It was all enough to make me tired, and the bed did feel good. Someone had opened the window, I presume in preparation for my coming, and a wonderful breeze from the gulf stirred the curtains. The room wasn't air-conditioned. Instead, there was a big old electric ceiling fan on the high ceiling above me—just like there used to be—but it wasn't turned on. Right now it was pleasantly cool without it. I looked at two framed needlework samplers on the wall. Had they been there when I was? Probably. I thought back to that summer; reverie blended with near-sleep.

In the summer of 1940—the only time, until now, that I had been back to St. Christopher's since I had left there with my family in 1927—I came here to do archaeology. I was a graduate student in 1939, and, toward the end of that year, I persuaded my professors at Harvard to support me for a season's fieldwork in Florida the following summer. The Indian mounds near St. Christopher's, of which there were a number, had fascinated me as a boy. Indeed, I suppose they had had something to do with my choosing archaeology as a career. Now, as a budding professional in the discipline, I wanted to go back and explore them properly.

That summer turned out to be a happy and successful one. I began digging with a small crew at the Bull Mounds, a site about a mile northwest of town. Named after an ancestor of Webbie's who had once owned the property, the Bull Mounds comprised a big site by Florida Gulf Coast standards, with a group of four tumuli. These had been partially excavated almost forty years before by an archaeologist named Clarence B. Moore, who used to travel the Gulf Coast and other southern waters and waterways in a stern-wheeler steamboat, pulling ashore when in proximity to an Indian mound and turning his boat crew loose on it with shovels. In spite of this rough-and-ready approach to excavation, Moore had published his results promptly and extensively, so that they were available to subsequent generations of archaeologists. I had become particularly intrigued by the pottery he had found at the Bull site and had illustrated in his reports. This led to my digging there, which, in turn, led me on to more digging in other sites in the region.

One of these was the mound on St. James's Island. It was one of the few burial mounds which Moore had not excavated when he came through in his steamboat. The reason for this abstinence was not any compunctions on Moore's part; instead—for whatever cross-grained reasons—my great-uncle

Major Charles Randall, and Webbie's grandfather Thomas Bull, then the co-owners of the island, had sternly refused Mr. Moore's request to dig there. As a result, it had remained one of the few untouched Indian mounds of the northwest Florida Gulf Coast, until I dug a part of it in the summer of 1940. This was the mound that Webbie had told me Charles now wanted to dig into in his search for family treasure. I had certainly seen no sign of such treasure when I'd excavated out there, although I had only dug about half of the mound.

As I relaxed on my comfortable St. Christopher House bed, I felt pleasantly content about that summer's fieldwork. My excavations at the Bull site, at the St. James's Island Mound, and at other sites along the Gulf Coast that summer had given archaeologists a new perspective on Florida prehistory. My results were incorporated into my doctoral dissertation and eventually published in a long, if somewhat tedious, monograph. Since then, my career had taken me away from Florida, to Peru and then to Central America, to Inca roads and Maya temples, but the romance of none of it compared with that first summer's digging on the outskirts of my old hometown.

I recalled, with some amusement, the attitudes of my relatives toward my activities that summer. Most of them left little doubt that they thought my choice of a career was utterly bizarre, perhaps bordering on insanity. Webbie was one of these. He used to pay me occasional visits at the Bull Mounds while I was digging. I could never convince him I wasn't engaged in some sort of a treasure hunt. Gold buried in such places—usually to keep it away from the marauding Yankee soldiers in the Civil War—was still very much a part of the local folklore. Charles, by contrast, was more understanding of my pursuits. But still another cousin, John Crawford, had actually objected to my activities.

He and Selena Randall had been married earlier that year and were living in New Orleans. She didn't come to St. Christopher's that summer, but John did, shortly after I started digging out at St. James's. He came over to the island

one day while I was digging there and looked around. He
didn't seem very friendly. Afterward, he went to both Webbie's father and Charles's mother—then the island's owners—and tried to get them to make me stop work. I didn't
know about this until afterward, when Charles told me. I
could never figure out why. In our early teens we had been
rivals over Selena, but that was long in the past, with them
now married.

I saw more of Charles that summer than of any of the
others. I often dined at the Randalls' house, with him and
his mother, and they, or sometimes Charles alone, joined me
in the St. Christopher House dining room. I should explain
that, prior to returning to St. Christopher's, and taking up
residence with his mother, Charles had gone to Princeton,
where he had acquitted himself well academically and joined
one of the better undergraduate clubs. I'd seen him in 1935,
at Princeton, shortly before his graduation from there and
mine from Harvard. He said his father wanted him to go on
to law school and come into the family firm, but Charles
had declined. I don't know what reasons he gave, or whether
this brought on a family row. He never said. When he talked
with me about it later, he merely told me that he had decided
to go back and live in St. Christopher's "in the way that a
southern gentleman should live in a place like that." I guess,
at that time anyhow, there was sufficient family money for
him to do this. I believed that Charles—who I always
thought had the temperament of a scholar—should have
gone somewhere to graduate school and studied history, but
in 1940 he told me that it was too late. He couldn't leave his
mother after what had happened.

What had happened had been his father's disappearance.
In December of 1939, James Randall went on a business trip
to New Orleans, but he never returned. Whether he had run
away, assumed another identity, and taken up a new life
somewhere, or whether he had been the victim of a crime
was never determined. In 1940 Charles's mother was still
suffering from the shock of this—and she never really recov-

ered from it. She died early in the war years, still hoping that her Jamie, as she called him, her "handsome Jamie," would come back to her.

Now, back in St. Christopher's in 1985, I wondered again about Jamie's disappearance. I could still see him, back in the 1920s—tall, dark, extraordinarily handsome, and imperially slim, like the Richard Cory of the poem, who "one calm summer's night went home and put a bullet through his head." Had Jamie Randall done the same thing, in some location other than home? Somehow I didn't think so. I could remember the talk when I was a boy about Jamie Randall drinking too much, chasing around after other women, and his too frequent trips to New Orleans. This was the sort of talk, between my mother and some of my aunts, that was hushed up when I came into the room. I doubted that he had voluntarily given up the pleasures of the flesh. Poor Aunt Marie—that was Charles's and Selena's mother—had had much to suffer from handsome Jamie. Aunt Marie was French, French from New Orleans. She'd been so beautiful, everyone said, but she had faded—and all because of Jamie.

Perhaps I dozed off. I roused myself and looked at my watch. It was only a few minutes after five. I lay back down and thought about southern families—parents, grandparents, uncles, aunts, cousins, that intricate yet highly important network of relationships. Charles, Selena, Webbie, John Crawford—all of them—they and their parents and their children, and their uncles, aunts, and nephews, were all some kind of relative of mine. Not first cousins or close uncles and aunts, but second cousins, second cousins once removed, great-uncles, or whatever. I couldn't have plotted it out on a kinship chart just how we were linked, but we were, and as a child these relationships were among the earliest things I had been conscious of and believed to be important. And, as I thought about it now, I suppose I still thought they had some importance. After all, I had been born and bred a southerner. That was why I was down here now— even after all this long time and after spending almost sixty

years transforming myself into a Yankee. I came because
Charles had asked me to.

I guess I had always felt that the Randalls were at the
center of this complicated familial web of ours. The first of
them had come here from Charleston in 1834. The eldest
of the Randall brothers, Alexander, must have had some
inheritance, for he was the owner, as well as the captain, of
a ship. St. Christopher's was just beginning as a seaport
then, but it prospered at the delta of a river system by which
cotton and lumber were brought down to the gulf from the
interior. The Randalls prospered with the town, carrying cotton to England and other commodities to the West Indies
and South America. They may also have traded in slaves,
although this was never part of the family lore that we
learned as children. During the Civil War—the War Between
the States—the brothers were blockade runners, and Alexander had a very colorful reputation in this regard, or so goes
the family history. They had some bad years during the Reconstruction period, but by 1880 they, particularly Alexander, were beginning to emerge as rich men, certainly the
richest in St. Christopher's.

All three of the brothers had children, taking local women
as wives. My mother, Genevieve Randall, was the granddaughter of one of Alexander's brothers. Alexander's eldest
son, Charles, survived the Civil War. I always thought of him
as Great-uncle Charles—Major Charles Randall. He always
led the Confederate Memorial Day parades in St. Christopher's. He had been wounded and spent some months in a
Yankee prison camp, so he had earned this honor, but there
was some political motivation in it, too; he was twice a
candidate for lieutenant governor of the state, although both
times defeated. I recall all this in contrast to my Grandfather
Edwards—Captain Edwards—who never said much about
his war experiences, never ran for office, and used to grumble
when Grandmother insisted that he march in the parades.

Great-uncle Charles Randall did not follow his father into
the shipping business or merchandising but after the war

went to study law at Virginia and came back to set up a practice. His father gave him substantial financial support in this, and when Alexander died in 1892, Charles was his only living direct heir and was left very well provided for.

Great-uncle Charles had only one child, James—Uncle James to me—the "handsome Jamie" to whom I have already referred, the father of Charles and Selena. James was just a little younger than my father. They both went to law school, James following his father at the University of Virginia while my father went to Harvard. For a while they practiced law together in St. Christopher's—Randall and Edwards. Jamie married Marie Desmoulins, of New Orleans, and my father married Genevieve Randall. I was born in March of 1913, and the twins Charles and Selena, in May of that same year.

I got up from my nap, or near-nap, refreshed and quite hungry. I was also in need of a drink. I unpacked my suitcases, hung my suits up in the closet, and put the rest of my clothes away in appropriate bureau drawers. I then undressed, showered, and dressed again, selecting a lightweight blue pinstriped suit this time and a dark gold tie. I thought I'd better call Charles pretty soon but then decided to put it off, maybe until after dinner.

Looking out the windows, I saw the sun was getting low. The clouds of an hour or two ago had disappeared without fulfilling that threat of an afternoon rain. The breeze had died down a bit. It was a nice, a restful, time of the day. I went downstairs, entered the little parlor-bar, and ordered a scotch and soda from a white-jacketed bartender. I sat at a little table facing a window looking over the waters of the gulf. It was extraordinarily peaceful in the otherwise empty bar. I was gradually suffused with the mild euphoria that a drink, after a tiring and somewhat nervy day, will produce. I ordered another scotch and asked the bartender if he would notify them in the dining room that I would be in in about twenty minutes. He brought me my second drink and kindly went off to oblige about dinner

Outside, the sunset was looking more gorgeous all the time. St. Christopher's. Home. Did I still think of it that way? It really could be very pleasant down here, couldn't it? Why hadn't I come back before? Except for that 1940 sojourn, when I'd had archaeology, and a beginning career, as an excuse, I hadn't often thought of the place, not very consciously anyway. Did St. Christopher's, and my leaving of it, still raise some bad memories for me, memories of Selena—even as young as we were then—that I would prefer not to confront? It must have, for I found my very asking of this question just a little disturbing.

Someone spoke, and looking up I saw the bartender at my elbow. "Sir," he asked, "are you Mr. Edwards?" I told him that I was.

"There is a telephone call for you. If you like, you can take it in at the desk."

I went out into the lobby. The desk clerk looked at me expectantly, nodded, and pointed to a telephone at the corner of the desk. I picked up the receiver and said hello.

For a second or two there was no response; then a woman's voice said, "Colin, is that you? I heard you were here." Did she sound the same? How could I know? How could I remember how she used to sound? She had been fourteen when we spoke last. A lot can happen to the human voice—and body—and soul, too, for that matter—in fifty-eight years; yet I knew it was she.

"Selena?"

"Yes, of course." Her reply wasn't impatient or brusque—just directly and clearly stated, the way she had spoken as a child. She waited a slight moment and then went on. "Colin, why haven't you called us?" I found myself embarrassed—and then cross with myself for feeling embarrassed.

"Well, I—I just arrived and have been getting—uh—shaken down, unpacked, and so forth. I was about to call you," I lied.

"Oh . . . I'd heard you got into town much earlier this afternoon" was her quick reply. Just what lines in St.

Christopher's grapevine had revealed my presence so prematurely? Did the Randalls have a spy in the hotel? Or had Selena peeked out from behind one of those drab shades of the Randall mansion and seen me as I drove past? Then I remembered Webbie. He must have spotted me after all and passed the word on to Selena.

"Well, not much earlier" was my lame answer to her intelligence. "I was a bit tired after the trip," I went on, "so I took a little nap." I changed the subject by asking about Charles.

"Charles is fine," Selena assured me, "and he is put out with you for not coming to stay with us—just like I am," she scolded gently. I could not imagine Charles expressing any such sentiments, but I didn't say so. "Colin," she went on, "is there any chance that it's not too late to ask you to come over and have dinner with us tonight?"

I prevaricated a bit on this, saying that I'd already started dinner but that, if it would be all right with them, I would come over after dinner, say about eight o'clock. Selena said they would like that but to try to get there a little earlier and have coffee and a brandy with them. Before I could agree she hung up.

I went back into the bar. A party of four, tourists by appearance and manner—loud in both dress and speech—had come in during my absence and taken a table next to mine. I finished up my whiskey, signed my tab, and went into the dining room.

The St. Christopher House dining room was where it had always been, situated to the rear of the lobby but entered from the hall. It was a large, high-ceilinged room, and the new owner—I was beginning to approve of him as a man of taste—had used restraint in his redecorating. He had eschewed such favorite Gulf Coast dining- and barroom touches as fragments of fishing nets, glass net floats, or swatches of something that was supposed to resemble seaweed. Instead, the walls, which had been painted in a darker tone than I remembered them, were hung with a number

of light and bright Winslow Homer prints. There were only
two or three other patrons in the room, seated at their separate tables.

The hostess came over to take my order, informing me that
the special that night was broiled red snapper. Was the food
still as good as I had remembered it? Such hopes usually go
unrewarded, but the red snapper, the corn bread, and even the
cooked greens were superb, better than they were in 1940. I
was tempted to go for a bottle of wine but confined myself to
a glass in view of my brandy date with Selena and Charles.

I was feeling very well disposed to the world by the time
the dessert, strawberry shortcake—real southern shortcake
made with shortening—was brought in. How would it be to
live in St. Christopher's again? Not all the time, but maybe
a part of each year? The place to stay, very obviously, would
be right here—up in Room 22. I could do a little writing,
have a desk and a word processor brought in. I was never
much for fishing, but I could play a little golf. There was the
local course and others not too far away. I might even do
some archaeology. There were students of mine, or students
of students of mine, teaching at the universities in both
Tallahassee and Gainesville. They might be willing to let me
in on some of their field activities. It could be a very pleasant
life. And I could always head back to Boston when I got bored
with it.

Who would I have for company? I had forgotten most of
my relatives, and they would have forgotten me. There would
be children and grandchildren among them whom I had
never seen or even heard of. Of the few I still knew, in the
sense of having seen something of them in the intervening
years, I supposed I would have to depend upon Charles as a
companion, unless he had changed as much as Webbie
claimed. And Webbie? Well, he was a bore, but I wouldn't
have to see too much of him. Selena? Was I looking forward
to her company? God knows what she was like now. But
then why get myself exercised about that—at least until I
had seen her.

I looked at my watch. It was twenty minutes until eight. I thought I'd better get going. It was only five or six blocks to the Randalls', an easy and pleasant walk, especially on this summer evening, but I'd let the time get away from me, so I decided to drive. It was almost completely dark now, the last faint glimmer of light showing above the dark water of the bay to the west. I walked out to my car in the parking lot.

A mosquito hummed familiarly in my ear. I slapped at it. I was back in St. Christopher's, all right. My mother used to be very concerned about mosquitoes. I could remember her telling me about the yellow fever epidemics of the past. The first great one struck in 1844, I think she said. Hundreds died agonizing, burning deaths. No one knew what brought the fever then. Night air? Rotting vegetation? Miasma from the swamp? There were other yellow fever epidemics later, lasting well into her young womanhood. By that time, though, scientists had discovered that the mosquito was the culprit, and they had set about destroying the kind of mosquito that brought the disease. But there were other mosquitoes, my mother warned me, carriers of malaria. Our house was screened, but even so I can still see our housemaid, Nellie, going from room to room in the evening after dinner, spraying vigorously before saying, "Good night, Miss Genevieve," and departing for her own screenless, sprayless home.

I got into my car—my rented, unfamiliar car—and fumbled around for a minute getting it started and moving the gearshift correctly. It didn't work quite like my Mercedes back home. What kind of car was it? I had no idea. To me, most of them looked alike now. It would take a used-car dealer, I thought, to distinguish among them. It had been different back in the old days. In 1918, my father had a Ford, which he regarded rather suspiciously, especially the cranking part. In 1919, we got a Buick, with a self-starter. That was really something. The Randalls were way ahead of us, though, with a Pierce-Arrow. Charles and I had been fascinated with the way the headlights rose out of the front fenders, and we used to sit in it, taking turns behind the wheel and providing motor noises with our mouths as we roared around the Indianapolis Speedway. The Bulls had a big Packard touring car, but Webbie wasn't any fun to drive in the Indianapolis with. He didn't have any sense of the event. He'd keep telling you how his father got the Packard "up to eighty" on his way to Pensacola.

I left the shore behind me, drove inland a couple of blocks, and turned down Palmetto Street—our old street. I passed the former Edwards house. There were some children playing in the street in front of it, and a woman came out on the porch and called to them, like my mother used to do with me when I'd play outside after dinner—or supper we called it then—until it got quite dark.

I pulled up in front of the Randall house. There were some lights on inside, although these shone only dimly at the front of the house. The porch light wasn't lit. I went up the long walk to the steps and climbed these to the porch. I pushed the bell. I could hear it ringing faintly somewhere inside. Two tall plate-glass panels flanked the door. I remembered I used to look through these, as a young teenager, to see who was coming to answer the door, in hopeful anticipation that it would be Selena. I also remembered the last time I saw Selena, when she had closed this door. I waited quite a while but refrained from peering in. Perhaps they were still at dinner. Then, quite suddenly—I had heard no approaching footsteps or latch turning—the door was opened. I couldn't see clearly at first. She was silhouetted, with the light at her back.

"Colin," she said.

▽

2

SELENA OPENED THE DOOR TO ME, and I stepped into the front hall. She must have turned on a hall light because we could now see each other better. Would I have known her if I had not been expecting her to be there? Would I have recognized her if she had been someone I came across casually at, say, a cocktail party? I doubt it. Fifty-eight years is a long time. Selena had an extraordinary figure for her seventy-two years—slender but very shapely. She looked at least ten years younger than her age. She put her hands up on my shoulders, and I bent down to exchange the kiss on the cheek. As we kissed, I noticed, looking down over her shoulder, that she stood on one foot, bending the other leg up at the knee, with the amatory exuberance one associates with much younger females. She stepped back then, holding me at arm's length.

"Oh, Colin, let me get a good look at you!" she exclaimed. "It's been such a long time! You are so handsome and distinguished looking, aren't you? What a lovely suit." She ran a hand over a lapel. "And a beautiful tie—but then you always did dress so nice. Aunt Genevieve brought you up just right," she added, with a hint of crispness in her voice. She blushed slightly, looked down and then up, with a little smile that I seemed to remember.

Was I being needled? Was there just a slight edge of hostility in that voice? Or was I being oversensitive, covertly hostile myself in remembrance of the last time we had stood at this door together? I had remembered Selena's voice as soft. Now it was stronger—perhaps the difference between the voice of a young girl and the voice of a mature woman— even, God help us, I reflected, an *old* woman. We moved farther into the hall, where the light was stronger, and I looked at her, at her green eyes. They were still beautiful, although tired and perhaps a little sad looking now. But whose eyes, I asked myself—other than those of an idiot or a saint—are not more tired and sad looking at seventy-two than at fourteen?

"Selena," I spoke at last, "how amazing and how nice to see you. You retain the beauty that was yours." Was I being a little too elegant, too stilted?

"Colin," she said smiling, "you haven't changed." She hooked her arm into mine. "We're in the library."

She led me down the hall to the library door. I suppose the house was much the same as when I had seen it last in 1940—or even in 1927, for that matter—only shabbier. Selena opened the door and said, "Here's Colin, dear."

Charles was at the desk, opening a bottle of brandy. There were brandy glasses, cups and saucers, and a silver coffeepot on a tray. Charles looked up from his task and got up from his chair. The lighting was subdued—only a lamp on the desk and another somewhere in the room—but I didn't think Charles looked well. He was haggard and yellow-pale, and thinner than when I had seen him two years ago. There was an unhealthy hollowness at the temples, over which parchmentlike skin was stretched tight. Perhaps Webbie was right. Yet, in spite of his physical appearance, there was no evidence in his speech of not being mentally alert and astute, nor any vacantness or madness in his eyes to justify Webbie's assertion that he was mentally deteriorating. He gave me his old wry, cynical smile that I knew so well and extended his hand with the greeting "Well, how are you, Professor?"

I replied that I was about as well as an aging academic could be. He chuckled, then wanted to know how the accommodations at the St. Christopher House were. When I told him they were up to old standards, Selena cut in and

chided me for not staying with them or at least coming over
and joining them for dinner. I partially countered this by
asking for a rain check on the dinner and suggesting that
they must be guests sometime in the hotel dining room.
Selena poured coffee into delicate eggshell cups of a pale blue
with gold rims—antebellum china, I had once heard Aunt
Marie tell my mother. Charles served us brandies. I was
seated on a sofa next to Selena, while Charles had gone back
to his desk chair—the old desk chair that Great-uncle
Charles used to sit in. I looked around at the books. They
were still there, or at least the shelves were filled like they
used to be. I caught a glimpse of a Marajó burial urn in an
empty corner space. It had been there when we were children, although I hadn't known what it was then. It was one
of those mysterious objects of the library that I used to ask
Great-uncle Charles to tell me about. I wondered if it had
been old Alexander, back in his sailing days, who had put in
at the island at the mouth of the Amazon and obtained this
pre-Columbian piece.

Selena politely asked me about my family—my daughters
and grandchildren. She had heard about Helen's death from
Charles. She was so sorry. She wished she had known her.
Why had I taken myself so completely out of their lives? "You
know, Colin," she told me, "you could have become a professor of archaeology down here in the South. After all, you
came down here once to dig things up—but then you took
them all back to the North. Charles should have talked you
into staying then. I'm sorry I wasn't here. Maybe I could
have convinced you."

"Oh, I had too many others to convince me to stay in the
North" was my mildly flippant retort. I hesitated to ask her
about her marriage to John and their divorce. I had heard, a
long time ago, that she had had a daughter. She must be a
middle-aged woman now, but I thought I'd wait and find out
more about her later. Selena and I chatted, rather self-consciously, for a while about various mutual relatives—the
great-aunts and -uncles, the second cousins once removed—

who still lived in St. Christopher's. Charles wasn't much help in all this, sitting silent and, I thought, covertly amused by our conversational struggles.

The doorbell came to our rescue. Selena got up to answer it and told me on her way out that it was probably Webbie. "I've invited him over to see you tonight, Colin," she called back over her shoulder.

Charles explained that Mildred, their servant, had the night off, and that they had to answer their own doorbell.

I could hear voices in the hall, and then I recognized the man's voice as Webbie's. There was a pause, perhaps broken by faint whispers. Then the door was opened, and Selena came in, followed by Webbie. He looked about the same as when I had seen him in Boston a few weeks ago—although perhaps a little glummer.

I got up, extended my hand, and told him it was good to see him. We shook hands. He mumbled some sort of greeting. Selena, I thought, looked flushed and angry. I wondered what had transpired between them in the short time since she had gone to answer the door. I struggled awhile to make conversation with little help from Selena and none from Charles.

Finally, Charles said, "Webbie, won't you have a brandy with us? I'm afraid the coffee has gone cold."

Webbie said, "Yes, thanks."

I inquired about Mabel, his wife, and told him to give her my regards, adding I hoped I would see them sometime during my visit. Webbie nodded. I wondered to myself if he had seen me in the afternoon as I drove past his house. He must have and told Selena, but he didn't say anything about it. After a few sips of brandy, Webbie announced that Mabel's brother, John, had driven in from New Orleans about an hour ago. I should note here that John was John Crawford. Webbie had married John's sister, Mabel. I felt I had to ask about John, even in Selena's presence. "Does John get over to St. Christopher's often? What is he doing now?"

Webbie said, "Yes, frequently," and then added, "John is still at Lockwood Galleries, in New Orleans."

I think that I had heard it from either Charles or Webbie, on some of their northern visits, that John Crawford had worked in a New Orleans art gallery for a man named Lockwood—Calhoun Lockwood—and that Lockwood had died some years ago. I asked if this was so, and Webbie verified it. The gallery now was owned, he told me, by a consortium, but a Tommy Fawnley, a former protégé of Calhoun Lockwood, was the manager, and John worked with him.

"Yes," Selena cut in, "Tommy Fawnley. He's such a great friend of Charles's. Charles is a member of the consortium. I do hope Colin will have a chance to meet Tommy. Is he coming over to St. Christopher's anytime soon, Charles, or do you prefer to get together in New Orleans?"

I don't quite know why, perhaps it was the tone of her voice, but I sensed a dirty crack of some kind. Charles didn't respond.

"How long will John be here?" I asked. "I'd like to say hello to him."

"Not long," answered Webbie. "I think he plans to drive back tomorrow." I had the feeling that he didn't want me to follow up on my suggestion of getting together with John, so I didn't pursue the matter further. We talked around a bit about trivial matters. I referred to his last visit to Boston, although not to the things he had told me then.

After a half hour of this, Webbie got up, saying that he would have to get back. He murmured something to me about us seeing each other sometime while I was here. The vagueness of his suggestion surprised me. I thought he might be wanting to see me in a more definite sort of way, to continue with what he had told me in Boston, but he gave no indication of it. Selena rose then and said she'd see Webbie out.

After they had closed the door, I asked Charles, "What's happened to the usually voluble Webbie? He barely uttered a word the whole time he was here. When he was up in Boston a month or so ago, he nearly talked my arm off."

"Yes, he was rather mute, wasn't he?" replied Charles.

"Maybe his tête-à-tête with Selena, on the way in, damped him down."

"Tell me about Selena, Charles. What's happened to her over all these years?"

Charles poured himself another brandy and started to get up to give me a refill, but I declined. He sat back down. "Oh, Sel," he said, using the old nickname that I never liked, "has had sort of a hard time of it. I've often wished she had married a fellow she had something serious going with back in Virginia, when she was at Sweet Briar, a chap from VMI. I think things would have been better for her if she hadn't come back here and married John."

He stopped for a bit, then went on. "John—John won't do, you know. He managed to graduate from Tulane, but then . . . then nothing happened. He wanted to go into business, but he didn't have any money of his own at first to get started. He got tied up with Calhoun Lockwood for a while. Then, about the time he married Selena, he came into some money—I don't know how much—but he must have invested it badly in some harebrained scheme. Anyway, he lost most of it. He was in the navy during the war, where, I guess, he did all right. But after that he was never much of a success at anything. He finally ended up going back to Lockwood Galleries, where he still is."

Charles stopped for a bit, then went on. "Selena had a child, you know, a daughter, born in 1944. Then she and John were divorced shortly after he came out of the service."

"What happened to the daughter?"

After a time, Charles said, "She died. It was after the divorce."

I said I was very sorry to hear this. How sad for Selena.

"Selena continued to live in New Orleans," Charles went on. "She had a job as a secretary in a law office. I saw her occasionally on my trips over there. She didn't remarry, but I suppose she, well, amused herself. She never came back here until last Christmastime, when she suddenly appeared and announced that she was going to stay."

As Charles was telling me this, I felt some surprising little surges of jealousy at his references to his sister's liaisons—the "chap" from VMI, the "amusements" in New Orleans. "Why did she come back here to live?"

"Oh, I don't think there's any mystery about that" was Charles's reply. "She had been informed of the prospective sale of St. James's Island, and I suppose she wanted to be on hand to look after her . . . her interests. I don't know what you've heard, Colin—from Webbie, Selena, or whomever—but Selena didn't come back here to St. Christopher's to look after me. I was doing fine on my own, as I have been ever since Mother died. No, my purposeful sister came back here because she wanted to." I thought he said this last rather grimly.

Then he grinned and told me, "Colin, Selena and Webbie have become great buddies in their old age. They have these long, confidential conversations, and they go out to dinner together and stay to all hours. I rather think they're having an affair."

"Does Mabel know about this?"

"I don't know. I hardly ever see her" was his reply. Charles poured me and himself another brandy and resumed his chair. Then he looked over at me and said in a loud whisper, "Webbie and Selena are trying to do me in, Colin! I think they're trying to kill me!"

It took me a couple of seconds to absorb the shock of this. I felt I was back in the conversation I'd had with Webbie in Boston. Was Charles making the same accusation, in reverse, or was he making a joke? I tried to counter his remark with a lighter one of my own. "Charles, I know Webbie has always appeared to want to bore us to death, but I never thought it was intentional."

"No, damnit, I'm serious! I've never liked him. I've never liked his fat, pop-eyed style, but I've always maintained a live-and-let-live attitude towards him. Now he's out to get me. Things have gone from bad to worse between us. Earlier in the spring we had a falling out over him telling me what

I ought to do. He came around here then, I'm sure at Selena's urging, trying to make me think I was going off my rocker and that I ought to go up to Tallahassee to see a psychiatrist. He's been going around telling people I'm losing my mind! But worse than that, he even tried to kill me! And I'm afraid my own sister is in cahoots with him in all of this!"

Was Charles going around the bend or was Webbie? Who was trying to kill whom? Who was crazy? I was shaken by the vehemence of Charles's statements, just as I had been by Webbie's in Boston. I was about to tell him that Webbie had been telling me that he, Charles, had been trying to kill him, but I heard Selena's footsteps in the hall, and she opened the door. She still looked flustered and angry. I wondered if it was the result of more conversation with Webbie or if she had heard anything of what Charles had been saying before she opened the door. So far, this had not been a very pleasant evening.

Selena apologized for being away from the room so long. "Webster," she said, "had some business to discuss before he left." Charles looked over at me very archly.

We talked for a time about what I would like to do and where I would like to go during my visit to St. Christopher's. And wouldn't I come over for dinner tomorrow night? I accepted with pleasure. Charles remained silent during this exchange. At last Selena stood up and asked if I would excuse her. She'd had a tiring day, but she looked forward to seeing me tomorrow evening. I looked at my watch at this point, but Charles saw me do so, frowned, and shook his head, forestalling any announcement that I had better depart now.

After Selena had left us, we sat for some moments as I waited for Charles to tell me more of what he had been telling me when Selena came in. When he didn't, I came out with it. "Jesus, Charles, tell me more! You can't say people are trying to kill you and then just drop the subject! What's happened?"

"I meant just what I said," Charles replied. "Webbie and Selena want me out of the way!"

"You'll have to explain," I told him.

"It's a long story," Charles began, "and it has to do with my asking you to come down here, to come down as an old friend and help me." Charles got up, went over to the door, opened it, and looked down the hall as though we might not be safe from eavesdroppers. Then he closed the door and went on. "It concerns St. James's Island to begin with. The state of Florida wants to buy the island—to set it aside as a recreational and wildlife area."

"So Webbie told me when he was up in Boston last," I informed him. "I hope you approve."

"It's all right with me," replied Charles. "It's inevitable. We'll have to let the island go sooner or later. It takes more money than we have to look after it. Anyhow, the state could take it by eminent domain, whatever our wishes. Fortunately, they are willing to give us a good price on it—ten million dollars. The deal's being completed now. Webbie is representing us legally, and he is being assisted in it by his brother-in-law, Harry Hedrickson."

I remembered then that I'd been told that Hedrickson—a poor redneck schoolmate of our boyhood—had come up in the world. He graduated from law school, in Gainesville, when Webbie did. Shortly after that, he married Webbie's sister, Lydia. It was just after the war. There had been opposition to the match at first on the part of the Bulls, but Harry had persevered in his suit—and in his upward social mobility—and the Bull family, including Webbie, was finally won over. Not long after the marriage, the Bull law office became Bull and Hedrickson.

Charles continued. "Naturally, those concerned want to see it move along as rapidly as possible."

"I think Webbie said that the island was held by some sort of trust between your two families. Is that right?"

"That's right," said Charles. "The trust is now composed of four members: myself, Selena, Webbie, and his sister, Lydia. Originally, the island had been purchased and held jointly by our great-grandfathers, Alexander Randall and Hezekiah

Bull. Eventually it came down to our fathers, James Randall and Webster Bull, Sr. In 1923, they set up a trust to be administered by their children, the four of us. I think, at the time, they hoped brother and sister would marry brother and sister. That is, I would marry Lydia and Selena would marry Webbie—all as a way of further consolidating the trust."

Charles looked over at me and laughed as he said this, took a sip of brandy, and continued. "As you know, the best laid plans of one's forebears have a way of going astray— thank God! In any event, the island was to be owned by the four of us. A fifty-fifty division between the Randall family and the Bull family was to be maintained as long as there was at least one of each family within the trust. Thus, if I predecease Selena, she will inherit my share, or vice versa, and the same arrangement holds for Webbie and Lydia. If there should be only two of us left, of whichever family, they would own the entire island, and if it came down to only one of us surviving, he or she would have the whole property. Of course, James and Webster Sr. figured that all, or at least some, of us would have children and that the trust would be participated in by them and by their children, on down the generations. But, as it has happened, none of us has left an heir."

I thought of Selena's dead child.

"Now it doesn't matter so much," he went on. "The future of the island is taken out of our hands because its sale will dissolve the trust, and the ten-million-dollar proceeds will be divided evenly among the four of us."

"Well, that sounds nice."

Charles paused for a minute. Then he said grimly, "If I were to be eliminated, Selena would take my share. I think, Colin, that she and Webbie are trying to arrange for that. Selena has Webbie completely under her control now. If they get rid of me, they'll then go for poor old Lydia and her part. They'd have the whole ten million then."

I could only shake my head in disbelief. The accusation that his sister and Webbie were conspiring to murder him

sounded utterly mad, crazier than Webbie's insistence that
Charles was out to kill him. Certainly, the Webster Bull I
knew didn't have the kind of imagination and daring for that
kind of *crime passionnel*. I couldn't visualize him doing it
even with Selena in the role of a seductive Lady Macbeth
urging him on. Was he really having a late-autumn affair
with Selena, as Charles had said? I remembered Webbie as
being bewitched by Selena when we were boys, just as I had
been. After all, Selena had been a bewitching type, and even
now I was sure she still could be. I broke off these thoughts
and asked, "Charles, when exactly is the sale of the island
to come off?"

"Well, it could be as early as the first of July, that is, in
just a month," he told me, "and that brings up the concern
that led me to ask you, as a special favor, to come down here.
There is something I want to do on the island before the sale
goes through. I told Selena about it, thinking she would be
interested and supportive, but, to my great surprise, she
became extremely upset and objected strongly. I thought I
could at least trust my twin sister, but, instead, she revealed
my plans to Webbie to get his support in opposing me. Indeed, their attempts to harass me and, eventually, to get me
out of the way all started two months ago, just after I told
her what I wanted to do over on St. James's."

"And what do you want to do over on the island that is so
desperate or important that it prompts attempts at homi-
cide?" I tried to put my question in a casual, offhand manner,
but, following Webbie's warning of Charles's desire to dig on
the island, I thought I knew what was coming.

"That, my dear fellow, my dear professor," said Charles,
"is why I have asked you to come down. I need some professional advice, and professional advice from someone I can
trust, someone in the family who won't go around telling
everybody about it."

With a sinking heart, I opened my hands as though to
indicate my mystification. "I don't get it, Charles. Just what
do you mean by professional advice?"

"You're an archaeologist, aren't you?"

"Yes," I answered, "I've been identified as one for the past fifty years of my life. Why?"

Charles reached down and unlocked a desk drawer. Before opening it, he asked me, "Colin, do you remember a little gold figure that Grandfather Charles used to have in this desk and showed us when we were kids?"

I said I did. "What ever happened to it?"

"Dad sold it. I believe he sold it to the Lockwood Galleries, years ago, before he . . . before he left us," Charles said. "But what do you think of this?" He reached down and brought a small gold figure of an alligator or a crocodile out of the desk drawer and handed it over to me.

I hefted it in my hand. It was about five inches long and of solid gold. The gold was of good quality. The object was clearly pre-Columbian, like the little man had been, but I told him this specimen looked to be Panamanian rather than strictly Colombian.

Charles brushed over this archaeological erudition by asking, "What would you say if I told you that this came from our Indian mound on St. James's Island?"

"I'd say you were pulling my leg—or someone has been pulling yours—or someone has been salting a Florida archaeological site in a rather expensive way" was my quick reply.

Charles shook his head. "No, Colin," he assured me, "I found this little gold animal myself—in that very mound."

I asked him to tell me about it.

"It was earlier this year, in March. It was when the sale of the island to the state was being discussed seriously. One of the state people came to see me—an archaeologist. He knew of your former digging in the mound; he had read your report on it. He wanted to know what the mound looked like now, if it had been restored to its former size and shape, and if Harvard would be willing to loan some of the pottery and artifacts you found in it to the state of Florida for a tourists' museum there. He was aware that you had excavated only about half the mound and was considering the possibility of doing more work on the unexcavated portion after the state took over.

"While we didn't go over to the island when this fellow was here, I went over by myself a few days later. I wanted to check on our old summer cottage. We'll have to be clearing it out pretty soon. I suppose it'll be torn down after the sale. When I was there I looked at the mound. It's pretty much grown over now, of course, but your old excavations can still be seen. I was walking around on the part of the mound you didn't excavate, and the caretaker's dog, a pretty good-sized mongrel, was frisking after me when he saw a lizard and started chasing it. The lizard ran into a hole, and the mutt began digging after it ferociously. He'd gouged out a hole about a foot deep when I saw something shiny sticking out of the sand he'd thrown up. I reached down and picked it up, and it was this little gold alligator. Well, after that, I couldn't restrain myself. I went up to our cottage and got a shovel. I came back and dug around quite a bit near the spot, but I didn't find anything else. Of course, I didn't dig very deep. Anyway, I brought the little alligator back home, and I got down your book about your diggings over there. You didn't find anything like this, did you?"

"No, I certainly didn't."

"Then I got to wondering if the Indians here, on the Florida Gulf Coast, ever traded with the Indians from South America or Central America, or places where such gold things came from. Did they?"

I was gratified by Charles's sensible archaeological question. He would be way ahead of Webbie as a researcher in our field. I told him that we didn't have very much evidence for the kind of trade he was asking about, but I did explain that occasional Spanish galleons, of the sixteenth century, had been wrecked off the Florida Keys or the south Florida coasts, and that this had resulted in occasional gold items, such as South American ornaments or Spanish coins, being found by the Florida natives and, subsequently, placed by them in their burial mounds. Usually though, I said, these objects had been hammered into little nuggets, pendants, or beads by the Indians who found them and, to the best of my knowledge, no such superb piece as the alligator had ever been recovered from a Florida site, especially not from this part of the state.

Charles nodded. I thought maybe he'd be disappointed by what I told him, but he wasn't. Instead, he said, "That's what I thought. I don't think this"—and he indicated the alligator—"was left at our mound by any Indian. I think it was put there at a much later time."

I didn't know quite what to say at that point. If Charles was telling me the truth, he had found an unusually exotic item out there on the St. James's Island Mound. How had it come to be there? I waited for him to say more.

"Do you remember, Colin," he asked me, "how Grandfather Charles used to say that his father, Alexander, had brought back many more figures, like the little gold man that he kept in his desk, and that no one knew where they were?"

I said, yes, I did.

Charles dropped his voice to a conspiratorial tone, and said, "I know that Grandfather Charles told my father that there must be such a cache of treasure somewhere, a great many gold figurines and ornaments that Alexander had brought back from one of his Colombian voyages. Grandfather Charles had said that they were known as the Gomez Collection, after a Colombian family who owned them and who lived in Cartagena, an old Caribbean seaport city. There were almost five hundred items in the collection. Great-grandfather Alexander bought them from the Gomezes on one of his voyages down there, but there was some sort of complication about the deal. He was in it with someone else who was demanding a share, and Alexander didn't want to give it to him. That's why, according to what Grandfather Charles told my father, Alexander hid the gold the way he did. I guess he died before he ever got around to digging it up."

Charles hesitated, then went on, quite determinedly. "Colin, I think Great-grandfather Alexander hid that cache

of gold figurines in the Indian mound and that I was lucky
enough to find one of them. I want to go out there and dig
that portion of the St. James's Mound you didn't dig back
in 1940, really dig it—deep and thoroughly." He held up the
little gold alligator. "I think," he said, "that this piece somehow got separated from the rest when they buried the lot
and that there are many more of them out there. I want you
to help me, Colin. And I want to do it quickly, before the
island is sold to the state."

Well, I had it now, and it was about as bad as I had thought
it might be. "Charles," I said shaking my head, "this is out
of the question." And I proceeded to tell him why. "We'll
have to look it up in my report, but as I recall the St. James's
Island Mound was about seventy to eighty feet in diameter
and at least six feet high. That's a fairly substantial pile of
sand and earth. It took me a month, with a crew of ten
workmen, to excavate the eastern half of the mound. That
was forty-five years ago. Today, any archaeologist would be
severely criticized for going as fast as I did then. I think I
recorded about twenty burials and perhaps seven or eight
whole pottery vessels, plus a lot of potsherds, as well as a
number of stone and shell artifacts. I suppose most of the
pottery was in the eastern half of the mound. That's why I
excavated that side. Moore, in his many excavations along
the Gulf Coast, found this east side location of the pottery
offerings to have been a consistent trait of the Weeden Island
culture, and the St. James's Mound is very clearly a Weeden
Island I Period burial place. Possibly, or even probably, in the
digging of the western half we wouldn't find as much pottery,
but there would almost certainly be burials, and to clean
these off and properly plot and photograph them takes time."

"But, Colin, I don't want to do a scientific excavation of
the place. I want to see if the gold is there and, if it is, to take
it out. Then we can turn whatever's left of the mound over
to the state, and they can dig it some more, restore it, or do
whatever they want with it."

I had been up for sixteen hours at that time, and this, plus the trip and my sessions with the Randalls and with Webbie, had worn me out. I was going to have to wind this up and go back to the hotel and get some sleep. I gave a slight groan. "Charles," I said, "I don't think you can do it. You could get into some legal trouble by attempting it, and I, as an archaeologist, cannot participate in anything like this."

"Why not!" exploded Charles. "The gold is mine, isn't it? That is, it belonged to the Randall family, and we still own the island, at least until the deal goes through at the end of the month! All I'm asking is for you to give me a little help on it, for the family and for friendship's sake. You could dig there without anybody raising a fuss. You . . . you're one of the country's best-known archaeologists. Lots of people, even down here, know about you. Nobody would say anything if you dug over there!"

"Charles, things just don't work like that. I would place myself in a very bad position with all of my colleagues down here, and elsewhere, by doing that. Even if we did find some gold—and even if we could prove it to be old Alexander's Gomez Collection from Colombia, Panama, or wherever— we couldn't take it away surreptitiously. You know how word about anything like that gets around in a place like this better than I do. With a digging operation of the size it would take, people would know about it. If it is to be done at all, it will have to be completely open and aboveboard."

Charles was obviously very disappointed. He said, bitterly, "So you want to block me from doing it, just like Selena and Webbie."

"Charles," I told him, "I admit the finding of the little gold alligator out there is hard to explain, and I can understand your curiosity, as well as your desire to get your hands on a golden treasure, but, if anything, the presence of such a rare exotic in a Florida Indian mound is reason for a very thorough and large-scale excavation by qualified archaeologists, not for going out there and burrowing some secretive hold in the ground."

I paused at this point, and my mind went back to the way

Charles had come up on all of this in his conversations with me. "Tell me how all of this is related, as you seemed to indicate that it is, to Selena and Webbie trying to do away with you. And if it is, just what have they done, or are you exaggerating when you use a word like *murder*? Tell me specifically what has happened."

Charles sighed and suggested we have just one more brandy. I knew I shouldn't, but if I was to keep on listening I would need it. He poured us two more, then began his story.

"It all started," he said, "when I showed Selena the little gold alligator and told her what I wanted to do. I hadn't seen her much in recent years. After she came home at Christmas, I didn't find her as easy to talk with as she used to be. We got on each other's nerves, I suppose, and we hadn't been getting along together all that well. But when I said I wanted to go out to the island and dig in the mound, she hit the roof."

"What were her objections?" I asked him. "I mean, I can see some objections. I've just told you what mine are. But what were hers?"

"I don't really know. She just flew into a rage. You can remember what a temper she had as a kid? Well, she still does. She said it was an insane and crazy idea. It looked like she was willing to go to any lengths to keep me from going out to the island and digging. It must have been at about this time that she told Webbie. He came over, in his pompous way, and asked to see me about what he said was a very serious matter. He tried to dissuade me from going out to the island to dig. He said it would upset the negotiations with the state for the sale of the island. Then he went on to imply that I was losing my mind, that I'd better see a psychiatrist."

"When did this close relationship between Selena and Webbie start?"

"Oh, at about that time, I guess. He's been here at the house frequently, in the afternoons and evenings. They go out together for dinner, too. I don't know just where—Panama City or Tallahassee. Anyhow, after that visit of Webbie's, things got worse."

"How?"

"Somebody," said Charles very grimly, "and I think it was Webbie, tried to kill me. A week or so after that talk, I was sitting here in the study one evening. It was about eleven o'clock and quite dark outside. I heard a shot, and a bullet came through that window and buried itself in the wall there." He pointed to a window that looked out over a side lawn and then to what appeared to be a bullet hole in the paneling above his head. "I went out of the house and looked around, but I didn't see anybody. I came back in and called to Selena. She was upstairs. She said she had heard a shot but hadn't realized it had been fired at our house."

"Did you report it to the police?"

"Yes," said Charles. "I called the chief of police, Brad Ellis, the next morning, and he came over. I showed him the bullet hole in the window and the place where it went into the wall. He dug out the slug and took it down to the police station. But that wasn't the end of it. They tried again.

"About a week after the first shot, I was down here, and it was later this time, about midnight, and somebody fired another shot through the window, the same window. This bullet barely missed my head and hit the wall there." Charles got up and went over to the wall and, with a trembling forefinger, pointed to another hole in the woodwork. It was marred around the edges as if it had been enlarged by probing.

"I got Ellis back over here again and showed him the hole, and he took the second bullet out of the paneling. He said both of the bullets looked like they came from a thirty-eight revolver. He and one of his deputies came out the next day and ran a string from the bullet holes in the window to where the bullets had gone into the wall. His only remark was that whoever did it had only missed my head by about an inch on the second try. I think Webbie did it. I think he tried to kill me twice."

By the time Charles had finished telling me this, he had himself pretty well worked up and was breathing hard. "Take it easy, old man," I cautioned.

I was, to say the least, confused. Here was Charles telling me more or less the same thing that Webbie had told me up in Boston, except that now it was in reverse. Who was telling the truth? Somehow, I didn't think either of them was. It was all too bizarre. Someone else must be responsible, some nut or some wild kid trying to terrorize the neighborhood.

After a minute, I asked, "Did you voice any suspicions about Webbie's or Selena's possible involvement to Ellis?"

Charles said he hadn't.

I felt relieved. "Good," I told him. "I think you've done the right things. You had to call the police in. The whole business is disturbing, frightening. But, Charles, somehow I can't see Webbie doing such a thing. Selena and Webbie might not want you to dig in the mound out on the island, but to murder you to keep you from doing it strikes me as completely out of proportion. I must say, though, I don't blame you for being upset by what appears to be a homicidal night prowler. Don't the police have any suspects?"

He shook his head.

"Have there been any more attacks here like those you have told me about?" I asked.

He shook his head again.

When he did this, I felt I had to say something to him about what I was thinking.

"Look, Charles," I began, "Webbie told me just about what you've told me when I saw him up in Boston a few weeks ago, but in his story he was the victim. He said someone had fired a shot through his bedroom window at night. Don't you know anything about that? Didn't the police mention it when you called them over after the sniping at you?"

Charles had been looking at me, but now he avoided my eye. He looked down into his brandy glass before answering. Finally, he said, "I haven't talked with Webbie since our argument—until just now, tonight. I really don't know what's been happening to him."

"But didn't the police say anything? They must have—"

"Yes, yes," he cut me off impatiently, "they did mention

something about somebody shooting at Webbie's upstairs window."

"Well, don't you think that suggests that there must be some maniac or some oddly motivated prankster on the loose, and that this would be a better explanation than blaming it on Webbie? You know, I hate to tell you this, but, well, Webbie thinks you're the one who shot at him."

Charles didn't seem surprised by this news. He replied rather coldly. "How like Webbie. That's preposterous. You know, if it weren't so ridiculous, I'd consider it libelous." Charles sloshed a little more brandy into his glass and stared away, again, at the bookcases.

There didn't seem much point in pursuing this any further, but I asked, "Tell me, Charles, have you and Selena had further words about your St. James's mound-digging project?"

"Not at any great length. I think she knows the matter isn't settled yet, though. She knows that's why I asked you down here."

If she knows that, I thought, it's a wonder she was as pleasant to me as she was.

I looked at Charles sitting there in the dim light. He appeared frail and worried. I felt sorry for him. God knows what should be done about the midnight marksman. It didn't appear to be something that I could do anything about, although I wondered if I might not inquire around in the next day or so—maybe go to Chief Ellis's office and see what he could tell me about it. It would be good to have what might be a more objective report on these peculiar matters than the ones I had received from Cousins Webbie and Charles.

As to Charles's archaeological interests, I came out with a plan that I'd been running over in my mind.

"Charles," I asked, "how would it be if I see whether I can get hold of a metal detector? I'm sure the archaeologists in the department up at Florida State have one. I know one of the fellows there. I'll ask him if I can borrow it. We'll take it over to the island and see what it can tell us about the presence of metals in the St. James's Mound. There's no use in getting yourself, and everybody else, all excited about this treasure hunt if there is really no basis for it at all. What do you say?"

Charles didn't like the idea very much. "Colin, if we do that, we'll let outsiders in on what should be a family secret."

I didn't feel like arguing about it anymore that night. I stood up, realizing just how damned tired I was. I looked at my watch. It was ten minutes of midnight. It'd been eighteen hours since I arose from my bed in Boston that morning. "Charles," I said, "I'm dead tired. Thank you for asking me over, but I must go. Please thank Selena for me."

Charles got up, too. We shook hands. His felt feeble. Poor Charles, he couldn't have had a very happy life. Yet, I didn't know. It had been so long, so very long ago since we had really known each other. I knew so little of what he had done through the years—his pleasures, his sorrows.

He showed me out. I told him that I would be over tomorrow morning and that I would see what we could do about the metal detector next week. He nodded, as if in agreement, but maybe it was only through weariness, and closed the door behind me.

Out at the street, as I got in my car, I looked back at the old, dark Randall house, that house that had been so much a part of my consciousness when I was growing up—the long-abandoned playroom up there on the third floor, the high-ceilinged, dark halls and rooms, the magic of the library. I started the car and drove away, as quietly as I could, past all the other dark houses, through the streets lighted only by the single high streetlights at the corners.

What was happening? Who was threatening Charles or trying to kill him? Or were they trying to scare him rather than kill him? And what about Webbie's story? Were two old men intemperate enough, in their anger, to go about taking shots at each other in the middle of the night? Charles's rather silly, romantic desire to dig for treasure in an Indian mound on his own property, while perhaps an inconvenience to his relatives at the present time, hardly seemed to explain all the events that surrounded it.

And what was I going to do about that? Now that I as
away from him and by myself, it seemed more foolish than
ever. I was being asked to engage in the kind of thing that I
had disapproved of or joked about all my professional life.
Obviously, I couldn't do it, but I had to try to calm him down
in some way.

Back at the St. Christopher House all was quiet, and there
was only a single light over the outside entrance. The lobby
was dark except for a small night-light over the desk. A night
clerk, or porter, a young black man, dozed beneath it, although he roused and said good evening when I entered. He
gave me my key, and I climbed the stairs to my room. I
reflected back on the musings I had had as I sat at dinner
five hours before—those thoughts about coming to St.
Christopher's for a part of each year, putting up in Room 22,
and partaking of the excellent fare downstairs. It all seemed
like less of a good idea than it had then. I undressed wearily
and climbed into bed. My God, I was tired. Thoughts of
Charles, Webbie, Selena, and gunshots fired through windows of peaceful residences in the dead of night went
through my head. How very strange, the things that happen
in other people's lives. I fell asleep.

$\triangledown$

3

THE RANDALLS USED TO have a carriage house and sta-
bles—a wonderful domain—at the back of their house. This
was when they had horses, and I can remember old Major
Charles Randall being driven around in what, I guess, was a
Victoria, or one of those carriages with a coachman sitting
up front. The coachman was Edmund, a large and impressive
black man who, when he drove Major Charles, sometimes
wore a stovepipe hat. Oscar, a smaller, younger black man
who used to smell like medicine all the time, was Edmund's
assistant, but his duties seemed to be mainly harnessing and
unharnessing the horses, not driving them. The Randalls
also had a smaller vehicle, a buggy, which was pulled by only
one horse and had only one seat for two passengers.

These are just about the earliest things that I can remember, and these memories go back as early as 1917, when I
was four, or possibly even to 1916. It's difficult to be sure
what one really remembers and what one has been told about
one's childhood. What I am positive about, though, is that
I remember Mrs. Randall—Aunt Marie—driving down our
street once with Selena in the buggy beside her. Selena was
wearing a round straw hat, with the brim turned up, and it
had a big red ribbon around it. She waved to me as they
passed. This is the first image I have of Selena, although we
had been virtually raised together, by the black nursemaids
of our two families. That was when she impressed herself
on my memory.

It is from a year or two after this that I have a second vivid recollection of Selena, and I can date this time definitely because it was when she and Charles and I took part in the St. Christopher's Armistice Day parade in November of 1918. Sometime in the preceding year, the Randalls had switched from horse transportation to the motorcar, for all the horses were gone, but, until they tore it down and built a garage, they kept the new car—the fabulous Pierce-Arrow—in the old carriage house. Edmund, as I recall, failed to make the transition from horse to automobile, but the younger Oscar did, and he drove the Pierce-Arrow wearing a black cap with a visor and still smelling of medicine. In the Armistice Day occasion, Charles, Selena, and I were to be figures on a float, the float being the Pierce-Arrow swathed in patriotic bunting.

The Pierce-Arrow's top had been put down, and Charles, Selena, and I could be seated on the folded top at the back of the car, prominently displayed, as child symbols of America's victory. Charles was wearing a sailor's suit; I had on a khaki soldier's suit, which my mother had made for me; and Selena was in a white Red Cross nurse's uniform. We were to be made secure on our precarious perches by three comely young ladies—some of our younger aunts or older cousins, as I recall—who, sitting in the backseat, would hold on to our legs. I was already so placed at one corner of the folded top, and Charles was similarly seated in the middle. At the last minute, Selena had been brought out to the car by Georgia, her black nurse, who lifted her up onto the other corner of the car's top; however, as soon as Selena found herself there she would have none of it. "I doan' wanna be here in the corner," she complained, "I wanna be in the middle." She explained this disagreement with previous arrangements with the argument that "I should be in the middle 'cause everybody knows that nurses take care of both soldiers and sailors, and so they should be in the middle between them! Lemme be in the middle!" As this change of positions would have taken some shifting around, the young aunt or cousin who was to have Selena in her care tried to talk her out of it by telling her, "No, my precious baby, you come sit right here, and I'll hold on to you nice and tight." But Selena was not to be dissuaded by such specious endearments. Instead, she responded with a wail and a flow of tears. "No, I won't! It ain't right! Nurses should be in the middle!"

At this point, Great-uncle Charles, who was sitting in the front seat in his Confederate major's uniform, and in a fuming hurry to get started so we would be sure to get a well-up-forward place in the parade, cut in crossly in Selena's behalf. "Damnit, can't you ladies get that child settled so we can leave?"

This peremptory order resulted in a hurried changing of places so that Selena had her desired seat. I can still see her. She was smiling now, contentedly, the tear streaks drying on her happy pink face, which was framed by dark bangs and the little white nurse's cap with the red cross on it. She stuck out her tongue at Charles. Then she looked over at me, winningly, coquettishly, with those absolutely ravishing green eyes. So I fell in love with her then. I know that there are those who say that one does not fall in love at that age, but I did. After that, I would go to sleep every night thinking about Selena, making up all kinds of stories in which we would be together—playing, talking, reading, drawing pictures, going on fabulous trips in boats, in automobiles, or on trains. I would fantasize that Selena, a beautiful green-eyed princess, was being held in a wicked castle against her will, or being pursued by evil villains, or sometimes by dragons—and I, Colin Edwards, was always her rescuer.

On that Armistice Day, however, I also remember hearing Georgia muttering fiercely from the sidewalk: "They gives that chile her way too much! She always gotta be de charge of de world! They's gonna be sorry." Finally, much to Great-uncle Charles's relief, he was able to tell Oscar to put the car in gear, and we rolled off to join the parade.

After that, my relationship to Selena was changed. I never said anything to her about my feelings, at least I didn't for several years, but I think she realized what they were. As they say, women always know such things without being told.

I still went over to the Randalls' to play, and Charles and I continued as best friends. They had a giant sandbox, or it seemed giant to me, for it was much bigger than the sandpile I had in our backyard. Theirs was located out by the carriage house, and Charles and Selena and I spent a lot of time creating realms of sand castles in it. A third early memory was a sandbox incident, maybe a year or so after the Armistice Day parade. Charles was busy building castles at one side of the box, and Selena and I were at the other side, where I was constructing another set of castles. I kept making up stories of the kings, queens, and knights who lived in the various towers of my castles and telling Selena all about these wondrous persons as I worked away and she picked dandelions in the grass beside the box to decorate my creations. She—this adorable female audience—seemed utterly enchanted by what I was doing, and this undoubtedly encouraged me in my sand-and-word fantasies. Finally, she looked at me with worshipful eyes, those beautiful green eyes, and said, "Oh, Colin, you make the bestest sand castles of anybody in the whole world."

Charles had been quietly castle building on his side of the box, but he heard this. He got up from what he was doing, came over to our side of the sandbox, and began systematically stamping on and destroying the castles I had been making. He told me, quite imperiously, "All the castles here are mine, no matter who makes them, and I can do anything I want to with them." This grand seigneurial attitude on the part of my host resulted in a combination fistfight and wrestling match between us, which was pursued so furiously and noisily that Georgia had to come out of the Randalls' kitchen to break it up and send me home. Charles and I both sulked for a couple of days before we made it up.

In the fabulous playroom of the Randall house, Charles had an electric train and troops of lead soldiers. There were also huge piles of blocks with which we could build tunnels for the train or forts for our armies. Selena had an impressive array of dolls, which I came to know by name, but there were other rooms in the house, "grown-up rooms," which captured my imagination even more than the playroom. The front parlor had a somber dignity that held me in awe, with its chandelier, formal furniture, and portraits of Alexander Randall, builder of the house, and his wife.

More than any other room, though, the library came to symbolize the house to me. Its high walls were completely book lined—more books than I had ever seen in one place, more it seemed than in the St. Christopher's Public Library. Charles and I, and sometimes Selena, would spend hours poring through these, lying on our stomachs on the floor with the great tomes open before us. I loved it there on those occasions, with the light filtering in through shutters which had been partially closed to keep the heat out on summer afternoons. In our earlier years, we obviously didn't do much reading, but the books had wonderful pictures, which opened up distant and forgotten worlds, the sphinx and the pyramids of Egypt, tigers in India being stalked by cork-helmeted British sahibs, the histories of kings and queens. I particularly recall a reproduction of an engraving of the dashing and cocky King Henri IV of France. I suppose if I had been asked to tell you of the most important room I had ever been in anywhere, at, say, age eight, I would have said it was Great-uncle Charles's library. Great-uncle Charles lived in the house then, along with his son, daughter-in-law, and grandchildren, and he continued to live there until his death, in 1921. He had a separate bedroom suite on the second floor, overlooking the front of the house, and the library was also acknowledged to be his special domain. When he wasn't there, Aunt Marie was the one who would let us go into the library, but Great-uncle Charles was usually very tolerant of us when he was there. He would tell us stories of faraway and long ago places, fascinatingly romantic blends of fact and fiction as I now think back on them.

The library also contained things other than books. There were the Civil War memorabilia—the sabers, sashes, and torn battle flags—common to other southern big homes, but there were also strange-looking objects, including pottery vases and plates of peculiar forms and with exotic painted designs that were infinitely intriguing to an eight-year-old. Great-uncle Charles told me that his father, Alexander, had brought them back from countries and places where he had gone in his sailing ships. Years later, as an archaeologist, I remembered these and could identify them—in my memory—as being pre-Columbian pieces from the Amazon, the West Indies, Colombia, and Panama—regions and countries that Alexander Randall had visited in his sailing ships.

On one occasion when Charles, Selena, and I were in the library, Great-uncle Charles gave us a special treat by unlocking a bottom drawer of his big mahogany desk and taking out a small, brass-bound wooden box. He carefully unlocked the box with a key. Inside, resting on the soft black velvet lining, was a little figure of a man, about six inches in height, that appeared to be made of gold. This was the figure Charles had asked me about, years later, when he told me of his discovery out at the mound. The figure had funny squinched eyes and a pointed noise, and little loose ring as a nose ornament. Great-uncle Charles explained that it had been made by the ancient Indians of Colombia, long before Christopher Columbus ever set foot in America. Charles and Selena may have seen it before, but I was breathless with excitement. I wanted to know more about it. Who was the little man? Was he a king? An idol?

Great-uncle Charles let us take the little figure out of the box and hold it. I asked if my Great-great-uncle Alexander—Charles's and Selena's great-grandfather—had been the one who brought back the little gold man from Colombia. Great-uncle Charles looked a little stern at this question, and he seemed slower in answering it than he usually was with our questions. "Yes," he finally said, "he brought it back and many more like it." Where, then, were the others? We wanted to know, but Great-uncle Charles only shook his head, locked up the little box with its precious content, and put it back in the desk. In recalling the little gold man since then, I know that the figurine was in a style known archaeologically as the Quimbaya and that it came from a region of the Republic of Colombia from which thousands of other gold items of this style have been taken from ancient tombs by looters over the past two centuries. I wondered then what Great-uncle Charles meant when he said that his father, Alexander, had brought back many more like it and, if so, where they might be. And now Charles, with his discovery, had started me wondering again.

As we grew older, and went through grade school together, my secret passion for Selena never waned, although it revealed itself in very little except saving my pennies to buy her the most elaborate valentines I could find for classroom Valentine's Day exchanges. Charles may have suspected me of being sweet on his sister, but he never teased me about it. Selena was not without other admirers. Cousins Webbie Bull and John Crawford, who were both in our class at school, made the standard ten-year-old advances to Sel—such things as putting a small frog down the back of her dress, or pulling her hair ribbon. There were times when I felt that Selena enjoyed this form of preadolescent courtship too much, screeching with delight as she eluded her pursuers around the school yard, or suddenly turning on them with mock rage. Inwardly, I disapproved of such behavior on the part of my rivals. After all, it was an unseemly way for a knight to treat a lady. I also resented the nickname Sel, by which she was called by all her peers except me. I held Selena to be much more courtly and romantic.

There was another classmate who worshiped Selena from afar and in embarrassed silence. This was a gangling redhead named Harry Hedrickson, a boy then considered to be from the wrong side of the tracks. I can remember one of my aunts saying that Harry's grandfather had been a Yankee plantation overseer, an occupation that would have assigned him to something dangerously near to being poor white trash. I doubt if this grandfather was still around at that time, but

Harry's father worked as a foreman in the lumber mill owned by Webster Bull, Sr., Webbie's father. Unlike our crowd, who came to school in knickerbockers, clean shirts, and ties, Harry wore faded blue and patched bib overalls. I used to see him gazing at Selena with a devoted admiration that had a touch of awe in it. I can remember resenting it. No one had any right to feel so soulful about Selena, except me.

When we were twelve years old, I went to dancing classes with Selena and others of our crowd. We were getting to be of an age where we no longer played together, so this was my only opportunity to be with her, however briefly. When I would dance with Selena I would become tongue-tied, and when I wasn't dancing with her I was busy looking over the shoulder of my partner to see where she was and with whom. Things went along like that through my early teens, with all the anxieties and hopes that are the lot of most of us at that age.

Then, in the summer of 1927, my relationship with Selena took a sudden turn for the better, or I might say that she suddenly gave me special notice. I've never been able to explain this. In my vanity about my looks, I thought it may have had something to do with an improvement in my physical appearance. In the two years since the beginning of the dancing class ordeals, I had grown some and filled out a bit. It seemed to begin—this change in Selena—at a party at the Bulls', a birthday party for Webbie. All of our crowd was there, except Charles. He had gone on to a private school in Pennsylvania that fall. I missed him and knew that I would miss him still more in the coming school year. Also, without him here, it would be more difficult for me to visit the Randalls, where I could see Selena. That evening Selena seemed to stay near me all the time. She might have been doing it to distress Webbie. He had invited her as his "date" for the party, but, along about nine o'clock, Selena told him that she had to go home and that I was taking her. I remember poor old Webbie was quite upset. As it happened, I had not asked Selena to leave early, nor had she consulted me about it, so I was almost as surprised as Webbie. Inwardly, of course, I was elated.

I had the family car that evening, and, instead of going straight to the Randalls', we drove downtown to an ice-cream parlor and added a chocolate sundae to the ice cream and cake we had eaten at the party. Then we drove out along the shore and parked under some palm trees on a side road just a little off the highway. The moonlight on the waters of the bay was overpoweringly, achingly romantic. We talked of our ambitions. Selena said she wanted to go to New York some-day and become an actress. Her father said she would be good at it, but her mother didn't like the idea. I became rather long-winded about my intentions to be a great scholar, an archaeologist, who would study strange things, like those that were in her grandfather's library, and who would travel all over the world. After a while, Selena, perhaps finding so much self-involved discourse on my part a little boring, said, softly, "Colin, that would be nice," and she moved over very close to me in the car. I could just see the faintest moonlight reflected in those lovely Selena eyes in the darkness, and we kissed—very tentatively at first, and then not so tentatively.

That month—it was August—went by so quickly. I saw Selena every day. I was at her house for lunch; she came to ours for dinner. I think my mother always had her reserva-tions about Selena. She felt that she was spoiled. "Pretty is as pretty does," Mother would say, often with the unspoken implication that Selena didn't always do prettily. But I was immune to any criticism of my darling. Selena and I would spend the days going to the beaches nearby or sailing in the bay in a little sailboat my father had given me. Nights we would go the movies, and afterward we would park in se-cluded places for some protracted necking.

It was in the last week in August that Selena suggested we sail over to St. James's Island and take a picnic lunch. I was both excited by the prospect and a trifle edgy about what her parents and my parents would think about such an un-chaperoned trip. I presented the idea at home. My mother's immediate reaction was negative, but my father took my side. It would be perfectly safe, he said. We should check with radioed weather reports first. Then, if there were no hurricane or storm warnings out, we could sail along the shore to the west for a few miles, to the place where the open-water distance to St. James's was relatively short—less than a half mile. That way, even if a quick afternoon thunderstorm came up, we wouldn't be on open water for very long.

Even after this nautical advice and reassurance, my mother remained distressed. I could see that the natural elements hadn't worried her as much as the human ones. But with my father on my side, she finally gave in, and I telephoned Selena the good news. She apparently had had no trouble in obtaining parental permission for the excursion. Selena's mother seemed always to give in to Selena's requests, and her father was out of town on business—in New Orleans, where he often was.

The next day dawned perfectly, with no storm warnings. Our cook had prepared a lunch for us, and my father drove us down to the docks where my little sailboat was tied up. He helped us run up the sails, and he checked to see that the life preservers were on board. Before we pushed off, he gave me a small paper bag, which, I found, contained a pint bottle of brown liquid. "Corn whiskey," he explained, "it's for Jackson. Tell him it's a present from me—for his kidneys!" He laughed. Jackson was the caretaker on the island, an old Negro who lived alone there. He was very attached to my father, who had once, long before I was born, intervened with a lynch mob and saved Jackson's brother's life. My father pushed us off. "Have a good time! Be careful!" he called.

St. James's Island—unlike most of the offshore islands, which are long, narrow bar formations that sustain only low vegetation—is wider and less barlike. It measures about five miles across at its widest point and is equally long. There are nice stands of trees on it, and at its higher, or western end, it rises to as much as ten feet above the high-tide line. A lot of land birds nest on the island, as well as gulls and other seabirds, and, protected as the island is, rabbits and other small mammals are also numerous. The southern shore, which opens out into the Gulf of Mexico, has a wonderful wide beach with a booming surf for swimming, but on the northern, or bay side, the beach is narrower and there are no breakers.

The island ranked high in my fond childhood memories. We would go over there in the summer and often stay for a week or so at a time. The Randalls and the Bulls allowed relatives the use of the cottages. By the 1920s, the island was very heavily posted, with No Trespassing signs put up everywhere, especially along its bayside shore at the western end, where the channel separating it from the mainland was narrowest. In spite of this, even back in those days, when there were not so many tourists around on this part of the Gulf Coast, occasional trespassers would land there, break into the cottages, and camp for a night. To prevent this, Jackson was employed as a guardian. After a spirited tack along the coast, Selena and I arrived opposite the western tip of the island, where we could see Jackson's shack down by the bay beach, and we came about and headed for it. When we were about 100 yards offshore, Jackson came out of his house, shaded his eyes, looked at us, and finally waved. We put in to a little pier, and Jackson helped us tie the boat up. I busied myself bringing down the sails. "Miz Selena, Mistah Colin," Jackson greeted us. "How y'all? Y'all ain't been ovah heah in a long time. How's Mistah Robert?" he asked me, referring to my father.

"Jackson," I said, "he sent a little present over to you." I handed him the bottle in the bag, and added, "He said it was for your kidneys."

Jackson responded with a chuckle, "Yes suh, yes suh, thank you, suh."

"Jackson," I went on to explain, "Miss Selena and I have come over to have a picnic." I lifted the picnic basket out of the boat. "Could we have the key to the Randall cottage?" I asked.

"Sho nuff, sho nuff, come right along. I'se got it right heah in de house." We followed him up the beach to his wooden shack, supported by piles in the edge of the forest. Jackson went up the steps and disappeared inside, coming out in a minute with a key on a ring, which he gave to me. "Heah it is. How long you goin' to be?" I told him we'd return in time to sail back to St. Christopher's before dark. He nodded. "All right, y'all behave yo'selves up dere, now," he added. I felt a surge of guilt. Was Jackson voicing suspicions of what looked like an illicit escapade? I had been over to the island many times before, as had Selena, but this was the first time we had ever been there together alone. I had the impulse to explain to Jackson that we had our parents' permission to be there, but I stifled it.

Selena and I walked up a familiar path alongside Jackson's shack that led through a thick hammock of trees and then on up a ridge where it was slightly more open. Here, not far from the trail, I knew there was an Indian mound. It was hidden in the trees and the undergrowth now, although once, two summers ago, when some of us were over here, my father and I, with Jackson's help, had cleared some of the growth away so we could get a better look at it. I also knew that not far away, back down in the direction of the bay beach, there was an extensive series of shell piles where one could sometimes pick up bits of old Indian pottery.

After about five minutes more on the trail, Selena and I passed the Bull cottage. It was shut up, and no one was around. I was glad. It would have been awful to find Webbie or some of his family over here now. We continued on deeper into the woods. It was awfully still, and it was also lush and beautiful. There was a summer smell of grasses, weeds, and wildflowers. Butterflies danced in front of us. At one place a giant spider's web stretched across the path, its gossamer strands still wet from the morning's dew. Selena squealed and ducked, and I batted at the web's large yellow-and-black occupant with a stick. Then we emerged into an open but still largely shaded clearing. Over at one edge of it was the

Randall cottage, which was really a good-sized house. It was brown-shingled, which gave it a kind of magical "witch-wood" quality in its sylvan setting. I remember it had at least eight bedrooms, six upstairs for family and guests and two downstairs for the servants. We went up the porch steps and unlocked the front door.

It was still and musty smelling inside, so Selena and I opened some of the windows and shutters to let in the air and light. Selena found a dustcloth somewhere and brushed off a table and chairs in the kitchen. It was noon now, and, after our morning's sail and hike up from the beach, we were hungry. Selena unpacked the lunch I had brought. The cottage dishes and silver were all stored away, and we didn't want to bother with them anyway, so we spread all our sandwiches and whatever else we had out on the table and ate off the wax paper it had been wrapped in. I can't remember eating. I can only remember looking at her and thinking about her.

After our lunch, we wandered, hand in hand, through the house, the big, barnlike living room and dining room downstairs and then the bedrooms upstairs. There were dust spreads over the mattresses. Finally, in a room that Selena told me she always stayed in when the family came over, we opened a window and the shutters. We were high enough to see over the trees to the open gulf shore. I was trembling with excitement. We moved very close together. Selena looked at me very directly. I can still see that flower face and the lovely green eyes. Then she looked down—although this was never a reflex of embarrassment with her. She looked up again, and we embraced.

I remember everything these long years afterward—yet I remember nothing. The reality of it eludes me. There was the frantic fumbling, the undressing, the dusty bedcover, Selena's delicious little hands helping me, guiding me. After the fury of it, after the release, we lay there in that very still room, within the larger quiet of the house, for a very long time. Finally Selena said, rather crossly, I thought, "Colin, we must go. It's afternoon."

We dressed. I sat beside her on the bed. I thought she
seemed angry. I put my arms around her. "Selena," I whispered, "are you all right?"

She shrugged and didn't answer me.

"Selena," I asked again, "is anything the matter? Did I,
have I . . . ?"

Selena got up from the bed and started toward the door,
but she still didn't say anything.

I got up and followed her. "What is it, Selena?" I pleaded.
"Why are you angry with me? Selena, I'm sorry!"

"Why?" she asked, with her head still turned away from
me. "You did what you wanted to do, didn't you? There's
nothing to be sorry about."

I was confused and distraught. "But, Selena," I said to her,
"I love you. I'll always love you. You must marry me."

She didn't say anything for a while. Then, almost testily,
she said, "Colin, don't be silly. We're too young. We can't get
married. We're only fourteen." I was silenced by the adult
truth of this simple declaration. She started downstairs, and
I followed her.

I got the picnic basket and found the key to the cottage
on the kitchen table. She walked a bit ahead of me as we left.
I locked the door, and we started back down the path toward
the dock. The sunlight was coming through the trees from
the west now, and, as we walked along in silence, we could
hear the singing of the cicadas, that saddest of late-summer
sounds. When we got to Jackson's shack, we found him
dozing in a chair on its little porch. I wakened him and gave
him back the key, telling him that we had left everything
clean and neat, just as we'd found it. He seemed sleepy and
less willing to talk than he had been that morning; perhaps
he had taken some of the kidney medicine my father had
sent over and was in the throes of recuperation. But he came
down to the dock with us and helped me run up the sails
and cast off. I waved to him across the growing space of open
water, and he waved back.

Jackson. Thinking back on it, I realized I was never to see

him again in this life. But he remains a part of that memorable day.

We arrived back at St. Christopher's in much less time than we had taken to go the island in the morning, or so it seemed. Selena had remained silent during the trip, trailing her hand now and then in the water as we swept along, and not looking at me. As we docked, I felt more desolate than ever. We walked home from the dock. I tried some conversation, but she didn't seem interested. When I left her at her front door, I asked her if I could see her tomorrow. "Why not?" she responded, without much interest, and turned away. I said good-bye and left.

When I reached home, I was beside myself with guilt. Apparently what I had done had made Selena deeply unhappy, had alienated her from me. Besides, my activities of the day were a profound source of suppressed guilt in the presence of my parents. My mother asked me if we had had a good time. I said yes, everything was fine. My father inquired about Jackson. My mother thought maybe I didn't look too well, perhaps I'd had a little too much sun. I said no, I was well. I went to sleep worrying. Perhaps Selena would become pregnant. I would marry her then, immediately. Or perhaps her father would shoot me—for ruining his daughter? Or maybe Charles would have to take over this task? I had a hard time envisioning either in the role of the family avenger. My own family would probably disown me. I went to sleep on such thoughts.

The next day, early, I went over to the Randalls'. When Georgia came to the door, I studied her face for signs that might reflect the household's corporate displeasure at my existence, but I could see no evidence of this on her impassive countenance. "Miz Selena's done gone ovah to St. Andrews with Miz Mabel," Georgia told me. She further informed me that they would be gone for the day. Was Selena trying to avoid me? I wandered on back home and spent the day reading, or trying to read.

That evening my father dropped another bombshell on

my world—although this one was different. He brought
home the news that we would be moving to Boston in September, moving for good, leaving St. Christopher's. He had
been offered an excellent opportunity in a Boston law firm
by a former fellow law student at Harvard. My mother was
both upset at the thought of such a major change in our lives
and, at the same time, pleased at this opportunity for my
father. She was extremely ambitious for him. I can see now
that my father was an unusually courageous and daring
man. None of his legal contemporaries in St. Christopher's
would have changed their careers at the age of almost fifty,
breaking with their southern heritage to venture out into
that larger world of the North. Of course, if it came to that,
none of them would have been invited to do so. My father
was a very able man, as his subsequent career would dem-
onstrate.

Naturally, I was excited by the prospect of the move. For
one thing, I would now have the opportunity, I was told, to
go to the kind of school that Charles was going to. In fact,
Mr. Warren, my father's friend in Boston and his law partner
to be, had a son my age who was entering a New England
preparatory school that fall, and Mr. Warren had written the
headmaster there, on my behalf, for a fall entrance. We
should have word in a day or two about this. If I was admitted, it would mean that I would have to leave for Massachusetts in a week. My father would come with me and help me
get installed in the new school as well as attend to some
business of his own in Boston. He would return to Florida
later to help my mother wind things up here in St. Christopher's for their move north.

But the prospect of our leaving had its tragic side. It meant
that I would have to leave my love, my darling Selena. I would
have no chance to close the rift that had so suddenly, and to
me mysteriously, opened between us, to somehow win her
back. It was with these thoughts churning in my head that
I went to sleep that night.

It was not until two days later that I finally had a chance

to talk with Selena. She had gone somewhere else the next day with Lydia Bull, and the day after that her mother had taken her to Tallahassee. I was definitely being avoided. By the time I did see Selena, letters had come through from the headmaster stating that I had been admitted provisionally, pending receipt of my grade record from St. Christopher's. As I was a good student, there didn't seem much doubt that I would be going, and it was with a heavy heart that I went to tell Selena about it.

We sat in the Randalls' porch swing that night, and I told her my news. With tears in my eyes, I swore that no matter what had happened between us, I still loved her and would always love her, and that I would come back to her and that she must wait for me. Selena simply said, "You have to go away. There's nothing you can do about it."

I asked her if she still loved me, if she had forgiven me, if she would love me forever as I loved her. All she answered was that there was "nothing for you to be forgiven for." I was to leave two mornings later, and I asked to see her again the next evening. It would be my last chance to be with her—to say good-bye. The best she would do was to say, "Maybe."

I went over to the Randalls' that next evening, my last before my departure, and rang the bell. I watched anxiously through the glass panel by the door as Selena came to open it, but she didn't come out on the porch or ask me in. She said, quite calmly, that she would be busy that evening, that John Crawford was coming over and that they were going out. I pleaded for just a few minutes. She shook her head, saying that John would be along any minute and that it would be better for me to go. I started to leave, then hesitated at the top of the porch steps and looked back, hoping for a last-minute reprieve, or at least a last wave, a last glance. But Selena had closed the door.

My first years in my new environment were all-engaging and challenging ones. But I suppose this was a good thing. It kept me from thinking about Selena, those last few days together, and her shattering rejection of me. I made a good friend in Ted Warren, the son of my father's friend and, eventually, my roommate both at school and at Harvard. Through him I met others and was taken into a club in college. I became a creditable athlete, something of a track star. As it happened, this gave me the opportunity to travel down to Princeton and to the Penn Relays with the track team on two occasions during my college years. I saw Charles in Princeton on these trips.

Charles had grown tallish and slender. He was not as handsome as his father, although there was an ascetic refinement about his face that was arresting, even distinguished. He moved, I thought, too languidly, and he seemed to play at being an aesthete. He told me he was trying to decide on whether to concentrate in English literature or art history. I told him that I was already concentrating in archaeology. I think he found this seriousness on my part amusing and, possibly, a little vulgar. Wasn't I being a bit of a grind? I asked about Selena. He told me that she was at Sweet Briar, where she was flourishing, "living in a gay social whirl" was the way Charles put it. The others—his mother and father, the Bulls, the Crawfords—were all fine. Webbie was going to the University of Florida, which, in Charles's estimation, was about right for him. John Crawford was attending Tulane, in New Orleans, where he was a basketball star and "dazzling and seducing all the girls between games." I felt a residual twinge of jealousy on hearing John's name.

I can't quite remember what my feelings were about Selena by that time. They certainly weren't overpowering. I had fallen in love at least once during my prep school days, and, at the time of this conversation with Charles, was enjoying, or suffering through, this condition again. Selena was a memory. Still, it may be too easy to pass these emotional storms of our early youth off as inconsequential, of no lasting importance.

But when I decided to go back down to St. Christopher's for a summer's archaeological fieldwork, I'm certain that thoughts of Selena never entered into the decision. I wanted to do Florida archaeology for my doctoral dissertation, and I thought St. Christopher's would be a good place to do it from. Moreover, I was emotionally secure by being in love with Helen. She and I were engaged, and we were to be married on my return from Florida in September. Besides that, Selena had married John Crawford and had moved to New Orleans early in 1940. It would be unlikely that I would see her.

When I arrived in St. Christopher's at the beginning of June, Charles was still very much concerned with his father's disappearance of the previous winter. It seemed that James Randall had set out from St. Christopher's for New Orleans, by car and by himself, the day after Christmas of 1939. He had a business engagement there with Calhoun Lockwood, the art and antiquities dealer. According to Lockwood, and also to John Crawford, who was then in Lockwood's employ as a gallery attendant, James came to new Orleans on the evening of December 26, Tuesday, and put up at the St. Charles Hotel. The hotel records and testimony from employees verify that he spent the night of the twenty-sixth there, checking out shortly before noon on the twenty-seventh.

Lockwood stated that the last time he saw James Randall was when they lunched together the twenty-seventh at Antoine's. Crawford was also at the lunch, and he verified this. They parted after lunch, and it was Lockwood's and Crawford's understanding that James was then going to drive back to St. Christopher's. They said they never saw him again, nor were there any other reliable sightings of James Randall after that day. His automobile was eventually found parked on a side street in Pensacola. Presumably it had been there for three or four days.

Investigations into James's business with Lockwood yielded no clues. James had represented him on various legal matters involved with the import of art objects from Europe and Latin America. Just how the Lockwood Galleries of New Orleans had happened to pick as their representative a lawyer from a small and out-of-the-way place such as St. Christopher's was explained by Calhoun Lockwood, who said that he had met Randall through Crawford, and through Randall's daughter, Selena, Crawford's fiancée.

Charles had pursued his father's disappearance with the police and with various missing persons bureaus for several months, but, by the time I saw him that summer, he was beginning to get discouraged. No sign of James Randall had come to light, nor had any useful clue as to what might have happened to him been reported. He had no known connections or associations with Pensacola that would explain his car being found there. In New Orleans, through gossip sources, they learned the name of a woman he had been seeing off and on for the past ten years, but he clearly was not with her, and she professed to know nothing of his whereabouts. It looked like an unsolved case for the files.

Helen and I were married in the fall, after my return from St. Christopher's, and we began a family of our own in Boston. The war then intervened for all of us. Right after the war—on one of his trips up to the Northeast—Charles gave me the Randall family news: his mother had died and Selena had had a baby. Later, on another trip, he informed me that she and John had divorced. After that, I don't think I heard of her until Webbie, on his last trip to Boston, had said she had come back from New Orleans to live in St. Christopher's and "look after" Charles, and Charles had confirmed this— not the looking after part, which he had vehemently denied, but her presence in St. Christopher's—by saying that Selena was there with him and adding that "she looks forward to seeing you after all these years."

$\triangledown$

4

I AWAKENED TO BRIGHT SUNLIGHT, which came in slant-ingly through my windows and bounced off the walls and the ceiling. In the distance, I could hear church bells. I re-membered then that it was Sunday. I had slept soundly and dreamlessly and felt enormously refreshed. Then, lying there for a while, I indulged in memories, childhood and adoles-cent memories in which Selena figured so centrally.

Now, as I got up, things didn't seem so depressing as they had last night. To be sure, the shots fired through the win-dows at night were not something to be taken lightly, but I couldn't see Charles and Webbie exchanging nocturnal gun-fire over an imaginary treasure on St. James's Island. At least, I supposed it was imaginary; strange, though, the little gold alligator. But the miscreant responsible for the gunshots must be some local nut or juvenile delinquent. I hoped the police had a line on him. I felt better about Charles's scheme to dig over on the island. He couldn't go about it as he wanted, but I felt I'd be able to talk him into a more sensible way of proceeding.

While I shaved, I thought about breakfast, my favorite meal of the day. I firmly disapprove of the continental break-fast, adhering, instead, to the more ample English tradition. Could the St. Christopher House provide me with a half grapefruit, ham, two eggs lightly fried, toast, marmalade, and coffee? And grits on the side? I was sure they'd have hominy grits. I hadn't had any since I last left.

Downstairs, I picked up a Tallahassee paper and went into

the dining room. The waitress, after a friendly good morning, took my order. Yes, they did have grits. My breakfast developed as I had anticipated, but I resisted the temptation to add a side order of hashed brown potatoes to everything else. Sitting there contentedly, after I had enjoyed my morning repast, I looked over the Sunday paper. The national news coverage was slight, so, after the sports page and the comics, I turned to the editorial section and read a couple of dull statements generated by the doings of the state's legislature. Then I happened to glance up and saw two shirtsleeved, holstered, and side-armed police officers standing in the dining-room doorway, talking to the desk clerk. They were looking over at me in what I thought was a rather hard-eyed way. The desk clerk whispered something to them, and one of them said something I couldn't hear in reply. The policemen then turned and left the doorway, and the clerk came over to me.

"Mr. Edwards," he said in a hushed voice, "Chief Ellis, of the St. Christopher's Police, and Sheriff Larrabee would like to have a word with you as soon as you are finished. They're waiting for you out in the lobby."

I was, I must admit, surprised. A parking violation? I couldn't think of anything else I might have done since my arrival that would bring me into conflict with the law, but that hardly seemed sufficient to muster out the principal law enforcement officer of the city and his county opposite number. Could this have something to do with Charles's scheme to dig on the island? Had Selena or Webbie set the law on me well before the crime had been committed? Somehow, this seemed unlikely, too. I told the desk clerk that I would be right out. I signed my check and went to the lobby.

The chief and the sheriff were standing over in one corner, near a front window, carrying on a quiet conversation. Chief Ellis was of my height—medium—and of youngish middle age. He had, though, lost the waistline battle, the buckle of the belt which held his holster and revolver being well below the navel. Had he partaken too generously, for too long, of hominy grits? Sheriff Larrabee was a big man, taller than

Ellis, and flat stomached, but older. They both wore cowboy hats. The chief introduced himself with a soft-voiced southern politeness, first calling me Mr. Edwards and then asking if I wanted to be addressed as "Professor." I told him mister would do just fine. He then introduced me to Sheriff Jess Larrabee, who didn't say anything but gave me a hardfisted grip. It passed through my mind that he must be a kinsman of the late Miss Connie, the former proprietress of the St. Christopher House.

I invited them to sit down, and we did, on a sofa and a couple of overstuffed chairs which composed a little circle around a coffee table in that part of the lobby. I noticed the desk clerk, back at his post behind the reception sign, staring at us. He looked away in hasty embarrassment. Was he wondering if he had taken a criminal into his hotel? I asked my guests if they would like some coffee brought in. They both said that would be good, so I caught the clerk's attention, and he found a bellboy and gave him the order.

Chief Ellis removed his light gray ten-gallon hat, putting it down on the floor beside him. "Mr. Edwards," he said, "you arrived here in town yesterday afternoon?"

I confirmed this, and he went on. "Last night you paid a call on Mr. Charles Randall and his sister at their house?" I told him I had.

"And Mr. Webster Bull was also there?" I nodded and told him that, yes, Mr. Bull had stopped in for a part of the time I was there.

He frowned and then said, "Well, sir, I'm going to have to ask you some more questions, but before I do I better explain that there has been a . . . murder."

"Whaa-t?" I gasped. "Who? Was it Charles?"

"You mean Mr. Charles Randall, sir?" asked the sheriff, eyeing me critically. "No sir, Mr. Edwards, it's not Mr. Randall. It's Mr. Bull, Mr. Webster Bull, who was murdered."

To say I was bowled over would be an understatement. At that moment, the bellboy brought in a tray with our three cups of coffee, sugar, cream, and paper napkins, and served us on the coffee table. I waited until he had gone before asking my interrogators to tell me more. "My God!" I said. "What happened? Where?"

The sheriff left it up to the chief to answer me. The latter took a sip of his coffee and said, "Mr. Bull was shot last night, shot and killed at the front door of his house. We don't know who did it. Yet."

"When was this?"

"I think, maybe, Chief," said the sheriff, "that Mr. Edwards better tell us now just what time he left the Randall residence."

"Why, I left there . . . That is, I got up to go . . . We were in Mr. Randall's study . . . It was just ten minutes before twelve o'clock. I looked at my watch then. I suppose I drove away from the house at about twelve." I felt terribly guilty. Was I under investigation?

The sheriff took out a notebook, looked at it, and said, "Well that checks. The night boy here said you came in a twelve-ten A.M. You drove back here?" I said that I had.

The sheriff nodded and put the notebook back in his shirt pocket. "Mr. Bull was killed at twelve-forty A.M., give or take a minute or so. Mr. John Crawford, his brother-in-law, who was staying at the Bull residence, heard the shot, was awakened by it, and looked at his watch at the time. He went downstairs and discovered the body just inside the front door. He called an ambulance and the police station. The ambulance and one of the chief's deputies got there at the same time, sometime before one A.M. Mr. Bull was taken to the local hospital in the ambulance, but he was dead by the time they got him there. He'd been shot through the heart at close range."

Poor old Webbie. Why did I feel so guilty? Was it because I had never really liked him, and now he was dead?

"Mr. Edwards"—the voice of the sheriff roused me from this introspection—"just a moment ago, when the chief told you there had been a murder, you asked if Mr. Randall had been the one who was murdered. Why did you think that?"

He waited, with his calm, steady gaze upon me.

How much should I reveal, I asked myself, of what Charles had told me? Then I remembered Charles had said that Chief Ellis had been advised of the bullets being fired into the library. So I told them what Charles had told me about these incidents and explained that that was why I had reacted as I did.

Sheriff Larrabee said, "You may not have known, Mr. Edwards, but Mr. Randall is not the only one who has had bullets fired through his windows at night in the last couple of months."

I explained that Webbie—Mr. Bull—had told me some weeks before that someone had fired through his window at night.

"Yes," the sheriff told me, "a shot was fired through Mr. Bull's upstairs bedroom window one night a little over a month ago, and last week a bullet broke the window and hit the wall near Mrs. Harry Hedrickson as she was sitting in her living room at night." He went on to explain something that I already knew—that all of the these residences, including the Randalls', were within a block or two of one another—and added, "It appears that there may be some kind of nut trying to terrorize that neighborhood."

The sheriff continued with his questioning. "Would you mind telling us, Mr. Edwards, why you are down here in St. Christopher's?" It was not asked in an unfriendly way, but it made me feel, again, like the outsider that I was here.

"I came down at the suggestion of Mr. Charles Randall," I answered. "We have seen each other, off and on, on his visits north in the past years, and he has suggested more than once that I ought to come down to St. Christopher's and stay awhile. I lived here, in St. Christopher's, you know, a long time back. As I'm retired now, I thought I'd follow up on his invitation and come for a visit."

The sheriff nodded and said that he did know I came from St. Christopher's originally, that his granddaddy had known my father.

We had finished our coffee by that time, and Larrabee and Ellis got up to go. I walked out to their car with the officers. I asked about Mabel—Mrs. Bull—and they told me she was under sedation at home. John Crawford, her brother, was there, too, they added. I wanted to know more about Webbie's death, but I didn't know what to ask, or whether they would tell me if I did.

Back in the hotel, the clerk said to me, "It's a shocking business, isn't it, Mr. Edwards?" I agreed. He asked me if I'd known Mr. Bull for a long time, and I told him yes, for a very long time.

I went up to my room, looked up the Randalls' number, and dialed it. I wanted to talk to somebody about the murder. Selena answered the phone. She must have recognized my voice because before I could do more than ask for Charles, she said, "It's shocking, isn't it?"

"It's god-awful. I've just learned about it. The police chief and the sheriff came around to see me, here at the hotel. I presume they've been by to see you. They knew I had been at your house last night." Selena said yes, they'd been there and had a long talk with both Charles and herself.

"Selena," I asked, "I feel that I, that we, probably, should go by to see Mabel. What do you think? Do you know how she is?"

Selena didn't answer for a minute. Then she said yes, that probably the three of us should go over to the Bulls'. She had heard that the doctor had Mabel under sedation, but that was last night or early this morning. Maybe by this afternoon she'd feel like seeing someone. She, Selena, would call the Bulls' and see if we could pay an afternoon call. Then she added, "Why don't you stop by here, Colin, at, say, about three-thirty this afternoon, and you, Charles, and I can go over together. And, don't forget, Colin, you'll be having dinner with us afterwards?"

I agreed on both counts.

It was only ten o'clock in the morning, and I didn't feel like staying in my room, so I decided to go for a walk. I went downstairs and out of the hotel, strolling off in the residential direction and, eventually, toward the cemetery.

Poor Webbie, poor Webbie—I wished I had liked him better. But who in the hell, I asked myself, as I walked along, would have done Webbie in? The police hadn't really told me very much, had they? I supposed that was their way. Play it close to the vest. Suspect everybody. Was I a possible suspect? Maybe they thought that my return to the hotel at 12:10 A.M. was simply a blind, and that, after coming in and establishing my alibi, with the aid of the sleepy-eyed night clerk, I had dashed down a back fire escape somewhere, got back over to Webbie's, by car or on foot, drilled him at his front door by 12:40 A.M., and vanished into the night before the law arrived. But no, they couldn't be silly enough to believe that. For one thing, what would have been my motive?

It struck me then that the principal difficulty in solving the "murder of Webster Bull" might very well be the lack of a motive—or at least a visible motive—for the crime. Who could be the chief suspects in the slaying of one of St. Christopher's leading citizens in the doorway of his own home? Would Charles or Selena be on the list? What would be their motives? Charles's irritation at Webbie for trying to keep him from pursuing his treasure-hunting scheme on St. James's Island still didn't seem a sufficient reason for firing a shot through his window or murdering him at his front door. Selena? But she, according to Charles, was hand in glove with Webbie in all kinds of ways. Why would she kill off her own accomplice, or, if Charles was right, her lover? Or could this be some kind of crime of passion, with Selena slaying her lover for some hidden reason? Thinking of Webbie, the idea seemed too ridiculous to consider.

What about the island and the ten million dollars, soon to be paid to its owners? Webbie was one of them. This might be a motive for bumping him off. Who would benefit? Would this help Selena or Charles? No, not if I had understood both Webbie and Charles correctly on the nature of the Island Trust. According to what they had said, the surviving Bull

and Randall heirs would benefit equally by family, five million to the heirs, or surviving heir, of each family, at the time
of the sale, presumably a month from now. Charles and
Selena had their five million secure, and Webbie's death
didn't increase their share of the sale price.

Whose share would it increase? Certainly not Mabel's.
Her only share had been through Webbie in the first place,
and now he was gone, out of the tontine before he could take
up his two and a half million to leave to any heirs. John
Crawford's only chance to have benefited would have been
through his sister's share, which now she wouldn't receive.
She would, however, inherit Webbie's estate, undoubtedly
the largest in St. Christopher's, even without the proceeds
from the island sale. That might be a motive for murder for
someone as feckless as John seemed to be, at least judging
from Charles's remarks about him. Even so, though, John's
possible source of revenue here would have to be mediated
through his sister, not the kind of prospect for coming into
wealth that would tempt one to murder.

But whose share of the island's sale did Webbie's death
increase? Lydia's, of course. Webbie's only surviving sibling,
his sister, Lydia Bull Hedrickson. Lydia's portion would now
go from two and a half to five million dollars. Here, on paper
at least, was a motive. Would sister kill brother for this?
Would fat, unattractive Lydia have rubbed out fat, unattractive Webbie for an additional two and a half million dollars?

I hadn't seen Lydia for forty-five years, and I rather
doubted that her appearance had improved or her personality changed much in that time. But I'd have had a hard time
picking her as a murderess of her own brother. Hedrickson?
Harry Hedrickson, her husband? Of course! Here was the
ideal villain—redneck Harry, the man from the wrong side
of the tracks. Through Lydia he would now come to control
five million dollars of the island's sale price. Or one would
assume he would. (There was no use developing these suspicions by halves.) So there it was. Or was it? As I walked
along, I wondered if the police had thought of Harry Hedrick-

son—thought of him, that is, following my brilliant line of deductive reasoning.

How about a more or less complete stranger as the murderer? With robbery as the motive. But that didn't make much sense in Webbie's case. A robber wouldn't wake someone up in the middle of the night by ringing his doorbell, then shoot him at his front door, and not rob him or the house. Maybe it wasn't robbery. The police had said, hadn't they, that there might be some nut going around. I wondered, again, if the police had any line on St. Christopher's eccentrics like this.

I had walked now to the edge of the cemetery. It was a beautifully shaded old place, the live oak trees festooned with Spanish moss. I followed along the crushed-shell roadway leading into it. The burial grounds, naturally, were more extensive than they had been in my boyhood, but here, in the old part, were the familiar graves and tombstones. The Randall lot had a large obelisk marking the graves of old Alexander (1812–1892) and his wife. Nearby were Great-uncle Charles—Major Charles (1840–1921)—and his wife. I could remember Great-uncle Charles's funeral. There were still some Civil War veterans around then, although, as I recall, they were too feeble to fire a volley over the grave of their departed leader. This was done, instead, by some World War I veterans. I had sat by Selena at the graveside burial service. Not far away was the Bull lot, dominated by the stone of Hezekiah, Webbie's great-grandfather and the contemporary of Alexander Randall.

A little farther along I came to the Edwards lot, where my Grandfather Edwards—Captain William B. Edwards, CSA (1842–1922)—and his wife were buried. All the stories I remembered about Captain Edwards were sensible ones, including his dislike of his military title. My father was sensible, too. He was buried in Cambridge, Massachusetts, as was my mother. As I walked back through the cemetery, I thought that I was not as sensible as my Edwards forebears. Had their hard common sense been diluted with Randall strangeness in my case? My mother, though—Genevieve Randall—had always been considered one of the more sensible of the Randalls. Maybe that, together with the no-nonsense Edwards genes, would save me—although salvation now, at my age, would be something to be enjoyed largely in the afterlife.

I got back to the hotel a little past noon and went into the bar. I thought I'd partake of a bit of dry vermouth and soda before lunch. There were two men at a table in one corner. One, gray haired, had his back to me and was talking in hushed, earnest tones to the other, who was facing me. The latter was, perhaps, in his forties, swarthy, dark haired, and tough looking. He didn't say much but nodded, now and then, at what his companion was telling him. I ordered, and the bartender brought me my drink. After a bit, the men at the other table appeared to have finished their one-sided conversation and got up to leave. The younger, tough-looking guy passed by me first, then the older man. The latter was much taller than his companion, well over six feet in spite of a stoop. He also looked familiar. He recognized me first, though, turned back, and asked, "Colin Edwards?" I acknowledged that I was, and he said, "I'm John Crawford. It's been a long time."

I stood up, and we shook hands. The last time I had seen John was in 1940 when he had come over to the island while I was digging there—and had not been very friendly. John had been very good looking then, with a blond handsomeness that also had a kind of blankness about it, a blankness of the eyes and the expression of the face. I can remember thinking of him as being like a Greek statue, a blank-eyed Greek god. Now, the face was lined and haggard, from, I supposed, age, dissipation, disappointment, sorrow, and God knows what. But, in thinking this, I realized that John and I were the same age and that I wasn't all that youthful looking either. John was wearing an open-necked shirt that was both ragged around the collar and not altogether clean.

He turned and called to his companion, who came back

to where we were, and John introduced him as Pierre Mc-
Govern. We shook hands. I nodded a how-do-you-do to
McGovern, and he responded with a surly look. He was
dressed like some kind of boatman, in a dark, turtlenecked
jersey and stained white cotton pants, and he carried a dirty-
looking yachting cap. McGovern, John explained, was the
caretaker out on St. James's Island; this, then, was the owner
of the dog who had dug up the gold figurine that Charles had
shown me last night.

I wanted to talk with John about the details of what had
happened at Webbie's, and this seemed like an opportunity,
but I didn't relish the idea of having his companion in on
our talk.

"John," I asked, "is there any chance of our getting together for a meal? I'd like to have a chance to talk. It's been
more than forty years." John hesitated and looked at Mc-
Govern. Maybe he gave the latter some sort of a signal, for
McGovern muttered something about having errands to run
"before he went back"—I presumed he meant to the island—
and took off. This seemed to clear the way. "Why can't we
make it lunch—right here—today?" I wanted to know. He
agreed, and we went into the dining room.

After we had ordered, we carried on some polite conversation addressed to catching up on each other's lives and activities over the past forty-five years, but it was obvious to
both of us that there was something more pressing to talk
about. I began: "Tell me, John, about this horrible business
of Webbie's death. The police were over here to see me this
morning, but I didn't get many details. I take it you were
there on the scene or close to it?"

He didn't seem loath to talk about it. "Yes, I was there in
the house, as you've probably heard," he told me. "I got into
town about seven last evening. I'd driven over from New
Orleans and hoped to be here sooner, but I had to go over to
the island to see McGovern. He's staying over there in the
Bull cottage."

Previous caretakers had stayed down on the bay beach,

where Jackson had had his shack. I also wondered why John seemed to be so much involved with the island's caretaker. I presumed that he was still paid jointly by the Bulls— Webbie and Lydia—and the Randalls—Charles and Selena. Maybe John had been deputized in some way by Webbie to check on him. I didn't inquire.

"I had supper with Webbie and Sis," John went on. "Webbie took off right after this to go to the Randalls' to see you. I stayed home with Sis. Well, hell—I didn't want to see Selena—not that I'd been invited. I suppose it was a little after ten o'clock when Webbie got back. He said he was tired, and went on up to bed. Sis and I followed later. Sis and Webbie have separate bedrooms on the side of the house away from the street. I was in a guest bedroom on the street side. I must have gone to sleep fairly early. All I know is that I was awakened by a shot—a hell of blast—but I was right over the front door. For a moment, I wondered what it was. I looked at my watch. It was twelve-forty. I looked out the window, but I didn't see anyone. I couldn't see the front door, which was right below me and covered with a little porchlike roof, but I could see that the porch light was on. I didn't hear anyone else moving about in the house, but I thought I'd better go down and investigate. As I came down the stairs into the living room, I could see Webbie lying in the entrance hall, just inside the door. He was in pajamas and a bathrobe, and when I got there I could see he had been shot, right in the chest. The door was open, but the screen was still latched. I could see the bullet hole in the screen. Well, I called the hospital—although I didn't think there was much hope for Webbie. He was awfully still. And I called the police."

"You never heard a doorbell ringing, before the shot?" I asked him.

John shook his head. "No," he told me, "and neither did Sis. As a matter of fact, she didn't even hear the shot, but she was farther away from it than I was. I suppose, though, that the bell must have rung, that Webbie must have heard it, and that he went down to answer it. There is a peephole in the front door, and he could have seen who it was. He'd turned on the porch light. But when he opened the door they must have let him have it."

"Had the porch light been left on, or did he turn it on?"

"No," said John, "the porch light wasn't on when Webbie came back around ten. He must have turned in on to answer the door."

"Then it sounds as though he must have recognized or known the person," I murmured and then went on. "I have heard, from both Webbie and Charles, that someone has been going around shooting through the windows at night in that part of town. It had happened to both of them, and the police told me this morning that it had happened to Lydia Bull—Lydia Hedrickson. I don't suppose the police have any idea who it could be?"

John didn't comment on any of this but glumly shook his head.

"Well, I'm terribly sorry," I told him, "and please convey my sympathies to Mabel. Incidentally, the Randalls and I— that is Charles, Selena, and I—may stop by this afternoon. Selena said she was going to call Mabel sometime after lunch and ask if it would be all right."

John didn't reply but assumed a grim expression. Our plates were taken away. Dessert was served, and we ate in silence for few minutes. Then John looked at me, in an accusatory way, and said, "I hope you haven't been encouraging Charles in this damn-fool scheme of his to dig in the Indian mound over on the island."

I must admit that I didn't take this too well. What business was it of his? Presumably, his late brother-in-law could have been legitimately concerned, and I supposed, so could Lydia, but the only other people to have a private proprietary interest in the matter were Charles and Selena. I could hardly imagine the state of Florida's interests or archaeological ethics to be concerns of John. I told him all of this, and he got mad. Then I went on to tell him that I would advise Charles about the matter as I saw fit and that on the archaeological aspects of the question I was better qualified than he, or any member of the families involved, or anybody else in St. Christopher's, for that matter, to advise. He didn't like it.

We got up from the table in silence. I walked to the hotel entrance with him and he left without saying thanks for lunch or even looking back. I saw him drive away in an old, green, beat-up-looking four-door sedan.

What the hell? Why was he so steamed up about that damned mound? Here John's brother-in-law was murdered. His sister was in shock. But John didn't seem as concerned about those things as he was about giving me unsolicited advice on archaeology! I suppose my academic *amour propre* was offended. Simmer down, Professor, I told myself.

Upstairs, in my room, I had a rest, took a shower, and changed clothes, then I set out to meet Selena and Charles for our call on Mabel. I walked to the Randalls', and when I arrived Charles and Selena were waiting for me in wicker chairs on the porch. Selena said that she had telephoned the Bulls' earlier in the afternoon and that a servant had told her that Mrs. Bull would expect us at four. As we still had some time, I sat with them on the porch for a while.

"What a business," I said. "Who would want to shoot Webbie?"

"Oh, I suppose lots of people" was Charles's facetious reply. "He did get on one's nerves."

"Still, it was rather bad form," I said.

Selena suddenly lashed out at us. "You both disgust me! You've always acted so damned superior to Webster! And now that he's dead . . . you . . . you . . . Oh, you're both in such bad taste! He was much nicer than you'll ever know!" Those lovely vixen eyes flashed. She was wearing a green silk dress that matched them. I could see her—well over sixty years before—in a green pinafore, in the sandbox, out by the Randall carriage house, furiously putting Charles and me to rights over some sand castle transgression.

I felt one of those quick flashes of jealousy at her affectionate remarks about Webbie. Poor Webbie. Guiltily, I tried

to make amends by steering the conversation in a more serious direction. "The police were around to the hotel to see
me this morning," I told them. "They didn't tell me many
particulars, but I saw John Crawford at the hotel, at lunch,
and he told me his story. Apparently, Webbie and gone downstairs to answer the door, in the middle of the night, and the
visitor shot him. He may have known the person."

"How do they arrive at that latter conclusion?" asked
Charles.

"Well," I said, "it appears as though Webbie turned the
porch light on, and very likely looked out through the peephole and saw who it was before he opened the door."

"What a surprise for the poor old boy" was Charles's response.

To forestall another outburst by Selena at what still appeared to me to be unseemly levity on Charles's part, I
quickly said I'd understood that the police had been over to
see them, too.

Charles said they had and concluded by adding, "It looks
as though they have oceans of suspects. Either Selena or I
could have nipped over and done it; John or Mabel could have
gone down their back stairs and come around to the front
door, let Webbie have it, and been up the back stairs again in
the winking of an eye; and even you Colin, are not altogether
in the clear. It's less than a half mile from the Bulls' to the
hotel, and you used to be pretty fast on your feet."

"Charles," I asked him, ignoring that last bit, "why didn't
you tell me that a bullet had been fired through Lydia's window, too, when you were telling me about what had happened to you and we spoke about it also happening to
Webbie? Sheriff Larrabee said that Lydia had been subjected
to a similar scare just a week ago."

Selena said, "As you may have noticed, Colin, my brother
is never terribly interested in what happens to other people,
only to himself."

"Why, Sel, how can you say that? I'm absolutely fascinated by all the things that happen to other people. You must

know that. Think how curious I am about your various nocturnal comings and goings."

Selena didn't say anything to this. I looked at my watch and said we had better be going. We walked the block or so to the Bulls' house. At their front door, I noticed the bullet hole in the screen. A uniformed and aproned young black maid met us and admitted us to the living room. Unlike the somewhat dilapidated decor of the Randall abode, the Bull living room appeared to have been appointed and decorated relatively recently, undoubtedly by a professional, perhaps someone down from Tallahassee, or more likely up from Miami. John Crawford was already in the room. Since lunch he had put on a wrinkled seersucker jacket and a necktie, which made him look even more bedraggled. Selena gave him an unsmiling "Hello, John," which he acknowledged with a glum nod before offering perfunctory handshakes to Charles and myself. He still looked put out with me, presumably as the result of our disagreement at lunch.

Mabel came down the stairs then. I had remembered her as a young woman, in 1940, as tall and blond, like John. She, too, had had that blank, dead-eyed, Crawford handsomeness, which had aged even less well with her than with him. She was dressed in black and had been crying. I felt sorry for her. She was alone now. I went forward and took her hand, and she did the same with Charles but not with Selena. She asked us to sit down, and the maid brought in a tea tray and put it on a table before Mabel.

It didn't take long to see that our visit was not going to be an easy one. I expressed my deepest sympathies to Mabel and said how shocking the whole business was. She looked at me like she was going to cry some more, but she didn't say anything. The maid passed tea, cream, sugar, lemon, and little sandwiches around. Everyone stirred and sipped in silence. I asked about the service and was told by John that it would be on Tuesday, at St. Luke's Episcopal Church. Were they expecting relatives from out of town, I inquired. I can't remember what the answer was to this or to some of my

other questions in the same vein. Whatever the responses
were, John gave them; his sister sat silently, staring at nothing.
This was heavy going. I looked over at Selena and
Charles in a silent appeal for assistance, but they avoided
my eye.

Somehow we got through it, although I doubt we were
there more than a half hour. Selena brought it to a close by
getting up, putting her cup back on the tea tray, and saying
to Mabel to please let her know if there was anything she
could do to help in any way. That, I guess, brought it on.

Mabel, without rising from her chair, and with a sudden
look of intense hatred on her face, virtually spat out at
Selena: "You bitch, don't ask me if there is anything you can
do! Haven't you done enough already? You brought on
Webster's death! You seduced him! You ruined his life . . .
you . . . you Jezebel!"

I was stunned, and John was, too. We both got up. He
went over to Mabel and put his arm around her shoulders.
Mabel put her head down and started to sob, but I felt more
protective of Selena. Before I could say or do anything,
though, she turned on her heel and, with a frozen look on
her face, walked out the front door, slamming it behind her.
Charles was the only one who seemed more or less unaffected.
He didn't get up from his chair right away. I don't
know quite how to describe his expression except to say that
he didn't register any particular shock or surprise. I did the
best I could. I told John to let us know if we could do anything,
thanked him for the tea, and said we would see him
at the service. Charles got up then, and he and I left.

We caught up with Selena, who was walking swiftly toward
home. I told her I was awfully sorry about what had
happened. I felt some responsibility for it all in that it had
been my idea to pay this courtesy call. Selena didn't say
anything but walked along with her head held high, staring
straight in front of her. When we got to the Randalls', I
wondered if Selena might not want to cancel the dinner to
which they had invited me. I was about to suggest this, but

as soon as we were on the porch, she turned to me and said, "Colin, wouldn't you like a drink? Scotch? I know Charles and I want one." I must say, the idea more than appealed to me at that juncture. We went back to the library, Charles brought out a bottle, and Selena asked the maid to get us glasses and ice. We drank in silence for a while.

Finally, Charles looked over at me and inquired, "Have you recovered now, dear boy?" And then, "I have never seen Cousin Mabel quite so animated in my life, have you? She obviously misses the departed, strange as it may seem."

Selena went over to the table, put some more ice in her glass, and poured herself another drink. Not till then did she say, "Stop it, Charles! The poor woman is crushed. If she wants to take her grief out on me, let her do it."

Selena made no attempt to explain anything in Mabel's denunciation of her, not that these topics—sexual seduction and, I guess, murder—would have made for easy conversation. What did Mabel mean, I wondered, by telling Selena "you brought on Webster's death"? Was this a direct accusation of murder? I suppose it was close enough. I found myself studying Selena. She was, even now, an extraordinarily beautiful woman. Did she know how well the green dress set off that beauty? Of course she did. James's daughter, and Marie's, she had inherited beauty from both sides, and she was not averse to heightening it. For me, her attraction went beyond sheer beauty, though. I couldn't explain it. It went back too far in my life.

The servant, a nice-looking, middle-aged black woman named Mildred, who was both cook and maid to them, told us dinner was ready, and we went into the old, dark dining room. I can't recall what we had to eat. During the meal, I remember asking Charles about Pierre McGovern. Where did he come from?

"Oh, he's someone John dug up for us, some Irish-Cajun tough, I guess—someone that he knew in New Orleans" was Charles's first reply to my question. But he went on to explain, "Webbie had been looking after the island caretaker matter for some time, and John recommended McGovern to him. I think McGovern had been some sort of heavy-work employee, or something like that, at the Lockwood Galleries. Just why he was willing to take on this kind of job, I have no idea. His salary, of which I pay half and Webbie the other half, isn't much. Given his gangsteresque appearance, it may well be that he wanted to get out of New Orleans for one reason or another."

"How long has he been on the job?" I asked.

"Oh, not very long," said Charles. "Probably replaced Thompson about three years ago. He had the job for over forty years."

I remembered Thompson, a young and obliging black man with a wife and two or three children. They'd rebuilt Jackson's old shack into a larger and more comfortable little house. "When did old Jackson leave? Wasn't it just before I came down that summer?"

"Yes, a few months before. In the winter, I think. Don't you remember? I told you about it when you were here then. Jackson just wandered off, disappeared. His dory was found over on the mainland, where he'd left it when he'd gone over there, but he never showed up again."

"You never heard anything more about him? No one made a search? Didn't he have any relatives?"

"None that we ever heard about," answered Charles. "No one inquired."

"Didn't anyone ever inform the police?"

Charles said he didn't know, probably not. I thought of the South, as it used to be, in 1940.

We finished dessert and had coffee in the dining room. I refused a brandy and left early. Charles and Selena saw me to the door. I said to Charles that I would give him a ring in the morning, and they said good night. It was still light out, some minutes short of eight o'clock, and I walked back unhurriedly to the hotel. On arriving there, it had been my intention to go directly up to my room, read a bit, and go to sleep, but the clerk at the desk told me that I had a visitor.

I reflected that I was becoming a very popular man on my second day back in my old hometown. This was my third visitation today, counting the lawmen and John. This time the visit was not to leave me in a very good mood. The desk clerk added that my new guest was in the bar.

I went into the bar, where, except for the bartender, there was only one person, seated at a table in the corner, facing me. He got up as I walked toward him. He was tall and thin and had what can best be described as a *boiled* complexion, lobster red and pockmarked. A few strands of sandy gray hair were plastered sidewise over a high, balding dome. He was dressed conservatively in a dark gray suit and a nondescript tie. His shirt collar was much too big for his turkeylike neck. He had small, pale blue, unfriendly eyes. He extended his hand as I came over to him; I shook it—a large, knobbly, bony hand—as he said, "Well, it's the great Harvard professor, isn't it? Come back to pay us country folks the courtesy of a visit."

It was a voice with malice in it. I could feel myself freezing. I'd had a hard day, at least according to my standards, and it was not the time for such a confrontation. I didn't say anything. He was drunk and swaying slightly. He continued, in a slurred, country-southern speech. "You don't remember me, of course, do you? I'm Harry Hedrickson. We went to school here together, but I wasn't one of your kind." He gave a mock-formal bow, pulling out a chair for me at his table. "Please sit down, Professor Edwards."

God! I thought. We must have rubbed it in when we were kids to make him carry a load like this for over sixty years. I was about to walk away, and I should have. Instead I accepted his offer and sat down. He sagged back into his own chair. Well, so this was Harry Hedrickson, old redneck Harry. This was what Lydia—poor, fat, homely, rich Lydia—married. I'm sure the disgust on my face was not well disguised. Redneck Harry leaned forward across the table and said, "What are you coming down here for, Professor? To help your high and mighty and sissy friend, Charles Randall, carry out some nonsense over there on St. James's Island? If you are, you shouldn't have bothered. Let me tell you something, Professor. My wife, Lydia, controls half of that island now, and I represent her. You're not going to dig an Indian mound over there without my permission, and I'm not about to give it to you." He belched, put his head down, and then looked up at me with boozed-up, pale blue eyes.

"Mr. Hedrickson," I replied, "from what I understand, that island will soon be the property of the state of Florida. I am quite sure that their archaeologists are fully competent to make all the decisions about that mound."

"Look here," he said, "I'm not without political influence in this state. I'll go to the governor, if need be, and he'll back me up. I know what's best for Florida . . . not you!"

At this point, I am afraid I lost my composure. "Hedrickson," I said, "you have one hell of a presumption to challenge me about any of this." I got up and walked away from the table. The next thing I heard was a crash behind me, including the splintering of glass. I turned and saw Hedrickson sprawled on the floor. The bartender told me later that he had started out after me, but in his drunkenness he had tripped on a chair leg and fallen flat, knocking his drink off the table. I saw the bartender helping him up; Hedrickson was staggering and waving his arms, with the bartender half-holding him back and half-holding him up. "Lemme at the son of a bitch, the high and mighty Harvard son of a bitch," he was muttering. "He can't talk to me like that. This is my country down here, not his!" The desk clerk, with an alarmed look, came into the bar, presumably in response to all the noise.

"Are you all right, sir?" the clerk asked me. I told him that I was, that Mr. Hedrickson had fallen. I said I was going up to my room and left. As I climbed the stairs, I thought I was probably lucky redneck Harry hadn't done me bodily harm. The titanic battle of the septuagenarians! What an edifying sight that would have been!

After I got into my bed that night, I wondered, again, what

was the matter with these people. In one day, I had been given serious advice, or warning, was more like it, by John Crawford and now by Harry Hedrickson, not to help Charles Randall dig into an Indian mound. One would have thought that Harry, at a time like this, would have been too concerned about his brother-in-law and business partner's death to come over to the hotel and carry on to me about something so relatively minor. Something was worrying them—and worrying Selena, too. Was it just the matter of disputing the island's sale to the state? I supposed it could be. But I went to sleep wondering about it.

$\triangledown$

5

THE MORNING AFTER MY near-fight with Harry Hedrick-son was Monday, the third of June, and it dawned cloudy, although rain didn't seem to be imminent. I hadn't slept quite as well as I had the night before, and I didn't feel as optimistic about Charles's intended adventure on the island as I had yesterday morning. What I wanted to do now was to go to St. James's with Charles. This seemed like a good time to make a preliminary trip and look things over. I got up, put on some light khaki chino trousers, a pair of heavy brogues, a shirt and neck scarf, and a cardigan sweater. I had breakfast right after the dining room opened at six-thirty. Then I went outside and walked around, going down near the shore. It was cooler than it had been yesterday, and my sweater felt good at this time of the morning. I went back to my room and read until eight-thirty, when I thought it would be all right to call Charles. This time *he* answered the phone.

I said, "Look, Charles, I thought it might be helpful if you and I went over to the island today and spent some time looking around. It's been a long time since I was there. I'd like to see the place again and, particularly, to have a look at the mound. I think we should do this before I try to bring in any archaeological colleagues. This would be a good time to do it. The funeral isn't until tomorrow."

Charles said sure, he thought it could be arranged for us to go over. He'd have to see about getting a boat, but that wouldn't be too difficult, and we could leave by about ten. Then he said, "Colin, what do you mean about 'bringing in archaeological colleagues'? I haven't agreed to anything like that."

"I know you haven't, Charles," I told him, "but it's only fair to make it clear to you, if I am to be associated with you in any digging, that we'll have to bring someone else in eventually." There was only silence, so I continued. "We don't need to settle the exact nature of their, or my, participation now, Charles. We can do that later, when we, or you alone, decide what you want to do. All I'm suggesting now is that we go over and have a preliminary look around."

Charles said all right. He would have to make a phone call to arrange things but would be back to me. I asked him to bring along a copy of my book, *Archaeological Excavations at St. Christopher's, Florida*. I knew there should be a copy in the Randall library because I'd sent him one when it first came out.

Charles called back in about a half hour to say that he had arranged for a boat, which was being readied for us down at the dock. He'd had to rent one. There was one that belonged to the island, that is, to the Randall and Bull St. James's Island Estate Trust, but McGovern must have been off in it somewhere, because Charles hadn't been able to raise him on the phone. I asked about the phone, and Charles said yes, the island was connected now by phone, and the phone was in the Bull cottage, where McGovern lived. I said I was impressed with this march of progress.

As I was about to hang up, Charles surprised me by asking, "Will it be all right with you if Selena comes along? She'll bring a lunch for us."

I assured him I would be delighted, although I thought to myself it was the last thing I'd have expected, given her role, at least as described by Charles, as the sworn enemy of his mound project. What was the relationship between these two? Could Charles really believe that Selena was trying to have him done away with? Or had the two of them gotten into such a brother-sister tiff that Charles had lost all sense of proportion? Whatever, I was pleased because I wanted to see more of Selena.

They picked me up shortly after this at the hotel, in a little sedan, with Selena driving, and we drove down to the waterfront. When we got there, Charles went into a small boathouse and came back with the proprietor, who led us down a wharf to a small inboard motor launch. "It's all gassed up, Mr. Randall," the proprietor told us. Then he commiserated with us, briefly, on Webbie's death. "Terrible thing about Mr. Bull, wasn't it? Right in his own home. I hope they catch whoever did it."

We got into the boat, with Charles at the wheel, and roared away on our western course. I was sitting up front with Charles, with Selena in a back seat. She was wearing slacks, in which she looked amazingly trim, a dark blue, nauticallike jacket, and a bright kerchief tied over her head. I looked back at her. She smiled at me, but her eyes were hidden behind dark glasses. I wondered if she could be remembering that much slower trip we had made in the little sailboat so many years ago. Probably not. Women, I reflected, are much less sentimental than men. The sound was calm that morning, and we made good time. Charles, in spite of his ascetic and not altogether healthy appearance, looked at ease and happy behind the wheel of the boat, which he handled with competence.

By ten-thirty we were in the narrow channel separating the western tip of the island from the mainland. Viewed from across the water, the caretaker's cottage looked about the same as it had the last time I'd seen it. We turned our boat in toward it and the little dock below. There was another boat—the island's boat, Charles told me—tied up at the dock, but no one was in sight. Charles gave our horn a number of blasts, but no one appeared. Then he cut the motor as we drew closer and got out a boat hook to bring us alongside the dock. The island's boat, which was tied up ahead of us, was larger than the one we had come in and looked like a much more expensive craft. I couldn't help but wonder why they—Charles and Webbie, I presumed—had purchased it. It was my impression that neither of them spent much time on the island anymore.

I climbed out onto the dock and helped Charles secure our boat. The old caretaker's cottage was the construction that had been new in 1940, when Thompson and his family had lived in it. It was locked up, and a look through the windows showed it to be unoccupied and dusty. "I don't think McGovern uses it much," explained Charles. "As I told you, he lives in the Bull cottage now." I wondered to myself, again, why he did and why Charles and, I presumed, Webbie and John, had provided this roughneck with such superior quarters.

We started up the path that led through the woods toward the mound and the cottages. I was walking in front, Charles at the rear, and Selena in the middle. Suddenly a dog began to bark, and a large mongrel came bounding down the trail toward us. Then McGovern appeared on the path ahead of us armed with an AK-47, or some kind of automatic rifle, which was pointed directly at me. There was the noise of someone walking on the path behind him, and John Crawford came into view.

"Easy does it, Pierre!" he said. McGovern kept the rifle up a few seconds more—longer, I thought, than was necessary—and gave me a hard grin. John walked around McGovern and came up to us. "Sorry. Pierre heard a boat coming into the landing, and he thought he better go see who it was. We've had quite a few trespassers pull in here lately, now that summer's coming."

I thought the AK-47 seemed a little excessive as a defense against the occasional motorboating tourist who might stop off to have a picnic or a look at the island, but it wasn't my island, and I didn't say anything.

John seemed a little annoyed to see us. "I didn't know you were coming over today, Charles," he said.

"Oh, we just decided to at the last minute," Charles told him. "We wanted to take a look at the Indian mound. I telephoned this morning, a little before nine, but I couldn't raise anyone."

John, scowling, said, "We had to go off somewhere for a

while. That's probably why we missed the call." Then he asked, somewhat suspiciously, "How long are you going to be over here?"

Charles ignored the question and asked one of his own. "The Indian mound lies off to the left here somewhere, doesn't it?" And he pointed off into the bush in that direction.

Just as Charles asked this, we heard footsteps on the path behind John and McGovern, and two more men appeared, walking single file. The one in front was scrawny looking and middle aged, with a high, hook-shaped nose. He was carrying a heavily packed duffel bag. He was followed by a tall, very muscular, light-colored black man, wearing a dark leather jacket dotted with metal studs as well as silvered, opaque sunglasses in the style of the Tonton Macoutes. This second man carried a carton, of liquor-case size, on one shoulder. John heard them and turned around. He looked both annoyed and embarrassed. The he said, indicting the hook-nosed white man, "This is Hebert," and followed this by introducing the big man in the silvered glasses in a similarly brief and perfunctory way as "Tiger." Neither of the newcomers, who had halted on the path, said anything, nor did we. Finally, John said, "Well, we'll leave you for a while. Pierre has to take Hebert and Tiger over to the mainland, and then he's got some business in town. I've got to get back there, too," he added, "so I may not see you here again today, but McGovern will be back later this afternoon . . . if you need anything."

I puzzled over what the villainous-looking McGovern could do for us. Fire a few rounds at our feet to jolly us up? With John leading the way and the other three and the dog following, they continued on down the path toward the dock.

When they were out of sight, I said, "What unusual people you meet over here, Charles. Where do they come from?"

Charles laughed. "Oh, they're business associates of Selena's ex-husband—from New Orleans, I'm told."

I looked over at Selena, but she avoided my glance. I half-expected her to come back at Charles in some way, but she didn't. As she had been behind me when McGovern confronted us, and then John and his companions came along, I hadn't seen her immediate reactions to them. Had she seen these characters before?

I decided not to go into the matter and, instead, to turn to archaeology. I went on up the trail and then bore off to the left, picking my way through the palmettos and higher bush. In a few minutes we came to the mound, climbing up the west slope of it. It was, as I had told Charles on the first night I saw him here, a sizable little mound, at least six feet above the surrounding ground level. In the distance, we could hear the motor of the island's boat starting up. McGovern, John, and their friends were departing.

My old excavations were still plainly visible. I had, in effect, sliced away the eastern half of the original mound, piling the dump dirt in back of me in a low, spread-out ridge as I had gone along in my profiling or slicing operation. I asked Charles if he had brought my old monograph, and he took it out of the picnic basket he was carrying and handed it to me. I hadn't looked at a copy for a long time, but, as I opened it and read some of my familiar sentences, the experience of writing it came back to me, as did the fieldwork on which the writing had been based.

I turned to the chapter on the St. James's Island Mound, a substantial section of the more than 500-page book. I read over my résumé of the recent history of the mound, or what little we knew of it. Moore's was the first definite reference to its presence. It was not clear if Moore had actually seen the mound or merely heard of it, but he was quite specific in saying, with some pique, that he "was unable to obtain permission to excavate there by the owners of the Island, Messrs. Thomas Bull and Charles Randall, gentlemen whose dedication to science was less than mine," to quote his words.

I read over my description of the mound as it had been when I had examined it in the summer of 1940, detailing the mound's diameter and height and general appearance.

I read on. What was this? I had noted that

> although there has never been any archaeologically
> reported digging in the St. James's Island Mound, and
> we know that Clarence B. Moore did not excavate here,
> there are, nevertheless, signs of what look like a rela-
> tively recent excavation on its western slope. Here, on
> the central axis of the tumulus, there is an area mea-
> suring approximately 3.00 meters (up-and-down slope)
> and 2.00 meters (across slope) which looks as if it had
> been disturbed recently.

I had forgotten this observation. At the time, I probably
didn't think much of it. Most Florida sand mounds had been
dug into, at one time or another, if not by Moore, by un-
known diggers, treasure hunters or pot hunters. Moore had
been denied access to the St. James's Mound, but it looked
like someone else had had a go at it—probably trespassers
in a quick dig of a day. I suppose one reason I didn't excavate
in this western half of the mound was this apparent disturbance; however, the knowledge, gleaned from a reading of
Moore's *Certain Aboriginal Remains of the Northwest Florida Coast* (1901, 1902), that the principal ceramic deposits
in these mounds were most frequently found on their eastern side had been my main reason for excavating there.

I walked back down the slope of the mound in an attempt
to locate this old area of disturbance. The grass and weeds were
about knee high, but there were three or four places where
some very recently excavated small holes, of a foot or so in
diameter, had fresh sand piled up around them. Charles explained that these were the places where he had done some
limited digging on the day he had discovered the gold alligator
figurine. "The little alligator," he told me, "came from here,"
and he indicated one of the holes with his foot. I was interested
to see that this location was within what felt like a very shallow
depression about halfway up the mound slope. I mentioned
this to Charles, and I also showed him the passage in my book.
After he read it, he passed the book over to Selena.

I wanted to be sure about the apparent surface depression, and to do this we'd have to get rid of some of the vegetation. I needed something to cut away the grass and weeds. Charles said that there might be a scythe or a sickle up at one of the cottages. We left Selena seated under a tree, reading my book, and Charles and I walked back to the trail and followed it on up toward the cottages until we came to the Bull place.

As it was another ten-minute walk to the Randall cottage, Charles suggested we see if there was any kind of a grass-cutting implement around here. We tried both the front and back doors, but they were secured with new Yale locks. Mc-Govern must be very security-conscious, I thought to myself—but then his AK-47 told us that. Charles said that there was an area under the house that was used for storage, and we found the door to it, which was unlocked and opened at ground level below the porch.

The space inside was just about head high, so we had to duck to enter it. It was dark inside, but by leaving the door wide open, and propping up some of the wooden, hinged windows, we let in enough light to make out various objects—a wheelbarrow and some rusted garden tools. After rummaging around for a while, Charles came up triumphantly with a rusty sickle. While he was dusting this off with a rag he had picked up somewhere, I happened to notice, on one of the big, squared wooden posts that held up the flooring above, some ancient graffiti. There was an outline of a heart, which enclosed the large capital initials, SR and WB. Not really? Selena Randall and Webster Bull! My own heart beat faster, and my gorge rose. The carving looked like it had been there for a good many years. Did it go back, say, to 1927? I turned away from the post quickly, before Charles could catch me examining the inscription and come over and look at it himself.

I said to Charles, taking the sickle from him, "That looks like it will do the trick." I helped him close the windows, and we left the cottage and started back down the path to the mound. I walked ahead of Charles. He may have tried to make conversation, but I was in no mood to listen. I was back in the past. Webbie Bull! My God! My rival! Fat, ugly Webbie. God damn him! I mused, with cynical bitterness, that if only I had carried a pocketknife on that long ago magic day in August, and had commemorated Selena's and my love after the fashion of Webster Bull, my darling might not have forsaken me as she did. But I hadn't a pocketknife, and even if I'd had one, I wouldn't have done as Webbie had. I would have thought it unspeakably vulgar. Then my rage subsided, and I couldn't help laughing at myself and my anger at ancient history. Charles and I walked along, turned off the path, and found our way back to the mound. Selena was sitting there under the tree, still deep in my book.

I whacked away at the grass and weeds with the dull sickle and finally cleared an elongated area about eight by six feet. Sure enough, there was a rectangular depression there where the ground seemed to have settled two to three inches below the surrounding surface of the mound.

Charles looked at it and asked, "How long do you think it's been there?"

I told him it was hard to say, but I thought it was the same disturbance I had recorded in 1940. Then, if anything, the surface of the area was mounded up slightly higher than the surrounding ground level, presumably as a result of relatively recent digging and refilling, but in the intervening forty-five years, I explained, the soil had settled a bit to form the slight depression that we saw now.

Charles interrupted me by saying, "You see, Colin, I think I'm on to something. Somebody buried something out here, buried it a long time after the Indians were here. Don't you think so?"

I said maybe. "But don't get too excited. There's been a lot of random digging by pot hunters in a lot of Florida Indian mounds, and that's all this may amount to," I concluded, stamping my foot on the depression in the mound slope. Selena had come over to us by this time and been listening to our conversation.

Charles said, "Sel, this is where the dog found the little gold alligator, just there"—he pointed with his foot again—"and Colin says that this is an old disturbed area in the mound, a place where somebody's buried something long after the Indians were here—in fact, relatively recently."

"A place where somebody's dug a hole and filled it back in, Charles," I corrected. "We don't know that they buried anything there."

"Well, how did the gold alligator get there then, if somebody didn't bury it? Unless the Weeden Island Indians buried it—and you tell me that's unlikely. Somebody put it there since. What I want to do," Charles exclaimed to us, "is to dig here and find some more like it."

"I know you do," I told him, "and I've also suggested the next proper step to take before you, or anyone else for that matter, go rooting around in this mound." I explained to Selena my idea about the metal detector. If results with it were negative, Charles could forget about it. But, if they were positive, then Charles should wait for the state's archaeologists, or someone from one of the local universities, to come in and do the job right.

"Colin," he said, "do you have any idea how much those gold figurines, such as the little alligator, sell for now? At least a thousand dollars apiece. It's not just gold bullion value, as it was a long time ago. These are very valuable as antiquities as well. I know, because the Lockwood Galleries have some for sale. They have one of those little god men, like Grandfather Charles had in his desk, that has a price tag of ten thousand on it. If . . . if, Colin, there are five hundred of those little figures down here in this mound, where Great-grandfather Alexander put them, why then that would be at least five million dollars' worth of antiquities, antiquities that legitimately belong to us, the Randalls. I don't think we should have to share that with the damned state government or anyone else! It's ours! It's not Florida archaeology. You said that, yourself. No ancient Florida Indians put it there. My great-grandfather put it there!"

It was a moot point. Certainly, it was not archaeology native to Florida. Would it have to be treated as Spanish gold, such as that found in wrecks off the Florida coasts? I seemed to remember that for those discoveries the finders had some rights to a portion of the treasure, that there was a division between those who discovered the stuff and the state, although I wasn't sure of this. Maybe it would be different if Charles could prove it was old family property. All I knew for sure was that it would be a lot better if whatever it was that was in this mound was properly excavated by a trained archaeologist and, in view of the upcoming sale, preferably under state supervision. And I went over all of this again with Charles.

Selena sided with me. Of course, she would, I said to myself, if she was really as opposed to Charles's digging here as he had claimed she was. But there was also a practical-sense side to Selena, which Charles lacked. I thought back to our childhood. Their differences in personality—in spite of their being twins—had been apparent then. Charles was always sort of strange, even fey; Selena was more down to earth. I looked at her as she stood there beside me. The sunlight, coming through the pine trees, was glinting on her hair. It was gray now, not the dark brown that it used to be, but it was still very pretty.

Charles would have none of my argument. "Damnit, Colin, this is a family matter! Why should I have to bring everybody and his brother in on it? I'm sorry that I ever told you anything about it. I should have gone ahead and done it on the quiet and not said anything to you, Selena, or anyone ese!"

"You mean get someone like McGovern and those two hoods he had over here to handle it?" I said. "You'd be lucky to come away with your life, let alone get any of the gold."

Charles ignored my reference to the caretaker and his friends, but we went on at it, back and forth, for another ten minutes or so. At last, Selena broke in. "For God's sake, why don't you two stop quarreling? Let's go up to the cottage and have lunch."

The three of us walked back to the path that led to the cottages. Selena was carrying my book. Why do you call these Indians that used to live here the 'Weeden Island people'?"

"Oh, that's the name of the archaeological complex or culture that pertains to these Gulf Coast burial mounds, like this one here on the island," I told her. "It refers to a style, or styles, of pottery that were made here back in that period and also to burial customs, as represented by what we find in these mounds—single skull interments, bundle burials, partial cremations, and so forth. The name Weeden Island comes from a burial mound of this type that was excavated down at Tampa Bay, back in the 1920s, by a Smithsonian archaeologist named Fewkes. Later on, another Smithsonian archaeologist, Stirling, used the Weeden Island site as what we call the "type site" for the culture; and then, in my book, I extended the use of that name and concept up this far north and west—in fact, as far west as about Mobile—to similar pottery and burial practices. Indeed, some of my archaeological colleagues have felt that I extended it too far. There are, as is usually the case, regional and chronological variations in things like this."

I was warming up to my subject in a professional way, and I went on. "You see, the Weeden Island culture lasted from about A.D. 200 until 1000. We didn't know that back when I was digging here and when I wrote that book, but since then, radiocarbon dating has allowed us to fix absolute dates to these Florida cultures. The mound here on St. James's belongs to the earlier part of Weeden Island, what we call the Weeden Island I Period. While this particular mound has never been directly dated by radiocarbon means, we know that the pottery assemblage found here is diagnostic of Weeden Island I, which at other sites has been dated to between A.D. 200 and 600. The assemblage is characterized by the association of the Late Swift Creek Complicated Stamped type with the earlier Weeden Island Incised type, and—"

"The professor's really letting us have it, isn't he, Sel?"

Selena repressed a smile, then looked up at me, I thought
rather sweetly, and said, "Oh, Colin, you poor thing—you
know so much."

We walked along in silence for a while, passing the Bull
cottage. The commemorization on the house post of her
tryst with Webbie rose before my eyes. Did she think about
it now as we walked by? Did she think about another hot,
dusty, panting afternoon? But Selena's thoughts were elsewhere, that is, if what she said next revealed them.

"Colin," she asked me, "what tribe of Indians built these
Weeden Island mounds?"

I extinguished, at least temporarily, the fires of jealousy
in the cooling depths of the archaeological past. "We're not
sure, Selena. The Indians that the Spanish found along this
coast were the Apalachee tribe; however, we associate them
with the Fort Walton archaeological culture, which is dated
between A.D. 1000 and about 1600. It may be that the
Weeden Islanders were also Apalachees or it may be that they
were Timucuas. The Timucuas," I went on to explain, "were
a tribe that occupied the Florida Peninsula farther down the
Gulf Coast. But," I finished up, "whoever was responsible
for the Weeden Island culture, it is the most distinctive, and
the best known, of all the archaeological cultures of the Florida Gulf."

"Professor," asked Charles, "can class be dismissed now?"

I ignored this crack, as did Selena. She walked along in
silence for a while. "Colin, Weeden Island is the best known
of all your Indian cultures, or civilizations, in this part of the
state, right?" I acknowledged that it was, and she continued.
"There's been a book written on the Weeden Island Mound,
down on Tampa Bay, no? Then this Mr. Moore excavated
almost a hundred other Weeden Island–type mounds, didn't
he? You say so in your book anyway." She waved it at me.
"And you, yourself, have dug still more Weeden Island sites,
haven't you?" I admitted to this. I was impressed and curious; what was it leading up to?

She stopped on the path and faced me. "Why is it, then,

Colin, if your Weeden Island culture is so well known, and has been dug up so much, that it is necessary to dig this one more poor little mound on St. James's Island—one which you've already half-dug? Why can't you archaeologists—as well as Charles with his silly treasure-hunting ideas—just leave it alone?"

"Well, Selena," I tried to explain, "it's not quite like that. You see, archaeology changes. New techniques of study and analysis are developed all the time. We are interested in asking new kinds of questions, exploring in different ways. The things that have been written on the Weeden Island culture in the past only give us a part of the story. Our excavation methods have changed. For instance, neither Moore nor Fewkes ever came up with detailed plans of the old surfaces beneath the mounds that they excavated. There are hints that many of these mounds may have covered old wooden structures, probably 'houses of the dead,' or charnel houses, where corpses were left to rot so that the skeletons could be disarticulated and buried in the mounds at special ceremonies."

"Ugh," said Selena, making a face.

"Oh, Professor, Professor, what a distasteful line of work you are in," Charles added.

I went right ahead. "If the old surfaces under the mounds were carefully scraped and studied, we could probably find post molds, places where house posts that are now decayed, or had been burned, had been put into the ground. This would give us some idea of the shapes of these buildings. When I dug the St. James's Island Mound, I didn't do this, but I'm sure that this would be one of the things the state archaeologist, if he excavates the remainder of the mound, would be interested in . . . the old premound surface. Besides, there are all kinds of other things to look for, to pay attention to, that archaeologists weren't formerly aware of. Did you know, for example, that archaeologists, by studying the shells recovered from refuse, can tell you what season of the year these shells were gathered in, and that this, in turn, has a bearing on seasonality of occupation, and this on our understanding of the subsistence system, so that a processual perspective may be—"

"Not really, Professor! God, how interesting can you get!" exclaimed Charles.

Selena held up her hand. "Stop, stop, dear Colin, before I brain you with your own book," she said, threatening to do so with her other hand.

We came out into the old clearing and saw the Randall cottage. I thought it looked much the same, but Charles said that they had made a number of renovations after the Second World War. There was running water and plumbing now, as well as electricity. The power came over from the mainland, like the telephone lines, and they had their own septic tank, as did the Bull cottage. Both cottages were served by wells, which had been there back as far as I could remember, but these had now been equipped with electric pumps. Charles had a key with him, and he let us in the front door. Expectably, the place smelled musty and looked dusty. He ran a finger across the surface of the table in the living room and remarked that McGovern, who was supposed to see that a cleaning person was brought over from the mainland every so often during the summer, to clean both houses, hadn't been on the job. As he told me this, I wondered just what job McGovern was on.

Selena unpacked our lunch. I thought of her unpacking another lunch for us in this cottage, but from the brisk efficiency of her movements, I was sure her thoughts now were completely in the present.

We talked of one thing and another as we ate. I purposefully avoided the controversial subject of digging the mound, and Charles also seemed willing to leave it alone. I said I'd try to do something about the metal detector the day after tomorrow. Tomorrow was Tuesday, the day of Webbie's funeral, and we would all be going to that. I inquired about the time, and Selena told me that it was at eleven.

Partly to make talk, but partly from real curiosity, I

brought up the island's caretaker and his strange companions. Charles told me, again, that McGovern was someone John had introduced him to at the Lockwood Galleries. He'd been a kind of watchman-janitor, or something like that, in the galleries, and he had been looking for a job that wasn't so confining, that would get him out into the open more, because he liked the outdoors. Thompson had wanted to retire, so McGovern was taken on. It wasn't easy anymore to get a younger man around St. Christopher's to take such a job. For one thing, complained Charles, they all demanded too much pay; for another, they, and their families, if they had families, didn't want to be marooned on an island all the time. Not that it was a long trip, especially if one went directly across the sound to the mainland, but even so it was trouble, as well as expense, to run the boat back and forth all the time. I recalled, from my experience here in 1940, that such short-range water commuting could get pretty tiresome.

Thinking of water transport, I remarked to Charles, "That's quite a boat that McGovern has now, a considerable improvement on what Thompson used to ride about in. I should think a boat like that, and the operation of it, would run into money."

"Well, I guess it does," Charles answered me, "but, actually, I don't know much about it. Webbie has looked after most of the finances for the island in recent years, including the boat."

"Don't tell me that he assumed the full cost of the boat and all of McGovern's wages?"

"McGovern doesn't demand much in the way of salary. That was one of the advantages in taking him on, and Selena and I do pay for half of that. As to the boat, I'm not sure what it did cost originally or what it costs to operate. John, acting for Webbie, arranges everything like that now, and I'm not sure just how it was paid for."

It all sounded pretty strange. McGovern didn't strike me as the type who would be willing to go without pay just for

the advantages of the open-air life on St. James's Island. I
wondered what was going on, and I think that Selena was
sensitive to my misgivings.

"And, Tiger and Hebert? Had you ever seen them before
today, Charles?"

"What? Oh, those chaps. Well, I might have, although I
don't know either of them at all well. As I told you, they seem
to be friends of John, and McGovern, too, I guess. I may have
seen them in New Orleans, helping John, probably around
Lockwood's."

It wasn't any of my business, but I began to wish I knew
more about the Lockwood Galleries. John's long employ-
ment there, or connection with them, struck me as somewhat unusual. At least I had never thought of John as being
in any way an arty type; however, that might not be a re-
quirement for someone in the antiques trade. The name
Lockwood still had a bad resonance with me. I associated it,
of course, with James Randall's disappearance. Charles had
had some links with Lockwood, as well. I recalled that he
had gone over to New Orleans two or three times when I was
here in 1940 and frequently had referred to Calhoun Lockwood. He'd been the one who had been around on that last
day anyone had seen James Randall. Now that Calhoun
Lockwood was dead, what was the name of the fellow they
said was running the Lockwood Galleries?

As if she had read my thoughts, Selena said, "I think
they're a couple of gangster types who do dirty things for
Charles's friend, Tommy Fawnley. I think Fawnley is in all
kinds of . . . of business, isn't he, Charles?"

Charles gave her a cold reply. "Tommy runs an art gallery
and an antiques business, and, as far as I know, he does it
on the up and up." He turned to me and said, "Don't pay
any attention to Sel when she gets catty like that. She doesn't
like Tommy."

Selena said, "No, you're right, I don't."

I was hesitant to bring up bad memories, but thinking
about the Lockwood Galleries and Lockwood led me to do

it. "Charles," I asked, "has there ever been any word about your father's disappearance? I know, of course, that you've had no official word, but have there ever been any rumors about what might have happened?"

I saw Selena tighten up, but she didn't say anything. Then Charles said, "No, nothing really, nothing of any importance. Not even any salacious scandal. His lady friend, there in New Orleans, died about twenty years ago. He certainly never came back to her."

Selena suddenly roused herself. "It's almost three. Maybe we should think about getting back." She began to clean up the remains of our meal, putting some odds and ends back into the picnic basket.

When we went outside, it was still overcast, but there had been no rain, and I didn't think there would be now. We went across the clearing and down the path. At the Bull cottage there was no sign of life; everything appeared as tightly locked up as it had before.

Down at the landing, our boat was awaiting us, but the island's boat had not come back, nor could we see any sign of it on the sound. I looked across at the nearest point on the mainland shore where a dock was visible, but I couldn't make out anything that looked like a boat.

Going back, the waves were slightly choppy, but there was a nice breeze behind us. This time Selena was seated up front with Charles, but she frequently turned and looked at me. I marveled, as I always did, at the perfection of her features. She had her kerchief tied tightly under her chin, and this nicely framed and supported her face. A woman to remember, I thought. Or, a woman it was impossible to forget? How nonsensically romantic was this. After all, I had forgotten her for forty-five years. So far, in this short stay in St. Christopher's, I had exchanged only a few words with her and all of these when someone else was present. What would it be like to have a more uninterrupted talk with her, to talk with her alone? As we bounced along on the waters of the bay, she still seemed to be watching me. When I stared back she would drop her eyes, then raise them again.

It was just four when we arrived back at the boathouse in St. Christopher's. The proprietor helped us tie up and then said to Charles, "Mr. Randall, Sheriff Larrabee and another gentleman have been here for a while, waiting for you. They'd like to talk to you."

I guess both Charles and I looked surprised at this. I was curious, but, assuming this invitation for an interview did not include me, I turned to talk with Selena, to tell her how pleasant the day had been and what a good lunch we'd had. I restrained myself from adding, a little maliciously, *just like old times*. But I could see Selena looking over my shoulder in the direction of the boathouse. I turned around and saw Sheriff Larrabee and a younger man, in a tan-colored suit, coming toward Charles.

"Mr. Randall," said the sheriff "let me introduce Agent Clancy of the federal Drug Enforcement Administration. He'd like a word with you."

Clancy looked the part of a competent federal agent of some kind—an FBI type, compact, self-contained, neatly dressed. He shook hands with Charles and then glanced over at Selena and myself. Perhaps he wanted us to move on off and let him confer with Charles in private, but, before we could do so, he said, quite pleasantly, "I understand that the three of you have spent the day on St. James's Island." We confirmed this. Then he asked us, "You didn't happen to see a man named Hebert over there, did you? A Raymond Hebert?" Before we could answer he gave us a thumbnail description: medium height, thin, about fifty years old, with a high-bridged, hooked nose.

I waited for Charles to reply and thought he seemed slow in doing so. Finally, he said, "Yes, we did pass someone by that name on the path this morning as we were going from the landing up to the family cottages."

Clancy continued, "Was there another man there, a big, light-colored black man, who goes by the name of Tiger Westcott?"

Charles nodded and looked around at me for verification, saying, "There was someone like that over there, too, wasn't there, Colin?" I said yes there was, that he had been referred to as Tiger, but that I didn't hear the name Westcott.

Clancy then wanted to know why they were permitted to be there. Wasn't the island private property? What was the nature of their business over there? Charles explained that they had been in the company of Pierre McGovern, the care-taker on the island, but that he, Charles, didn't know what their business was. He had assumed that they were friends of McGovern who had been brought over probably just to see the island.

Clancy said, yes, he knew McGovern, in a manner that made it pretty clear that he knew him and didn't think well of him. He wanted to know if Hebert and Westcott had come in their own boat. Charles told him no, that, apparently, they had come over in the island's boat with McGovern. Clancy then asked what time we'd seen Hebert and Westcott, when they had left, and where they had gone. Charles hemmed and hawed around on these questions, but finally, with prompting from me, it came out that we'd met them shortly after our arrival, which must have been at about ten-thirty in the morning, that they were coming from the Bull cottage at that time and were on their way, with John Crawford and McGovern, to the boat dock. We said we'd heard their boat start up about ten minutes after this. But as to where they'd gone, none of us had any idea. Clancy made a few notes, squinted at us, and asked, "John Crawford was with them, then?" We said yes. Clancy thanked us, conferred with the sheriff briefly, got in his car, and drove away.

I asked the sheriff if he could tell us what this was all about, but he said he wasn't at liberty to tell us anything right now.

We thought we were dismissed, but just as we started to walk over to where Selena had parked the car, Larrabee stopped us by saying, "There's just one more thing, Mr. Randall. This will interest you. We've just received the report from the state police ballistics laboratory in Tallahassee. The thirty-eight revolver bullet that killed Mr. Bull matches up with the bullets that were fired into Mr. Bull's bedroom some weeks ago, into your study, and into Mrs. Hedrickson's living room last week. All of them were fired from the same gun." Having dropped this on us, he tipped his hat to Selena. "Good afternoon, ma'am. Good afternoon, Mr. Randall, Mr. Edwards. You'll probably be hearing from me again." With that he climbed into his car and drove off.

We got into the Randalls' car. I invited my companions to join me later for dinner at the hotel, but Selena declined, saying she had another engagement. She seemed distracted now, not paying much attention to me, certainly not looking at me in the intent way she had done on the boat coming back. Charles thanked me, too, but said no, he felt rather tired, and, if I didn't mind, he would go on home, eat a small bite, and go to bed early. They let me out at the hotel, where I thanked them, again, for a nice day and a nice lunch.

I went up to my room, rested, bathed, dressed, and went down to dinner. It was a quiet evening at the St. Christopher House. The desk clerk nodded to me politely. On this third day here, I was relieved that I had no messages and no visitors.

$\bigtriangledown$

6

ON TUESDAY, THE DAY of Webbie's funeral, I awoke at my "old man's time" of 4:00 A.M. I had long decided, unlike many distinguished senior citizens of whom we read, that I would not get up at this unreasonable hour and turn to productive work or even read, but that I would continue to take advantage of God's dark and stay in bed. So I used this time to ruminate about life.

I thought of Webbie—the late Webster Irving Bull, Jr.— and I wondered why hadn't I liked him better. In the old days, when we were boys, here in St. Christopher's, I could imagine a psychoanalyst (not that there were any around St. Christopher's then) arguing that Webbie was unsure of himself, anxious for people to like him, eager to bolster his own ego, and that all this made him like he was. At least this sounds like the kind of diagnosis that is current these days, when psychological counseling is dispensed like hamburgers at McDonald's. But aren't most of us unsure of ourselves, anxious about the opinions others may have of us, eager to bolster our own egos? I know that I was. That I still am.

Of course, in looking back on it, I don't think I was such a god-awful bore as Webbie. I don't' really know, though. Perhaps it depends on the audience, on the "borees." As I turned over to assume a more comfortable position, it struck me that bores might be classified into two basic groups: passive and active. I suppose there are more of the former than the latter. I would have to be classed as a passive bore, one of those, for instance, who falls silent during cocktail party chitchat and leaves his conversational partner and himself marooned in an embarrassment of silence. In contrast, the truly great bores, I reflected, are the active bores, the aggressive ones. Webbie had been one of these. After telling myself this, though, I had to admit that the last time I saw him—indeed, it was the last time I would ever see the poor old boy—Webbie, as a bore, had been under wraps, extraordinarily muted. I still wondered why.

What thoughts to have, I chided myself, before attending a service for "the Burial of the Dead." We are all, in our weaknesses and our sins, equal in God's eyes. Lord, accept thy servant Webster. And forgive, too, the Cain who has slain his brother, Abel. Who could it have been? What were the undercurrents beneath the placid surface of small-town life here in St. Christopher's? I wondered if someone like Sheriff Larrabee knew about such undercurrents. Certainly, there must be some.

I rolled over again. Sleep now, before dawn, I knew, was no more than a ten-percent possibility. What about all those criminal-looking types we'd seen yesterday over on St. James's Island? As I recalled, St. Christopher's used to have its normal small-town share of crooks, or near-crooks, but they were far less professional looking than Messrs. McGovern, Hebert, and Westcott. Suppose those guys were running drugs, I asked myself. If so, what was John's relationship to their enterprise? And had they had some connection with Webbie? Charles had said that Webbie had been handling all the finances involved in the Island Trust. This, presumably, would have meant some dealings with McGovern. Or was it all mediated through John? Maybe Webbie and John had been in on it together? Perhaps St. James's Island had been turned into some kind of a distribution node in the cocaine traffic. Had Webbie lost his nerve and threatened to squeal? Was that why he'd been rubbed out? Had these gangsters put the finger on poor old Webbie? Wasn't that what they did? I realized that my lingo in describing and visualizing such activities dated back to the

1930s gangster movies I'd seen, with only a slight updating from modern TV series. The more I thought about it, too, the harder it was for me to conceive of Webbie, old establishment Webbie, the town's former leading citizen, being a part of big-time crime.

Was Webbie killed for money? I had asked myself that question before, and had come up with the answer that Lydia—and, indirectly, Harry—had stood to gain the most by his death. Harry Hedrickson. Of course, in my prejudiced eyes, Harry was more of a favorite now for the role of chief suspect than he had been the other day. I am afraid I detested the man. Where was he the night Webbie was shot? I daresay the chief or the sheriff had checked on that and found that Harry was appropriately asleep, undoubtedly in the marital bed with Lydia. Would a wife lie to protect her husband from being accused of her brother's death? I supposed that it would depend on the wife, and I really knew nothing of Lydia's relationship with her husband—or her brother. As a matter of fact, just about everything I knew today about people's relationships with one another here in St. Christopher's came from Charles, or Charles and Webbie, and, probably wisely, I had been hesitant to put too much reliance on what either of them had told me.

Was love, frustrated love, jealousy, or rage deriving from these, the motive behind Webbie's death? It seemed unlikely at his age. I would have had a hard time envisioning Webbie being done away with in a torrid love triangle even in his prime, let alone now. Yet we never know, do we? The paired initials, which I had seen on the post in the Bull cottage cautioned me to heed that old warning that one should never underrate another's proclivities in matters of the heart (read sex). If Webbie had been carrying on an affair with Selena, as Charles had alleged, would the injured Mabel have shot her husband? If not, would her brother, John, have done it for her to avenge the honor of the family? Or, better yet, maybe John arranged for someone like McGovern, or Tiger— the wonderfully sinister-looking Tiger, with his opaque sunglasses—to serve as the triggerman? It was no use. Every way I turned, my restless predawn reasoning brought me face to face with the ridiculous, the corny, the melodramatic stuff.

And what of those shots that had been fired through the windows? At Webbie? At Charles? And the one at Lydia? Both Charles and Lydia were also members of the Island Trust and beneficiaries of the upcoming sale. This didn't sound like either drug running or love, but money.

More immediately, and practically, before going to the funeral I thought I'd better call Florida State in Tallahassee, or maybe the state archaeologist there, to ask about a metal detector and, if possible, someone to come over and run it. Also, I wanted to explain the St. James's Island matter to someone like Joel Chandler, an archaeologist at Florida State. He'd been a student of a student of mine, and, although I knew him only slightly, he seemed like a sensible young fellow. He could introduce me to the state archaeologist, and maybe together we could work out some scheme to protect Charles's family treasure interests.

I heard a bath being drawn somewhere in the hotel. A little while after this someone started up a car in the parking lot. I looked at my watch: six o'clock. More sleep was out of the question. I'd get up and go for a little morning walk before the dining room opened for breakfast. I put on a dark suit and a somber tie, appropriate for the upcoming occasion of the day, and went downstairs. The night clerk was asleep behind the desk. I opened the door, stepped out on the porch, and then walked out to the highway. It was going to be a clear day. Yesterday's clouds had passed over. I crossed over the highway and walked the short distance down to the shore. Gulls were squawking, fighting for bits of edibles on the narrow beach. The offshore bar islands were distant and blue-black. Farther to the west, St. James's Island was beginning to glow in the dawn. I enjoyed the scene for a while, then went back up the way I had come.

Just as I got to the highway, a car came down the main street from the center of town. It was a worse-for-wear green sedan. The driver stopped for the stop sign at the highway, then turned right, or west, and sped out of town with an angry screeching of tires. It was John Crawford. He didn't seem to notice me, or if he did he gave no indication of it. He had looked harried, I thought, even more so than on Sunday. Where was he off to at this hour? Surely he wasn't going home, to New Orleans, before the funeral? But he hardly looked like he was taking a drive just to get some fresh air. Was he going over to the island to check on McGovern and Hebert and Tiger? To tell them that the heat was on, that the Drug Enforcement agents were on their trail? But John had headed off in the wrong direction for the Riverfront Docks. I wondered then if it might not be quicker to reach the island by driving down the coast, to the west, for few miles and then taking a boat there across the narrows.

Back inside the hotel, the dining room had just opened for breakfast. While eating, I read the paper, which had a little story on an inside page about the continuation of the investigations into the "mysterious death of a prominent citizen of St. Christopher's, the well-known lawyer, Mr. Webster I. Bull, Jr. Police," it went on to say, are "following up a number of clues although, as yet, they have no definite suspects."

I wondered just what the clues were that the worthy chief and the sheriff were following up. I found myself wishing that I had some inside police connection, like those distinguished amateur sleuths in detective stories, those guys who, by the brilliance of their insights, help the officers of the law to a solution of the crime. But I didn't suppose Ellis and Larrabee would welcome a retired professor who would be willing to volunteer his services in solving the case through stimulating conversation. They might be particularly unwelcoming if the professor himself was one of the suspects. I left the paper on the dining-room table and went upstairs to my room.

I waited around until a little after eight and then dialed Charles. "Charles," I said, "I'm going to call up an archaeologist at Florida State, a competent and nice young man named Joel Chandler. I'm going to ask him if he can obtain a metal detector and bring it down here and go over to the island with us. What day would be good for you—tomorrow, if I can get him for then?"

There was a pause, and, again, Charles started to balk at bringing in anybody else. "Colin," he asked crossly, "why do we have to have outsiders nosing around in what I consider to be purely a family matter? Can't you run that contraption yourself? Besides, what kind of story would we tell this fellow?"

"Why, Charles, we'll tell him the truth," I answered. You feel there might be an old Randall family hoard of gold buried in the mound over there. Show him the little gold alligator. Tell him that you've talked it over with me and that I've suggested we check the location with a metal detector. Then, if it seems indicated, we'll ask him his opinion about digging. Maybe Chandler would be willing to take charge of the digging as a university project. Or perhaps we could arrange for the state archaeologist to come in and dig now. In fact, this might be the best. The state people could advise you of your rights on any 'treasure' that might be found in the mound."

There was a long silence, then Charles simply said, "I still don't like it."

"But, Charles, there is no way you are going to keep any digging over there quiet," I told him. "Think about it. McGovern seems very close to John Crawford; he'll tell John; and from him it will go on to Mabel and Lydia, and Harry Hedrickson. The latter, incidentally, and for what reason I don't know, is strongly opposed to your digging over there. He was here in the hotel the other night, carrying on to me about it in a drunken rage. Legally, at present—and forgetting the state authorities for a minute—you've got to have the permission of the owners to dig on St. James's Island, and that means three people: yourself, Selena, and Lydia Bull Hedrickson. As far as I know, you're the only one of the three in favor of it. Selena certainly has indicated that she isn't, and I would doubt if Lydia would like the idea, judging from the way her husband protested the other night."

"Colin," Charles said, "there are ways to do things. I can handle McGovern, and this could all be over and done with in a day or so. We're not excavating at Ur of the Chaldees, Professor. We're not really excavating with a capital *E* at all. It would be just a spot of quick digging in that place on the mound that you say looks disturbed. I'm sure that's where the stuff is."

I decided then that it was hopeless to continue to argue and wound up by saying, "Look, how about this? I'll get Chandler, and the state archaeologist, if I can, and have them here in St. Christopher's to talk to you tomorrow, or by Thursday at the latest. We can all go on over to the island, and they can run the metal detector over the mound and advise you from there. As a favor to me, just listen to what they have to say before you do anything foolish."

Charles didn't say anything to this. After a while, he told me he'd see me at the church, and we hung up.

At nine-thirty, I called Tallahassee, got through to the state university, and, eventually, to Joel Chandler, and explained that I was calling from St. Christopher's.

Chandler said that it was nice to hear from me down here in Florida and that he hoped he'd have the pleasure of seeing me during my stay. Then he politely asked, "Dr. Edwards, what can I do for you?"

"Well," I responded, "it's a bit complicated, but it has to do with a Weeden Island burial mound on St. James's Island, an island near here." He wanted to know if it was the one I had excavated a long time ago and reported on, and I told him it was. "A very good friend of mine, a cousin, in fact, and one of the owners of the island, wants to make some excavations in the mound. I've advised him against it, but he has strong—let us say, personal—reasons for wanting to do so."

"Isn't St. James's about to be purchased by the state?" Chandler asked. I told him it was, and he asked another question: "Wasn't one of the owners, a Mr. Bull, shot and killed just the other day?"

I confirmed this and said, "As I told you, it is one of the owners, Charles Randall, who wants to do the digging. He's not an archaeologist, and the reason he wants to dig into the mound—into that part of it which I didn't excavate back in 1940—is that, God help us, he thinks there is a cache of gold treasure in it that was put there by his great-grandfather in the last century. I'm embarrassed to tell you stuff like this, but I think you can understand."

Chandler chortled at this.

"What I've advised him," I went on, "is that the particular area of the mound where he thinks the treasure may be hidden should be checked with a metal detector. I think—or I hope—that if the results turn out negative, this will calm him down and he'll forget about the digging. Do you fellows up there have a detector? And could we borrow it? Or better yet, would you be willing to come down to St. Christopher's and run it and also help me talk some sense into my cousin's head as to the best way to go about all this?"

Chandler didn't say anything, so I continued. "Maybe you could bring the state archaeologist down, too. I think there are a number of questions here—some involving just when the state will buy and take over the island, and others pertaining to the landowner's rights to dig on his property prior to such a sale. In other words, if you and he could talk to Mr. Randall, I think it would clear up a lot of things for him. I'd consider it a great favor if you would, and I'd be more than happy to put you, or the two of you, up here at the St. Christopher House as my guests for a night or a couple of nights if that proves necessary. As an added inducement, I can recommend the bar and the dining room."

Chandler said it sort of sounded like fun, but he didn't know if he could get away. But, yes, they did have a metal detector at FSU and so did Bill Calvert, the state archaeologist. We could certainly borrow one or the other. Chandler promised to get in touch with Calvert. I suggested, then, that

I come up to Tallahassee tomorrow—Wednesday—after-noon. I told him that I would try to explain the whole matter to them in more detail. He said that he'd be there, for sure, and that he would try to get Calvert to come over for an appointment with me. We rang off.

At about twenty minutes before eleven, I drove over to St. Luke's. Cars were beginning to assemble, so I had to park about a block away. I met Selena and Charles just as I got to the church door, and the three of us went in together and were shown by an usher to a pew about halfway down the aisle. The coffin was banked heavily with flowers. Fortu-nately, I had remembered to send some that morning, when I was making my other telephone calls.

The prelude music was being played when the family of the deceased came down the aisle: Mabel, Lydia, John Craw-ford, and Harry Hedrickson. Mabel was in black and veiled, and you could hear her softly sobbing as she went by us. It was the first time I had seen Lydia since 1940. Like those of some homely women, her looks had improved with age. She was dressed severely in black, which gave her a kind of ele-gance, and her figure, which had always been stout, was not excessively so now. Also, age had given the rather dog-faced features of her youth a certain dignity. John Crawford had on the same unpressed seersucker jacket that he had worn when we'd called on Mabel on Sunday. He obviously had not been headed for New Orleans when I saw him on the high-way this morning. Harry Hedrickson, who had brought up the rear of the family group, had the angry, parboiled look that he had had the night he accosted me at the hotel. The four of them were seated in the pew reserved for the family at the front.

After an opening hymn and a lesson, Hedrickson came forward to read the eulogy. In the harsh, disagreeable voice that I remembered from Sunday night, he praised Webbie as a husband, a brother-in-law, a partner at law, and a civic leader. I think I tuned out on a part of this encomium, but my attention was recaptured when I heard him denounce "those who had killed this distinguished man." I wondered at his use of the plural *those*, rather than a singular *he*. Or *she*. Had Hedrickson some inside information the rest of us knew nothing about? Or was this a slip of the tongue revealing that he, Hedrickson, had done the deed, aided by confederates? His anger rising, Hedrickson excoriated the outsiders who had come into this pure and virtuous American community; I assumed that American, in this context, should be read as small-town southern WASP. He denounced "those aliens who had taken the life of one of the finest men that ever breathed the breath of life" and advocated that "they should be treated with the severity they deserve!" He sat down trembling with rage and righteous indignation. What kind of justice was redneck Harry calling for? An old-fashioned lynching? Was he a secret kleagle? Whom did he have in mind when he said "outsiders"? I wondered if he had ever seen Hebert, or Tiger, with his silver-bright insect eyes. Tiger certainly looked like an outsider, even a Martian. Or maybe Hedrickson had me in mind.

I thought the minister looked a little embarrassed when he resumed control of the service. While Webbie's death was deplorable, this call for vengeance, delivered as it was from just in front of the chancel, could have struck some as a little un-Christian—at least for St. Luke's Episcopal.

The service for "the Burial of the Dead" followed. Then six Bull relatives carried Webbie's casket down the aisle and out to the hearse. Before the concluding prayers, the minister announced that, following the graveside service, there would be a reception at the Bull residence, to which all those in attendance were welcome. At the close of the prayers, the family filed out, and Charles, Selena, and I followed when our turn came. In the vestibule, I offered my condolences to Mabel and to Lydia. I was also greeting the latter for the first time, as we said to each other, "in all these years."

As I was leaving the church, I felt a touch on my arm, and there was Selena. She had on a simple, dark blue dress which fitted beautifully, and she was carrying the scarf which she had worn over her head in the church. She looked exquisite. "Colin," she whispered, "won't you have lunch with me someplace? After what Mabel said the other day . . . well, I don't want to go to the cemetery or to the reception. You understand, don't you?" I didn't answer but cupped my hand under her elbow, and we walked off in the direction of my car.

"Where shall we go?" I asked her once we were in the car. "Would you like to go to the hotel? The food is really very good there."

She shook her head, turned and looked at me, and said, "No, I'd rather not. I'd rather go farther away, if you don't mind. I know quite a good place. It's just off the coast highway, about twelve miles west of town. It's relatively new. It's called the Cape Sands. They have good drinks, and lunch and dinner, too."

Following her instructions, I drove back out to the coastal highway, and we made the same turn that John Crawford had made that morning. In this stretch to the west of the city, the highway follows closely along the bay beach, and for several miles there is very little in the way of construction, or even vegetation, on the seaward side of the road. Eventually, one comes to a place where a little cape juts out and forms a tiny piece of land just off the paved road. Here there was a long, low, motel-type construction, about a hundred yards off the highway, with a large blue-and-white sign on top of it, Cape Sands—Motel and Restaurant-Bar. I drove down the side road that led to a parking place near the main entrance.

We got out, and Selena led the way into the lobbylike foyer, where a man at the desk looked up, smiled, and welcomed her as Mrs. Crawford. Selena called him Jerry and asked if there was a table for two for lunch. He came out from behind the desk and told her that it was always a pleasure to see her. He led us into a large, air-conditioned dining room, which had windows all along the side overlooking the sea. A bar took up the other side of the room. There were other patrons in the room, but the place was not crowded. Jerry signaled a waiter, and when he came up Selena asked him to seat us at a table for two by the windows.

After I had sat down and had a look out the windows, I recognized exactly where we were. Below us, about a hundred yards distant, was a small cluster of buildings—boathouses, storehouses, or whatever—and a dock at which a couple of small boats were tied up. Farther off, across a narrow stretch of water, was St. James's Island, with the old caretaker's house down at the shoreline. This, then, was the closest point on the mainland to the island, which lay only a half mile or less away.

We both ordered cocktails, to be followed by shrimp salad. After a first hearty taste of our drinks, Selena said, "I needed that," and I agreed that the morning had not been an easy one.

Selena said, "Colin, all this has been terrible for you, Webbie's death coming just after you got down here. I feel we all owe you an apology—although that doesn't make much sense."

"No, it doesn't," I told her, "but, I admit, we have had a trying time these last few days." After a moment, I went on. "Selena, do you have any ideas at all about who might have killed Webbie? Or who could have fired those shots at Charles and Lydia, assuming it was all the same person?"

"Colin, I don't," she replied with a gesture of hopelessness. "You know I've been away from St. Christopher's for a long time, too. I really don't know what's been going on around here, or what antagonisms or hatreds have built up. I hate thinking anyone we know did it. Don't you think it must have been, as Harry said, an outsider?"

"What does that mean, an *outsider*? And speaking of Hedrickson, does he always carry on the way he did today in church?"

I think she caught the critical note in my question, and it ruffled her. "Colin, Harry has had a very hard time in his life, and he can get very emotional at times, but he means well."

She told me this with such primness in her voice that I

was tempted to reply that the same could have been said of Adolf Hitler; instead, I studied Selena's face. She was looking down now, twisting the base of her cocktail glass round and round on the tablecloth. How very little I really knew this fascinating woman. Try not to quarrel with her, I cautioned myself. Try to get to know her again—if she will let you.

I looked out the window and saw a large boat, a cabin cruiser, coming along the shore from the west. As it neared the little dock, it cut to half speed, turned, and moved in toward the pier. The motor was turned off, and a man got out and secured the boat to the dock. After leaving the pier, he walked up the path toward what must have been an entrance on that side of the motel. He was wearing a yachting cap, and his face remained shaded by the visor until he got quite close to us. Then he looked up, and I saw that he had on silvered sunglasses. Well, well, I thought, our old friend. He appeared to have avoided the clutches of the law so far.

The ground on that side of the motel was lower than on the highway side, so he passed out of sight below me. He must have come in a door there, for shortly after this he walked into the dining room. Selena, who was facing me, had not seen any of this, but now she saw him. He looked our way for a moment; I wondered if he had recognized us. He turned and walked over to the bar, where, yachting cap still on his head, he ordered a drink.

"Ah, there he is, my dear," I remarked. " 'Tiger, tiger burning bright.' Should we invite him to join us?"

Selena smiled rather bitterly but took my flippancy in good part. "Don't tease me, Colin, I don't really know him or those other men—the ones we saw over on the island. They're people that John has brought from New Orleans, just as Charles said. I shouldn't be surprised if they weren't up to something like running drugs. It will serve John right if they do get caught. I only hope that Charles will not be blamed in some way."

With this mention of Charles, I changed the subject. "Selena, why hasn't Charles followed some profession? I

suppose it's none of my business, but, after all, he and I are
the oldest of friends, even though we haven't seen much of
each other in all these years. He is a highly intelligent man.
He could have done well in the law, or, even better, as I used
to tell him, in some scholarly pursuit, history, for instance."

She shook her head slowly before answering. "I really don't
know—other than to say that when he came back here after
college, and refused Dad's offer to go on to law school, he
seemed to change, or maybe he had changed before that. He
seemed sad, depressed, and cynical so much of the time. He
wanted to live in a kind of make-believe, to imagine that he
was a scion of a great family of the old antebellum South,
someone above work and menial pursuits. He looked down
on everyone else in town—but then he'd always done that,
even when we were children. After I married John and moved
to New Orleans, he used to visit us. He liked it there. Sadly,
I'm afraid, New Orleans and its French Quarter had a deca-
dence that appealed to him. For a long time, there was
enough money for him to live without working—not as
much as he would have liked, but enough. Now, though,
there is not so much."

I took the opportunity to switch the conversation to herself. "Tell me about you, Selena. Until now, I haven't had a
real chance to talk with you since I've been here." She didn't
respond right away, so I went on. "You're looking famously,
as I told you that first night when I came over to the house.
How good, or how bad, has life been to you since I saw you
last, back there in 1927?"

"Oh, like everyone, I suppose I've had my ups and downs.
You know that my marriage to John didn't work out. It was
a mistake from the first. He had such grandiose dreams. He
wanted to be rich and important, but he didn't know how
to go about it. We . . . we were beginning to come apart even
before the war. When he came out of the service, we tried to
make a go of it, but we couldn't. We were divorced."

"I'm sorry," I said, and then asked, "You had a child didn't
you, a child who died?"

"Yes," Selena answered, "I had a child." But she didn't go on. I presumed the memory of the rest of it must have been too painful for her to want to go into, so I didn't pursue the question. We were finishing up lunch. We declined dessert but lingered over another glass of iced tea.

Tiger still sat hunched at the bar, nursing a drink. He may have been able to see us in the mirror in back of the bar, although I don't know if he was particularly interested. Suddenly, I was surprised to see John Crawford slouch into the room. He had shed his seersucker jacket and was in shirtsleeves again. He looked as defeated as ever. He saw us and gave us a glum stare of dislike but no greeting. Then he turned his attention to the bar and the man sitting there. Going over to Tiger and putting a hand on his shoulder, he had a whispered conversation. Tiger put some money down on the bar, got up, and followed John out of the room, moving with an elegant, sinewy grace.

I didn't want my afternoon with Selena to end. I asked her if there wasn't something we could do for the rest of the day. She looked pleased at my suggestion. It was only a little after two, she told me. Why didn't we go for a drive? We could go and look at some of the places that I hadn't seen for so long. We could drive over toward Panama City and Fort Walton.

We went out to my car, and, as we were getting into it, I saw John and Tiger down on the little pier. Another boat was coming in to dock. This time I recognized it as the island's boat, and there were two people and a dog in it. When it drew in closer, we could see that they were McGovern and Hebert and the "archaeological dog," the one who had dug up the gold alligator for Charles. The smaller boat pulled alongside the pier, and Hebert got out. He was carrying what looked like a heavily packed duffel bag. He, John, and Tiger then got into the cabin cruiser, and they pulled away from the dock and headed west. After this, McGovern, who had been holding his dog by the collar during this transfer, turned the smaller boat away from the pier and headed back toward St. James's. "Well, well," I said to Selena, "the gang's all been here, and now some of them are off and away. Wouldn't you like to know where they are going?"

"Not particularly," she said.

As we drove out of the car park area, I noticed a beat-up green sedan there—John's car.

It was a nice afternoon for a drive. We didn't talk for a while but rolled contentedly westward on the coast highway. Shortly, we passed the cabin cruiser going along in our direction, about a quarter of a mile offshore. I recognized a few landmarks beside the highway as we sped along, but things had changed. We got to the St. Andrews Bay region in about an hour. I had spent some time surveying sites and making surface collections around here. Panama City looked bigger than it had then. We went through it and on through the adjacent small town of St. Andrews and then through little places like Point Washington and Santa Rosa before arriving at Fort Walton.

Back in 1940, I had stayed here for a week, making a number of tests in some shell middens located between a large, flat-topped pyramidal mound and the beach. I explained to Selena that Fort Walton is an important site in Florida archaeology. The ceramic sequence there, I instructed her, ran from pre–Weeden Island times on through to the Fort Walton occupation. In fact, the town's pyramidal mound is the "type site" for the late pre-Columbian Fort Walton culture. As I told her this, Selena got that tolerantly amused look on her face that she'd had the previous day in response to my professorial discourse over on the island.

A museum had been established near the Fort Walton Mound since I had been there, and we stopped and looked through it. There was a copy of my book in a display case. After our museum visit, we had a glass of chilled Perrier and a sit-down rest under a sidewalk café awning. It was after five by now, and I inquired of Selena where she would like to have dinner. She told me that there was a good place, out on the open Gulf Beach, just before we got to St. Andrews,

on our way back. It was quite new and handsomely decorated, with first-rate seafood.

The place she had told me about was a two-storied motel.
the restaurant-bar was dark and air-conditioned and attractive. We were fairly early—it was just about six o'clock—and
were shown to a comfortable, red-leather-cushioned booth.
Over drinks, Selena reached out and touched my hand.
"Colin, dear," she said, "doesn't it make you proud to come
back to your old scenes of triumph? You're so famous now."

She was teasing me about my book being on display in
the museum. "Selena," I responded, "archaeologists aren't
famous. At least, not many of them are, and I'm not one of
them. Ours is but a narrow corner of the great world."

"I love to hear you talk, Colin. I always have. You have
such a romantic way of saying things."

"Romantic, or stilted and pompous?"

She laughed. "Romantic, I think—maybe stilted and
pompous, too, but it doesn't matter. I like it. You mean well."

"Like Harry Hedrickson?"

"Don't, Colin," she said.

A waitress, miniskirted and tightly bodiced, with her am-
pleness well deployed both front and rear, came up and asked
if we were ready to order. After taking it, and an order for a
second round of drinks, she twitched off into the roseate
gloom in the direction of the bar.

Had my appreciative glance at the waitress stirred something in Selena's mind? "Colin, are you going to marry again?"

"I have no plans," I said, "but I should think the question
would be more apropos for you, my dear."

She looked down and then, without looking up, said, "I
have no plans."

"But you have been single all these years—since you divorced John. Hasn't there been anyone else?"

She didn't answer this second question. I supposed I was
being too prying, too personal. The waitress came by then
with our first course. I waited until she had gone, then asked
something I had often wondered about. "Speaking of mar-

riage, has Charles ever been close to getting married in all these years?"

Selena shook her head and chewed a few mouthfuls before answering me. "No," she said, "I'm afraid that Charles is gay. You must have realized?"

I told her that I didn't know, that I never thought of such things when we were boys, but that by the time we were in college, or just afterward, in 1940, when I was down here that summer, I had wondered.

"I don't know when it started," Selena said. "Now, they say that one is like that very early on, from birth. I don't think, though, that I would have known it from back when . . . when we were children. Charles was always strange, though. Not like Webbie or John . . . or you. You . . . you were more predictable than Charles but more unpredictable than Webbie and John. You were just right." She smiled and blushed.

"I'm flattered," I told her. Then I thought that I would ask it, ask that question that had bothered me for so long. "Selena, what made you turn away from me, so suddenly, way back then?" I could see that she didn't like the question, and I braced myself for some evasions and prevarications. They came.

"Colin, I don't know what you mean. I never turned away from you. You turned away from me. You went away—up north, to Boston. What could I do?"

Should I pursue this, or let it go, this now antique jealousy? I decided to pursue it. "No Selena, that won't wash. For a whole week after . . . after our . . . our day on the island, you went out of your way to avoid me. This was even before my father said anything to me about our moving to Boston. Then, when I came to see you on my last night in St. Christopher's, you closed the door in my face and told me you had a date with John Crawford."

Selena didn't quite face me. She said, after a pause, "I don't remember it that way at all. I didn't leave you. You left me. Did you expect that I wouldn't got out with any other boys ever again?"

I saw it wasn't going to do any good to pursue it further. I'll drop the subject, I thought. Our main course came, and we ate in silence for a while. Then I remarked on the food. "It is really quite good here, isn't it?" But there was no response from my dinner partner. I ate along in silence for a time and then looked up. Selena was looking at me with her eyes full of tears. I couldn't believe it. This woman who had been so composed, almost severely so at times, in the three days that I had been here, now dissolving into tears.

"Selena, Selena, what is it, my dear?"

She looked down, shaking her head, and got out a handkerchief to dab at her eyes. Finally, she spoke. "Colin, I've always cared so much for you. All those years when we were little—you were the one I liked to play 'make-believe' with the most. You always thought up such wonderful things. I thought about you the most. And then, then when we were a little older, I was so . . . so confused. Can't you understand?"

Her tears had embarrassed me. "Yes, I suppose so," I answered, although I didn't really. To change the subject, I went back to Charles. "Are you really as upset as Charles had told me you are about his wanting to dig over on the island?"

"I don't know how upset he has told you I am. I suppose he has told you that Webbie and I have been trying to murder him. I won't dignify that crazy accusation by answering it. Although now, after what happened to poor Webbie, it does look like somebody might have been trying to do the same to Charles. But, as to Charles's digging in the mound, as I told you both yesterday, I think it's all foolishness. It will just get us into trouble with the state about the purchase of the island."

"Well," I agreed, "I can see why you think Charles's ideas are foolish. Still, there's no use getting upset about it. When the state takes over the island, I am sure that, sooner or later, they'll excavate the rest of the mound—so it's all going to be done anyway."

She seemed disturbed by this and said she couldn't see

the reason, going back to her argument of yesterday, that archaeologists already must know enough about mounds like this.

But I returned to Charles. "Is he all right, Selena? Is he well? I know we're all getting older, but I thought he looked rather poorly, as they used to say back when we were children. Has he been to a doctor lately?"

Selena said she didn't know, that she had asked him the same question when she'd arrived in St. Christopher's last Christmas. Charles had promised her then that he'd go see a doctor the next time he was in New Orleans. She didn't know whether he had or not. I took it from this that Charles had been in New Orleans since Christmas.

"What does he do in New Orleans, Selena?" I asked her. "What is this connection with the Lockwood Galleries?"

"We first got to know Calhoun Lockwood through John, back at the time he and I were going together—were, in fact, engaged. John got a job in the galleries after college. He'd been at Tulane."

I nodded that I had heard this, and she went on. "Well, Daddy got to know Lockwood through us, and he acted as Lockwood's lawyer from time to time. Daddy was in New Orleans a lot—he had some woman over there. Charles met Lockwood at about that time. I think they had a . . . a relationship. Lockwood was a homosexual. He was rather well-known in New Orleans as one. Before he died, back at the time President Kennedy was killed, he had a coterie of characters hanging around the gallery, some of whom were even gossiped about as having had something to do with the assassination. By that time, I was long divorced from John, so I didn't see anything of Lockwood, but I think Charles kept in touch with him until he died. Tommy Fawnley, who took over the galleries after Lockwood's death, is now Charles's lover."

"And Charles goes to New Orleans to see him?"

Selena nodded. "Charles keeps an apartment over there. It's expensive. He really can't afford it. He's also one of the members of the consortium that owns the galleries and employs Fawnley, but I'm afraid Charles has lost more money in the galleries than he has made. He's deeply in debt now. That's one reason why the house here looks so run-down. It's a good thing the island sale is going through soon. He needs the money."

We passed up dessert and a brandy and left. I waved goodbye to the pretty waitress who had served us, and she bestowed a warm smile on me.

It was dark and slightly cool outdoors now. We walked over to my car. There was no one around. I brushed against Selena's softness, and then I took her in my arms and kissed her. I don't know how surprised she may have been, but if she was she recovered very quickly, and we kissed again. "Selena, my darling," I told her, "I want to be with you. Let's stay right here tonight." She seemed very happy at the idea.

We went into the lobby section of the motel, and I asked the clerk for a room. No, we were without luggage, I explained, we'd pay in advance. I don't know whether patrons, or would-be patrons, of hostelries are given arch looks anymore in such circumstances, but this clerk maintained an imperturbable countenance. Perhaps my aged appearance was enough to assure him that we were, in spite of any other circumstances, on the side of law, order, and morality.

$\triangledown$

7

I AWOKE THE NEXT MORNING, as they say, "in a strange bed." It was Wednesday, June 5, the day after the funeral of Webster Bull, and the day after my night in bed with Selena. I was in a motel, on the Gulf Beach, somewhere a little west of St. Andrews. Sunlight and shadow flickered on the ceiling above me. There were a few morning sounds—birds, a car starting up, someone walking by in the hall outside. Where was Selena? Here she was, in the bed with me, curled up on the other side. Was she awake?

"Selena," I asked, "are you awake?"

"No," came the monosyllabic answer. She got out of bed then and headed for the bathroom. I could not help but admire her nude figure. In a little while, I heard the shower running. Presently, she emerged from the bathroom, wrapped in a bath towel and with a smaller towel tied around her hair.

"It's seven-thirty," she told me. "Don't you think we should go and have breakfast?"

"All right," I answered, "but wouldn't you rather have it sent up here?"

"No," was her unequivocal answer.

I got up and went into the bathroom. Then I realized that I had no toothbrush, no toothpaste, no shaving things. I remembered I had a pocket comb in a trouser pocket, so I wrapped a towel around my middle and went back into the bedroom to find it. Selena was partly dressed now and was sitting at the mirror applying lipstick from her handbag. I went over, put my arms around her, and bent down to kiss her cheek, but she turned her head away. I went back into the bathroom, showered, and combed my hair. When I returned, she was fully dressed and staring out the window over the courtyard of the motel. I dressed quickly, and we went down to breakfast.

Sex, I thought—that basic human motivation, even for the elderly. Performance may be more limited, but its allure remains. I had enjoyed my night with Selena, but now she seemed in some way offended by the act of love. It was as though she had suddenly turned against me, just as she had on that long ago day of our lovemaking on the island.

Downstairs we ordered breakfast. The dining room was medium full and bustling. Our winsome waitress of last evening was not on duty, and we were served, instead, by a middle-aged lady, fully and unexcitingly clad in a plain brown uniform, and with a pencil stuck in her bouffant hairdo. I had a hard time catching Selena's eye during breakfast, and, finally to engage her in some talk, I asked her what she was going to do today. She shrugged and said, "What I usually do there in St. Christopher's—nothing."

She ate very little and was clearly out of sorts. I told her that I was going to drive up to Tallahassee, to see the archaeologists at the university there. Wouldn't she like to come along? We could have lunch someplace there, before I went to meet these fellows, and she could either come with me then or do some shopping or whatever. We'd come back early, well before dinner. She didn't give an immediate answer to my invitation. Instead, I could see anger rising in her.

"Colin, you just go along your own pontifical, conceited way, don't you! You know so much better than anyone else! You come down her and indulge Charles in all of his fantasies! I've asked you not to let him, or those people from the state, dig over there on the island, but you brush my wishes and my opinion off like they were dirt on your sleeve!" She was flaming now. Those green eyes could, to say the least, express displeasure, and I was now their target.

I could only restate my position. "Charles," I said, "has been giving me the same kind of hell from the other side. I am not encouraging him to dig the mound, Selena. I've told him to leave it alone until we bring in these people from Tallahassee. I'm hoping things can be worked out so that if there is any, shall we say, family property buried there, it can go to the Randalls in an open and completely legal way without stirring up some kind of hassle."

"Why, Colin, does anyone have to be brought in?" she asked with vehemence.

"Because someone *will be* brought in as soon as the island belongs to the state. You are going to sell the island, aren't you? The state will take it. You can't avoid it. I can't understand why you are so worked up about the matter."

She ignored this and said, "The state people won't bother to dig in the mound if you tell them that what you have done and written about it in that overweight book of yours is already quite enough. They'll be bound to follow the advice of someone in your position."

There was no point in me trying to tell her again that things didn't work like that in archaeology. In fact, there was no point in trying to argue with her anymore. I was upset, though. Everything between us, which last night had seemed so, well, so very nice, was now gone. I paid the breakfast check, and we went out, got into the car, and headed east for home. We made the trip without exchanging more than a half dozen words. I could feel Selena's antagonism all the way.

When we got to St. Christopher's, I took Selena directly to the Randalls'. I hoped I wouldn't see Charles. Somehow, I didn't want to advertise to him the fact that I had spent the night with his sister. When we pulled up in front of their house, there was no one around except a black man who was moving a lawn sprinkler to a new spot on their front yard. Selena, not waiting for me to come around and open the car door, jumped out and slammed it behind her. She walked swiftly up to the porch and disappeared into the house without looking back. I drove to the St. Christopher House in a bad mood.

It was ten o'clock when I got there. The clerk at the desk handed me some mail and told me that Sheriff Larrabee had called around earlier in the morning to see me. "You were away last night, weren't you, Mr. Edwards?"

I suppose I had a guilty flush when I responded that I had been. What did Larrabee want? Was he, on behalf of the God-fearing citizens of the county, running bed checks on the nocturnal habits of the aging patrons of the St. Christopher House? I asked the clerk if the sheriff wanted me to get in touch with him, but he said no, looked at the clock, and told me that he thought the sheriff would be back anytime now, that he had said he would return. I said I'd be in my room and took my key and went up.

When I got to the room, I examined my face in the bathroom mirror and decided I'd better shave. I also needed to change out of my funeral wear of yesterday. I'd shaved and was selecting a less formal suit when the phone rang and the clerk told me Sheriff Larrabee was in the lobby.

Larrabee was waiting for me at the foot of the stairs. It was warm, so we went out on the porch and took cane rocking chairs there. The sheriff took out a flat leather cigar case, courteously offered me a cigar, which I refused, and lit one for himself. "I was checking on something, Mr. Edwards, if you don't mind," he began. "Yesterday, after the funeral, you were out at the Cape Sands about lunchtime, I believe?"

I wondered if all my other movements of yesterday had been subject to some kind of keyhole scrutiny. How very embarrassing, I thought. "Yes, Mrs. Crawford and I had lunch there. We were there, I suppose, from about twelve-thirty to two. Why?"

"Did Mr. Crawford, Mr. John Crawford, show up while you were there in the dining room?"

"Yes, he did. He came in just for a minute and spoke to that fellow Tiger Westcott, who had come in earlier and was seated at the bar."

"Did they leave together, from the dock down below the motel, on a cabin cruiser?" the sheriff asked.

"Yes, they did. This fellow McGovern, who works on the island as caretaker, came into the dock on the island's boat about that time, and brought with him the man called Hebert, whom we saw the day before yesterday over on St. James's. Then Crawford, Tiger, and Hebert took off from the Cape Sands dock in the cruiser. McGovern, accompanied by his faithful dog, whose name I do not know, then returned in the smaller boat to the island."

"Did Crawford come to the Cape Sands by car?"

I said, "I think so. When Mrs. Crawford and I left, about two, Crawford's green sedan was there in the parking lot of the motel. I suppose he arrived that way, although I don't know for sure. I might tell you, too, that a quarter of an hour later, as Mrs. Crawford and I were driving in the direction of Panama City, we passed the cabin cruiser as it was going west."

The sheriff nodded, and said, "Thanks, that checks."

I couldn't restrain my curiosity. Maybe now I could have that insider's conversation with an investigator that would put me in the picture.

"Sheriff Larrabee," I asked, "does this have—do these fellows, McGovern, Hebert, and Tiger, have anything to do with the Bull death, do you think?"

The sheriff gave me an answer that would have been worthy of one of those TV serials that take place west of the Pecos. With his Texas cowboy hat tilted forward over his eyes, he took his cigar out of his mouth, studied it carefully, and said, "Mr. Edwards, we don't rightly know that. But you may be correct in that assumption, or, again, you may not."

I kept trying, however lamely. "Sheriff, do you have anything new on the Bull case? Has the gun, the gun that fired those bullets—the one that killed Mr. Bull and the other bullets that were in Mr. Randall's wall and in the Bull and Hedrickson houses—has that gun ever been found?"

The sheriff gave me a hard look after I got that out but

then told me, quietly, politely, "Not yet, Mr. Edwards, but you and all of the other citizens of the county will be informed just as soon as we do find it." With that, he thanked me for my time and departed.

I thought to myself that it didn't sound like they had much yet. Larrabee's interview with me had been focused on our friends, the putative drug runners. Could Webbie's death be linked to them? I constructed a mental image of the chromium-eyed Tiger ringing the Bulls' doorbell in the dead of night, then, when the master of the house came to answer it, pulling a "heater" from his waistband and letting Webbie have it. The scenario wasn't convincing.

When I got back upstairs, I read the letters that had come for me. They were from two of my daughters, telling me of family news and hoping that I was having a good rest and enjoying myself. What they had to say took me, for a few minutes, back into my real life and out of the unreal ambience in which I had been moving since my arrival in St. Christopher's. I thought back on my good life with Helen— Helen, who had that wonderful quality of *tendresse*—and then, as they always did, such memories brought on the blackest sense of loss.

But I went ahead with things. I got Joel Chandler on the phone. He said that he had arranged for Bill Calvert to meet with us that afternoon. I apologized for the fact that I might be a little late and said I hoped that a three o'clock appointment would be okay. Chandler told me he was sure it would be, then gave me instructions on how to find him at the university and where to park my car. I thought about calling Charles, just to tell him of my plans, but I decided against it. It would be better to confront him with Chandler and Calvert—presuming I could persuade one or both to come down here sometime tomorrow—rather than let Charles mull it over and think up new arguments against doing the sensible thing.

I ate a light lunch at the hotel, then headed for Tallahassee. I'd been over the Tallahassee–St. Christopher's route, but coming this way, only last Saturday. My God, I thought, I've only been here for four days, but seems like forever.

It was a little short of three o'clock when I got to the city limits of the state capital. I found the university with no trouble and parked my car following Chandler's instructions. His office was in the basement of a large building which served as both a museum and the quarters of the Department of Anthropology.

Joel Chandler was a tall, lean, friendly young man with glasses and a beard. His desk was messy with books and papers, and books had overflowed from his bookcase so that they were piled up in several places on the floor. We chatted for a while about what he had been doing recently. He told me he had been much interested in a historic period site, not far from Tallahassee, dated from around 1700. A metal detector had been used there with slight success, although metals had not been especially abundant in the site, which looked like a Spanish mission station with a small resident Indian population. Chandler brought out the metal detector and explained how to run it. He told me that Calvert would be along any minute, and almost as soon as he said that the latter appeared. Bill Calvert was also young, friendly, bespectacled, and bearded—but short and chunky rather than tall and lean.

Calvert asked me about the St. Christopher's murder and if I knew Mr. Bull. I told him that I did, that he was some sort of second cousin of mine. In response to a question about progress on the case, I had to tell him that I didn't know of any. Then we got down to business, with the two of them kidding me about being in the treasure-hunting line now. Was this what retired Harvard archaeologists got around to doing? I said that I was afraid so and that I only hoped they would bear with me in my predicament.

Chandler got down my book and opened it up to the St. James's Mound chapter. I had a map of the mound in it drawn in fifty-centimeter contours, and I showed them about where, on the west side of the mound, the depression, probably signaling an old refilled excavation, was located. It was somewhere around there, I told them, that my cousin, Charles Randall, aided by a lizard-chasing dog, had found the little gold alligator, an object very definitely in a Panamanian style. Chandler wanted to know about when this gold style dated in Panama. I told him we weren't sure, but somewhere in the range of A.D. 500, give or take a couple of centuries in either direction. Then, jokingly, he said that this dating would be perfectly compatible with the Weeden Island I chronological placement of the mound, and maybe the gold alligator was a true trade piece. I said that even though the dating ranges made such an interpretation compatible, I thought the chances of this being a legitimate pre-Columbian trade item, passed from Panamanian to Floridian Indians, were pretty slim. Calvert tended to agree with me.

I tried to tell them something of Charles's character and personality. "He's a very family-oriented sort of a man. The Randalls have been in St. Christopher's since his great-grandfather's day. He's got a bee in his bonnet about treasure being buried in the mound on St. James's, and he is convinced that the treasure consists of a large number of Colombian and Panamanian pre-Columbian gold objects, which this great-grandfather, Alexander Randall, is presumed to have brought back, or some way received, from Colombia in the 1880s. For whatever reason—and as you know, gentlemen, there is very little reason involved when it comes to dealing with buried treasure—this Great-grandfather Alexander is supposed to have buried the gold there. Cousin Charles's grandfather and his father were both convinced that Alexander had hidden the gold somewhere, although they didn't know where to look. Now, with the finding of this single gold artifact in a superficial location in the mound, Charles feels he's spotted the place. He wants to excavate it, as Randall family property, before St. James's Island passes over to the state—to the state Park Service. What do you say to that?" I concluded, turning to Calvert.

"Well, I'm not in the state Park Service. I'm only associated with them, off and on, as state archaeologist, but I'm
afraid that might bring on some trouble. Joel"—he motioned
toward his colleague—"has told me some of this, and I find
it hard to advise on. As long as it's privately owned land,
antiquities, here in the United States, belong to the landowner. Oh, I know there have been some attempts to frame
state laws that would protect antiquities as they are protected, say, in Europe, where anything like this belongs to
the state no matter whose land it is on. I'm not a lawyer, but
I don't think such laws would stand up constitutionally.

"On the other hand," he went on, "this is just the kind of
thing that could stir up a real mess, considering how close
the state is to taking possession of St. James's Island. If all
goes according to plan, it will probably become state property
by July first. The state is interested in the island's wildlife,
in protecting its environment, in developing recreational fa-
cilities for the public that will be consistent with environ-
mental protection, and in making available to the public
something of the island's history, which includes archaeology. I told Mr. Randall all this when I went down to St. Christopher's earlier this year. At that time, he didn't say anything
to me about wanting to dig over there before we took over."

"It was after that, Dr. Calvert, that my cousin went over
to the island and found the gold alligator in the mound."

"I understand, Dr. Edwards. But if a landowner goes rooting around in an archaeological site on his property in the
month before it is to be taken over by the state, that's going
to cause trouble. It's liable to mean litigation brought by the
state to reduce the size of the sum in the condemnation
settlement. I'd advise against it."

I thought that the threat of financial loss, and further
litigation, would make Charles unhappy, and, maybe, this
would be enough to make him give up his private digging
plans, but I wasn't at all positive. Every time I thought I had
talked some sense into him, he would break out again with
his old arguments. I didn't know quite what I was hoping

for now. I guessed it was either some kind of blessing from the state's representative that would have allowed Charles to do a limited amount of digging and keep all the anticipated treasure in the family, or, failing that, to have Calvert talk him out of doing anything before the island was taken over by the state. Whichever, I wanted very much for Calvert and Chandler to come to St. Christopher's and talk with Charles. I had hopes that they could convince him to follow some more sensible course than the one he now seemed anxious to embark upon.

To this end, I said, "Gentlemen, I would be deeply obliged to you if you would agree to come down to St. Christopher's and talk with my cousin. I think he would be influenced by your opinions. I've tried to talk some sense into him for the last four days, but I'm a member of the family, and I think that in this case an outsider's opinion might have more influence. Besides," I added, looking at Calvert, "it would be in the state's interests, too, to have this thing settled as smoothly as possible. As I said to Dr. Chandler over the phone, I would be more than happy to put you both up, with no expense to yourselves, at the St. Christopher House, where I am staying. Won't you try and make it?"

Chandler smiled and looked over at Calvert. "What do you say, Bill? Let's go down. I've always liked it at St. Christopher's, and I'd like to see the island and the site over there. Besides, this whole business intrigues me."

Calvert looked at me and asked, "When do you want us?"

"How about tomorrow? Could you come down early, so we could get over to the island before noon, if possible?" I thought once I had them there in St. Christopher's, Charles would be willing to go with them.

Calvert said, "I think I could shift some things around to make tomorrow clear for such an excursion, if that's all right with you, Joel."

Joel agreed and, turning to me, asked, "How would it be if we left here right after breakfast and got down there at, say, about nine-thirty to ten?"

I told them that would suit me fine, that I'd be waiting for them in the lobby of the St. Christopher House.

We talked on for a while after this. It was a relief to feel enfolded again into the profession after my stressful exposure to old friends and relatives. I reflected, then, as I had at other times in my life, that although archaeology isn't a very lucrative profession, there is a camaraderie in it. Even though I had been out of the Florida field for almost half a century, I was still interested in it and had continued to keep up on some of the literature so that I was current about a few of the things that were going on.

The whole matter of Weeden Island subsistence, for instance, was a frontier of investigation. Back when I was working down here, I had guessed that the Weeden Islanders were probably practicing some limited crop cultivation. Now, from various lines of evidence, it was appearing that this had been happening during Weeden Island II times. We talked about this and other matters. My hosts brought me up to date on local academic gossip—who was getting hired where, what people and institutions were getting what research grants. Time went by swiftly, and when I finally looked at my watch it was five o'clock. So I left, with the arrangement that I'd see them tomorrow morning in St. Christopher's.

I got back a little before seven. After a quick bath and a change of clothes, I decided I would call Charles, explain to him what I had done today, and get his promise to meet with us tomorrow morning. I braced myself for an argument, but I was determined that Charles listen to reason. The phone rang at the Randall residence several times, and I was almost ready to put the receiver down when it was answered by the servant, Mildred. I told her who I was and asked for Charles.

"Mr. Charles is not here. No, I don't know when he'll be back. He went over to St. James's Island early this morning."

This was curious—and disturbing—news. I asked if Charles had gone alone.

"Well, sir, I don't really know, but I heard him tell Miss

Selena that Mr. McGovern, the caretaker over there, was going to meet him in the boat down at the Riverfront Dock."

What was Charles up to? I was suspicious. Had he gone over there to retrieve the treasure before I, his unfaithful cousin, could bring in the forces of the state to thwart him? I asked if I could speak to Miss Selena.

"No, sir," the maid said, "Miss Selena is not here either. Mr. Charles, himself, was just trying to talk with her on the phone a little while ago, but I told him she'd already gone out to dinner with Mr. Harry Hedrickson. Mr. Hedrickson picked her up in his car just a little while before Mr. Charles called."

I was disturbed again. Selena going out with Harry Hedrickson? Was she just going over to the Hedricksons for family dinner? It seemed rather unlikely that she would be picked up in a car by her host for this. It was less than a couple of blocks from the Randalls' to the Hedricksons'; besides, Selena had her own car. Well, there wasn't much I could do about Selena, but maybe I could get in touch with Charles by telephone. I asked Mildred if she had the phone number over at the island.

"Yes, sir," she said, "just you wait a minute and I'll get it for you." She came back presently and gave me the number. Should I give Charles a call now? It was seven-thirty, and the dining room closed at eight. I'd better get downstairs and eat first. Any conversation with Charles would have me asking him what he was doing over there, and this would lead to a discussion about the treasure and undoubtedly to an argument when I told him I had invited the state archaeologist down here tomorrow. All this might take a while.

I went down to dinner, and, considering how late it was, I ordered my predinner cocktail in the dining room. There was only one other guest in the room, a gentleman I had not seen before, who was seated at the table next to mine. When I came in we both nodded; then he turned back to a book that he had open on the table beside his plate. He appeared to be near to finishing his dinner. I was enjoying my drink,

after having ordered my food, when he turned in his chair
and asked, "Aren't you Professor Edwards?" I acknowledged
that I was, and he said, "Well, I thought so. I'm Thomas
Fawnley. I've heard about you from your cousin, Charles
Randall, who is a good friend of mine."

Well, I thought, so this is the notorious Tommy Fawnley,
who—at least from Selena's remarks—was, indeed, a good
friend of Charles.

"Would you mind," he asked me, "if I brought my coffee
over and joined you?"

Actually, I did sort of mind. I wanted to worry in peace
about Charles and what he was doing over on the island, to
say nothing of indulging my jealousy about Selena and what
she was up to with redneck Harry. However, one can't be
rude, so I said, "By all means. Please do," and I stood up to
shake hands.

Fawnley was slender and slight of build. He was somewhat
shorter than I, but he stood very straight, excessively so, so
that he actually appeared to be leaning a trifle backward. He
had very even, cold features, with a long, pointed nose, which
he looked down with an expression of permanent arrogance,
as if he were playing the part of a French marquis at the
Court of Versailles during the ancien régime. He was extremely well groomed and cared for. His darkish blond hair,
only slightly streaked with gray, was abundant, immacu-
lately groomed, and styled to lie close to his elegant head. He
was dressed in a light gray, closely fitting Italian-cut suit, a
white shirt, a dark red necktie, and a matching handkerchief.
When we were seated, I noticed expensive-looking, heavy
gold cuff links in the spotlessly white French cuffs which
protruded from his jacket sleeves. I estimated him to be
about forty, but a carefully massaged and cosseted forty.

"This is a rather charming little hostelry, isn't it? I've
never been here before, but I've heard so much about if from
dear Charles. When one has to rough it, it's so nice to do it
in comfort, is it not?"

I felt that this patronization hardly did justice to one of

my favorite inns, and, in saying it, he put my back up. Fawnley spoke with some kind of accent, presumably British, but
I have a poor ear in such matters; it might have been an
affected overlay covering something much more local. We fell
silent for a while, during which time my first course was
served. After taking a few bites, I felt that I probably owed it
to Charles to do my part in some sort of conversation.
"When did you come in?" I asked.

"Oh, I drove over from New Orleans today and arrived
about five this afternoon."

"Have you come to visit Charles?"

"Yes, I have, and at his express wish, but now the terrible
fellow has gone off and abandoned me. After I arrived I had
a telephone call from him from that island of his, and he
told me that he wouldn't be over to pick me up until the
early hours of tomorrow morning. So there was nothing for
it but to put up here. I'm supposed to be down at the dock
by seven A.M., when he has said he'll come and rescue me.
Do you know this fabulous island, Professor?"

I told him that I did, giving him some background. Meanwhile, I was asking myself why Charles had invited this
individual down here at this time, and why, above all, he was
going to take him over to the island, especially now, when I
was trying to help him get things straightened out about the
mound-digging business. Was Fawnley being asked in just
to make it more difficult for us to proceed with the people
from Tallahassee?

The rest of my dinner came. Calm down, I told myself.
Helen had always told me never to eat when I was mad about
something. I began to address my food slowly. I found I was
hungry.

Fawnley, however, showed no inclination to leave me.
"You are in such a fascinating, field, Professor. I wish I had
had the opportunity to study it in greater depth."

To what depths, even the tantalizingly superficial ones
which were implied in this statement, had Thomas Fawnley
plumbed the mysteries of archaeology, I wondered.

"Did you ever know my mentor and former employer, Mr. Calhoun Lockwood?" he asked me. After I indicated that I hadn't known, but had heard of, Mr. Lockwood, Fawnley went on. "He was much interested in and very knowledge-able about archaeology. Mr. Lockwood traveled all over the world, you know—Greece, Egypt, places like that. His own background was an international one. His father was an American, but his mother was from Colombia. She was a Gomez, a very aristocratic and well-known old family there. Mr. Lockwood was a very remarkable man, very remarkable. He had a great interest in the occult as well. I have missed him ever so much since his death, yet there are times when I almost feel he is still with me. There was a great bond between us."

I had visions of Fawnley's great patron of archaeology and the occult communicating with his devoted and elegant pro-tégé from the other side, with table rapping, lights lowered, and ectoplasmic substances floating in the air.

"He was like a father to me," Fawnley confided. "He took me into the Lockwood Galleries when I was only eighteen. I owe everything to him."

I asked Fawnley when Mr. Lockwood died.

"It was in 1968. Unfortunately, his last years were made miserable by . . . by the persecutions of certain persons." He told me this with a somber and meaningful look.

But now Fawnley went off on another tack. "Tell me, how is the charming sister, Selena, since she has left New Orleans and settled here again? You must have seen her."

I told him that Selena was well and that I had seen her several times in the few days I had been here.

"I take it she intends to live here permanently now, even though it means abandoning her child to do so." This last was said with a chilling hardness, as though with an attempt to wound, and it took me by complete surprise.

"Abandoning her child? Why . . . why I had understood that her only child was dead."

I could see that Fawnley had taken satisfaction in dropping this contrary information on me. "Oh, goodness, no, her daughter is very much alive. She is, in one sense, no longer a child. That is, she is my age; however, she is a child, or even less, mentally. She is in a mental institution in New Orleans." Fawnley continued to look gratified. "I can't understand why Charles, or Selena herself, hasn't told you. Well, I suppose Selena is glad to be over here and away from it all for a while. One can hardly blame her."

I was beginning to have my fill of this little man. When the waitress cleared my plate, I told her I would skip dessert. "Well, Mr. Fawnley," I said, "you'll have to excuse me. I've had a long day, and I'm going to turn in. Have a pleasant excursion to the island tomorrow. Good night." I got up and left the table.

In my room, I sat on the bed in the dark, thinking about Selena as the mother of a mentally incapacitated forty-year-old daughter. How horrible. After a bit, I turned on the light and dialed the telephone number on the island. I let it ring about twenty times, but no one answered. I recalled Charles had said that the phone was in the Bull cottage. Maybe Charles wasn't staying there; still, McGovern should have answered it. Apparently he wasn't in.

My watch said it was a quarter to nine. I thought about a brandy, but I didn't want to go back downstairs for fear of running into Fawnley. I was about to call down and have one of the bellboys bring me up a drink when the phone rang.

I picked it up and said hello.

There was a pause, and then a woman's voice I didn't recognize asked, "Colin?"

I said yes, and the speaker identified herself as Lydia Hedrickson. "Colin," she went on, "I'm sorry to bother you at this hour, but I wonder if I could talk with you if I came down to the hotel." I wasn't used to how she sounded on the telephone, but I thought that her voice seemed sad and as if she were under a strain.

"Of course, Lydia," I told her. "When would you like to come?" I thought briefly of offering to drive over and see her, instead, but then I remembered my confrontation with her husband and thought I might not be altogether welcome in the Hedrickson household.

"If it's all right with you, I'll be there in about ten minutes," she replied. I said I'd await her in the lobby. I wondered what Lydia, whom I had no more than spoken to since my arrival in town, could want to talk with me about. Of all the girls of our circle in St. Christopher's in my boyhood, I think I had paid the least attention to her. I suppose it was because she had been fat and unattractive. I had danced with her at those dancing classes, but I can't remember ever saying more than a few words to her or thinking about her. But, after all, in those days all my thoughts had been reserved for Selena.

I went downstairs and took a chair in the corner of the lobby. I was relieved to see that Thomas Fawnley was nowhere in sight. In fact, both the lobby and the bar were deserted. I'd only been there a short while when Lydia came in from the veranda entrance. She was wearing a dark linen suit, which became her, and I thought, as I had in church yesterday, that she had become a rather attractive woman. I greeted her with a handclasp and showed her to a chair. I asked Lydia if she wouldn't like something to drink and said that I was going to have a brandy. I was surprised when she said that she would join me. After giving the bartender our order, I went back to my chair and looked at Lydia inquiringly. She smiled at me. Age had given her a charm I didn't know she had—or perhaps I had never looked to see before. There was a grace about her manner that her brother, Webbie, lacked. I gave her my sympathies again about his death.

She shook her head and said that it was terrible. When I asked her if there was any new information about it, she told me there wasn't. The bartender brought us our brandies. What could she have come to see me about? Was Harry filing some sort of legal document—I believe they call them restraining orders—to keep me from assisting Charles in digging in the mound on St. James's? Had she come, then, to appeal to my good judgment not to become involved in any such foolishness?

After tasting her brandy, Lydia looked at me and said, "Colin, did Harry come over here to see you the other night?"

I confirmed that he had, that he had called on Sunday night, and that we had had a discussion, as I put it, in the bar.

"Colin, I'm sorry that Harry behaved as he did. He had no right to talk to you like that. He wasn't himself." From this, I judged that Harry must have told her of some of the things he had said to me. My other reaction was that Harry had been too much himself.

"He was trying to keep you from digging over on the island, wasn't he?"

"Yes," I said.

"Colin, he has no right to tell you such a thing. I am one of the co-owners over there; in fact, since my brother's death, I own one half of the island. I want you to know that you, and Charles, have my permission to dig in the Indian mound over there, or anywhere else you want to on the island."

I was surprised by her concern. I wouldn't have expected her to be worried, or even to have known, about such matters.

"Lydia, this plan to dig on the island is Charles's idea, and, from an archaeological standpoint, a very amateur idea. He has asked my advice about it, and I have told him not to do anything until we have consulted the proper authorities. As things stand, I've arranged for a Park Service archaeologist to visit the island tomorrow and to discuss matters with Charles."

She took another sip of her drink. She looked as though she was trying to make up her mind to tell me something else—and then had decided to do so. "Colin," she said, in a slow, precise way, "Harry said what he did to you the other night because of Selena. She . . . she has an unfortunate influence over him now."

I thought that there were tears forming in Lydia's eyes. "For whatever reason, Selena seems very concerned about her brother digging in the mound over there. I don't know

why. Her opposition is her business, but it seems ridiculous
and out of proportion to the importance of the matter. She
talked my brother into her way of thinking, and now she is
exerting the same influence on my husband." Lydia paused,
looked away, and blinked. There were tears in her eyes now.
Then she continued. "Selena was taking Webster away from
Mabel when he was killed, and now she is doing her best to
take Harry away from me."

I didn't know what to believe, let alone what to say.

"The woman is like a sorceress, Colin, a vicious sorceress.
Ever since she came back here from New Orleans last Christmas, she has spread trouble in her wake. She seduced Webbie
to enlist his aid against her own brother. She has seduced Harry
to her own purposes. Both were old enough to know better. But
she has always been like this, ever since we were children. You
should remember." With this last she looked at me, I thought,
very accusingly. "She had you, John Crawford, Webbie, and
Harry—she had all of you—and she hasn't been good for any
of you. You were the luckiest. You got away early."

"Lydia," I began, "I don't know what to say. I—"

She laid her hand gently on my arm. "There isn't anything
to say, Colin. I suppose I have laid too much on you by
coming down here like this, but I wanted you to know that
Harry isn't the bad person that he may appear to be in your
eyes, after the way he talked to you the other night. He hasn't
been himself lately, not since he's come under the spell of
that, that she-devil." Lydia dried her eyes with her handkerchief and continued. "I know that some people felt I shouldn't
have married Harry, that he was too crude, not from our class.
You know what I mean. But he has been a good husband to
me, and I still love him." She was crying more openly now.

Lydia may have come to see me, in part, to apologize for
Harry, but I think her main reason was to let someone know
of her grief. I tried to be reassuring, although I am afraid I
didn't quite know how. I felt I was in a poor position to tell
her that Selena's motives might not be as she imagined
them, knowing as I did that Selena was out with Harry at

that very moment. Had Selena been ensnaring me in the same way—and for such a trivial purpose? What were Selena's reasons for going to such lengths to keep Charles or anyone else away from the St. James's Island Mound? Or did she just enjoy the exercise of her power, her role as a seductress, a "sorceress" as Lydia had called her?

Lydia drew herself together at last, looked at her watch, stood up, and extended her hand to me. "You've been very kind, Colin, to let me unburden myself to you like this." She smiled then, looked up at me, and said, "Did you know, Colin, that I was very much in love with someone when I was about fourteen?"

I didn't think she was referring to Harry Hedrickson. "No, I didn't. Who was that? John Crawford?"

"No, Colin. It was you."

I must have looked flabbergasted.

Lydia went on. "You were always so nice, Colin. I knew you didn't care for me, but you were always so gentle and polite."

Life, I thought, can be so extraordinarily sad at times. I pressed her hand good-bye and gave her a kiss on the cheek. It was still damp from her tears. She told me that she had to go, that she had a taxi waiting outside. I was mildly surprised at this. Perhaps she didn't drive; or did the Hedricksons have only one car and that one was now with Harry and Selena? I offered to give her a ride home, but she told me no, that she had someplace else to go first. I saw her into her taxi, which was waiting at the side of the hotel.

Back upstairs, I knew that I was terribly tired, as tired as I had been that first night here. I thought about what Lydia had said to me before we parted. So I had been polite those long years ago. A very modest virtue, politeness. Still, in one's old age, to be remembered for a second-best virtue is better, I suppose, than to be remembered for none.

Before I turned out the lights, I tried the telephone number on the island again. I let it ring and ring, but there was no answer.

$\triangledown$

8

THE GARDENS AND THE LAWN around the carriage house, and the sandbox where we were playing, were lighted by Japanese lanterns, which, suspended from the trees, swayed ever so slightly in the wind as they cast their lovely soft red, orange, violet, and green luminosity over us. In the house, where the grown-ups were having their party, we could see lights and hear the music of the foxtrot or mingled voices.

Great-uncle Charles came up the driveway, driven by Edmund, who wore his tall hat. Edmund stopped the carriage not far from the sandbox, and Great-uncle Charles got out and came over to us. He was carrying a gold-headed cane, and his face was ruddy and smiling above a wing collar and a broad, dark cravat with a pearl stickpin. "How are my darlings?" he inquired of Selena and Charles, and he bent down, lovingly, and kissed Selena as she squealed with delight. He turned to Charles, giving him a hug and a kiss on the cheek. Then he looked over at me, someone legitimately within the wider circle of the family, if not fully appropriate to the inner circle of embracement. At that point, I stood up, bowed, and extended my hand, saying, "Good evening, Great-uncle Charles." He responded with a formal handshake and said, "Good evening, my little man." Then he turned away and walked toward the house, disappearing into the dark that separated us from the music, the party, the talk, and the laughter.

It was late for us to play out, but this was a special occasion because our parents were at the party in the house.

Georgia had just brought us lemonade, a cookie apiece, and some sherbet, with the admonition not "to spill that all over yourselves." Having finished this treat, I was working on the biggest and most intricately romantic sand castle that I had ever conceived and constructed, and Selena was there beside me, watching and admiring. But then I felt a change come over everything. I began to be afraid. The breeze that had barely rustled the leaves above us grew stronger and frightening. Everything became darker, and the warm colors of the Japanese lanterns turned gray. I looked for Selena, and cried out for her, but she wasn't there. I saw Charles digging on the other side of the sandbox. I went over to him, put my hand on his shoulder, and said, "Charles, why is it getting darker, and where is Selena?" He didn't answer me at first, and then he turned and looked up at me. He looked awful. He was an old, wrinkled Charles with dead eyes, and he grinned at me in a horrible way, like a skeleton would. I turned and tried to run away or to scream, but I could do neither.

I woke up. I was sweating, trembling, with the residues of my dream still floating before me. I sat up and took a drink of water from a glass on my bed table. Then I looked at my watch. It was just 6:00 A.M., and it was beginning to be light outside. I heard the comfortable chirping of birds. I thought about my nightmare. I have rarely had any since I was a child, but that one was like some of the old bad ones. It had all been so beautiful in the beginning, but it had turned evil and wicked. I lay back on my pillow, in the cool of the morning, and tried to wish it all out of my head.

I remembered that last night, in the dining room, Tommy Fawnley had told me that Charles was coming over this morning at seven o'clock to pick him up down at the dock and take him back to St. James's Island. Should I get up now, dress and go down and try to see and talk with Charles when he came in? I thought about it awhile, but then I decided I wouldn't. He would resent my interference. I decided that I would call Charles later this morning and tell him he'd have to see the men from Tallahassee or stop asking me for advice.

If I still couldn't get him on the telephone, I'd take them over to the island on my own. After a little while, I fell into a light, early-morning sleep and when I finally awoke it was past seven.

Fawnley, of course, was nowhere to be seen when I went downstairs. I thought about Lydia's visit of last night and wished I could have cheered her up. It struck me that she and I were—in our affairs of the heart—the injured parties, she forsaken by red-faced, redneck Harry and I by the beautiful Selena. Harry's transgression was unarguably the worse of the two; he was, after all, her lawfully wedded husband, while to me Selena was—what? Some kind of unholy spirit from the past, bound to me only by my jealousy and my febrile imagination? I switched to Fawnley in my musings. I supposed that by now—it was ten minutes to eight when I looked at my watch—he was well on his way to the island, if not already there. Had Charles or McGovern come over to pick him up?

After breakfast, I ordered three lunches from the kitchen for us to take to the island. I got up from the table and went out to the lobby to see if the morning paper had come in, and who should be there but that morning regular at the St. Christopher House, Sheriff Larrabee, chatting with the desk clerk. We said good morning, and then, rather gravely, he asked if he might speak to me in private, for just a minute. Did the desk clerk register his usual slight alarm? Perhaps it wouldn't be long before I received a neatly typed letter from the management requesting me to vacate my room in view of the fact that other patrons had become uneasy associating with a member of the criminal classes.

The sheriff and I went over to our corner of the lobby, but, before sitting down, he asked me, "Mr. Edwards, did Mrs. Hedrickson come here to the hotel to see you last night, a little before nine, maybe?"

I confirmed that, indeed, she had been here.

"Well, sir," the sheriff told me, "Brad Ellis called my office a little while ago and informed me that Mr. Harry Hedrickson had telephoned him early this morning to say that Mrs. Hedrickson hadn't come in last night. As near as we can put it together, Mrs. Hedrickson called a taxi last night—this was while Mr. Hedrickson was out—and the driver brought her here to the hotel. He says—the taximan, that is—that he waited for her outside and that she talked with you here in the lobby. In view of Mrs. Hedrickson's disappearance, I wonder, Mr. Edwards, if I can ask you to tell me what she came here to see you about?"

This time I was glad to be able to clear the desk clerk of the charges of espionage that I had been levying upon him in my mind and to have the taxi driver identified as the informer. As to the sheriff's question, I decided to give him a limited version of my conversation with Lydia.

"Sheriff Larrabee, last Sunday night Mr. Hedrickson came to the hotel to see me, and we had a little argument here in the bar. It didn't amount to anything; Hedrickson had had too much to drink. We had been boys together here in St. Christopher's years and years ago, and we didn't get along very well then. Apparently, he still remembered it and was blowing off steam. Mrs. Hedrickson came by to apologize for the way her husband had behaved. That's what we talked about."

"And was that all you talked about?" He looked like he didn't believe me.

"Yes," I told him. I didn't feel that it was appropriate for me to go into Lydia's marital troubles; however, in a town as small as this, he may already have had some inkling of them.

As the sheriff turned to go, I asked him, "Was Mrs. Hedrickson's appearance here last night the last trace you have of her? When she left here, I had offered to drive her home, but she said that she had a taxi waiting and that she had someplace to go. Maybe the taximan can tell you where."

"I've asked the taxi driver that, Mr. Edwards. He told me that when Mrs. Hedrickson left the hotel she asked him to drive her out to the Cape Sands Motel. He says he left her in the parking lot, near the motel entrance, sometime between nine-thirty and ten o'clock. As far as we know, she hasn't been seen by anyone since. Her husband says he got home last night sometime after midnight and she had not come in by then. When he woke up this morning at about six and she still wasn't there, he notified the police." After telling me this, Sheriff Larrabee touched his hat and left, going directly to his car outside.

Lydia missing? Had she run away, left her erring Harry? Had she done away with herself as a way to end her sorrow? She had been upset last night, but I didn't have the feeling that she was on the verge of suicide. When she left me, she had some of her composure back and sounded determined, rather than undone by grief.

I went back up to my room and tried to call the island. The result was the same as last night—prolonged ringing but no answer. Where was everyone? I went back downstairs and looked at the morning paper. There was nothing about the Bull case and nothing about any of the suspects in what I had come to think of as the drug-running case. Come to think of it, I hadn't seen anything in the papers about any kind of a local cocaine connection since I had been here. Mr. Clancy's visit last Monday, together with his questions about McGovern and his associates, were the only evidences I had that something like that might be going on; otherwise, the drug running was a melodrama of my own concoction, stimulated a bit, no doubt, by remarks from Charles and Selena.

The time dragged by very slowly, and I gave the island phone another try—again, with no success. I have always been impatient, and old age had not made me less so. I picked up the lunches in the kitchen, where a nice lady wished me a nice day and a nice picnic. After that, I waited in the lobby, where I was looking out one of the windows when a pickup truck, with "Department of Anthropology, Florida State University, Tallahassee, Florida," painted on its side, turned off the coast highway into the side street by the hotel.

Chandler and Calvert saw me through the window as they pulled up to park. They came on in, and I introduced them to the desk clerk, who registered them for the night. While they were leaving some light luggage in their rooms, I asked the clerk if I could use the desk phone to make a call, and I rang the island once more. There was still no answer. It was now twenty until eleven. When Chandler and Calvert came back downstairs, I explained to them that I was determined to take them over to the island, even though I'd been unable to raise Charles, who had gone over last night.

When we got down to the Riverfront Dock in the pickup, I made arrangements with the boatman to hire the same boat Charles had taken out on Monday, and I asked him, "Did McGovern, the St. James's Island caretaker, come over here to pick up Mr. Randall yesterday morning?"

"He came over, all right, Mr. Edwards," he told me, "but then Mr. Randall took the boat back by himself. This fellow McGovern stuck around here for about fifteen minutes when Mr. Crawford and them other two all came up in the big cruiser, and McGovern went off with them."

Well, I thought, we'll just have to go on over and see who's there. I'm sorry if Charles objects, but, if he wants me to help him, he should keep me more up to date on what is going on. I thought then to ask about this morning. "Did a man named Fawnley come down here early this morning, and did Mr. Randall or McGovern come over in the boat from the island and pick him up?"

The boatman shook his head and said that he hadn't seen anyone here, but that he, himself, didn't get down to work until about half past seven. Maybe this fellow had arrived and been taken away in the boat before then.

Chandler and Calvert took the metal detector out of the pickup and settled it in the middle of the boat. Chandler had told me that he had had quite a bit of experience with motor crafts like this one, so I invited him to take over and relaxed and sat back with Calvert for our ride down to the narrows. When we got there, I recognized the island's boat at the pier, but the cabin cruiser was nowhere in sight. I felt some relief that we would not have Tiger and Hebert around to observe our upcoming meeting with Charles. Had McGovern gone with them? I hoped so.

After we'd tied up at the pier, I suggested to my colleagues, as they were unloading the metal detector, that it might be better to leave it down here by the dock house until we had tracked down Charles. I wanted to get his permission and approval before we went ahead and ran the gadget over the mound. Chandler and Calvert left it there, and, with me in the lead, we started up the path toward the cottages.

When we got to the place on the path where we turned off to go to the mound, I gave a "hallo" and then another. There was no human answer, but McGovern's dog came bounding and barking down the path toward us from the direction of the cottages. He calmed down quickly and started off through the bush toward the mound. We followed him. In a minute or so, we reached a point where the mound came into view. My heart sank. On the slope of the mound, facing us, was a large, jagged-edged excavation, and judging from the heaps of sand and clay piled up around it, it was a deep hole. Goddamnit, Charles! I said to myself. Now how are you going to explain this?

At first, I thought there was no one around. Then I saw Fawnley, seated on the ground and leaning up against a tree near the mound. He looked uncharacteristically disheveled and definitely unhappy. He was brushing sand off his trousers, which, although folded up almost to the knee, still showed neatly pressed creases above the folds. I guess he was so engaged that he couldn't be bothered to respond to my shouts.

Fawnley looked up and saw us, "Oh, hello there. I thought I heard a motor down at the dock." He returned to the task of making his trousers immaculate.

I wondered where Charles was, but just then his head and shoulders appeared above the edge of the hole, and he said, quite casually, "Colin, my dear boy, how good of you to come over and help us. Actually, you're just in time. We've come to a sticky part. An archaeologist is just what we need now.

And I see you have brought two others with you. How nice. There is work for all."

In spite of his jaunty tone, I thought he looked exhausted and unwell. He tossed a pick and a shovel up on the edge of the excavation. Pick-and-shovel digging was hardly the thing for a seventy-two-year-old, especially one whose health seemed precarious. I felt sorry for him, but at the same time I could have wrung his neck. I could remember him being like this when we were kids. If he was caught doing something he shouldn't have been, he'd try to carry it off with flippancy. While I was sure he was enraged with me for interrupting him like this, I knew he wouldn't let his anger show with strangers around. As I didn't see any treasure chest or outlays of gold objects around anywhere, I assumed that the digging, at least so far, had not been productive. It looked to me as if he had dug about where we had plotted the depressed area on the surface of the western side of the mound.

"Charles," I began, trying to keep a reproving tone out of my voice, "this is Dr. Chandler of Florida State University, and this is Dr. Calvert, the state archaeologist."

"Good morning, gentlemen," responded Charles. "Excuse me for not getting out of this hole promptly, but I'm really not very agile. However, I'm very glad to know you, Dr. Chandler. Dr. Calvert and I have met—earlier this year I believe it was—when he came down to St. Christopher's to talk about the island and its archaeology. As you can see, Dr. Calvert, I'm now engaged in a spot of archaeology myself."

"Charles," I said, "I told you on Tuesday that I was inviting these gentlemen down here to consult with you—with us—and that they would be here today. I was surprised when I learned that you had come over ahead of us. I tried to raise you on the phone last night, and again this morning, but to no avail, so I decided to bring them over here on my own."

"I do, indeed, recall our conversation, Colin, and I am desolated that I was not available to receive your calls, but, as you can see, I have been deeply occupied in what you gentlemen would call 'field research.' Alas, I must say that our results have not been positive ones. In fact, they have been rather ghastly, so much so that dear Tommy was sickened by what we have just found and has gone to sit under the shade of a tree to recover, as you can observe." After making this last remark, Charles climbed out of the hole, slowly and, as it appeared, painfully.

I walked over to the excavation and looked in. They—I presumed the diggers had been he and Fawnley—had gone down about four feet, opening a ragged hole perhaps seven by five feet. At the bottom of the hole were two human skeletons, partially and inexpertly exposed. They appeared to be the remains of two adults who had been buried in extended and prone positions, a burial position, it passed through my mind, not characteristic of the Weeden Island culture. Chandler and Calvert came up on each side of me and looked down, too.

"Well, Doctor," Calvert said to me, with a wry smile, "what do you make of it?"

Before I could answer, Charles piped up, "Colin, can't you and your friends take over and do what it is you do when you find something like this? I was loath to simply shovel the bones of the poor dead Indians out in my search for treasure. However, I am beginning to doubt that we will find anything worthwhile here, although, if these gentlemen have brought along their gold-seeking device, we might ascertain this for sure. I'm afraid, though, dear Colin, that I've come a cropper. It's been awfully hard work and lonely, too. I was digging here by myself all day yesterday. Tommy, bless his heart, came over to help me today, although Tommy's not much good at digging, are you, Tommy?" he chided, rather waspishly. Tommy didn't say anything in response.

"Charles," I told him "I don't think a metal detector is called for now." I turned to Calvert. "What do you think, Bill? Should we remove these burials now and box them up, or would it be better to fill the hole back in and leave them there until you, or whoever, excavate the remainder of the mound after the Park Service takes over?"

Calvert squatted down at the edge of the excavation and looked at the burials. Then he carefully climbed in. Charles had left a garden trowel, of a type definitely unsuitable for burial cleaning alongside the more exposed skeleton. Not having anything else, Calvert picked up this clumsy implement and began lifting earth and sand away from the skull, which was revealed to be in a good state of preservation. He looked up at me and said, "This fellow's mighty long headed for a Weeden Island Indian," and then, looking at the complete length of the skeleton, added, "and he's too tall for one. Don't you think?"

I agreed, and so did Chandler.

Calvert stood up then, and something caught his eye at the other end of the pit, in the area where the feet of the skeleton should be. He scraped there with the trowel and picked up something, then scraped some more and picked up something else. He stood up and held his hand out to me, palm up. There were the remains of what looked like two small, rusty nails in it. I took them from him, and he went back to searching around the area of the feet. After doing this for a few minutes, he showed me another three or four badly rusted nails. "If he's an Indian," Calvert cracked, "he was buried with his shoes on, and he had a good shoemaker."

I passed the rusted bits over to Chandler, who said, to no one in particular, "I think we've got a problem here." Charles looked at me questioningly, and Fawnley came over and joined us.

"Indians," I explained to Charles and his friend, "at least pre-Columbian Indians, didn't use iron and didn't have iron nails in their moccasins, or whatever it was that they wore on their feet."

Calvert went back to the skull and troweled away some more. After he had it fairly clear of the soft sand, he lifted it very gently and looked at the face. Then he took out his handkerchief and brushed lightly over the jaw area and teeth. He looked up at me, and I could see the excitement on his face. "This individual has had some modern dental work. This is no Indian burial. I'd say it's a matter for the police."

Chandler climbed down in the pit, too, and with a pocketknife and his hands began to help Calvert in cleaning off the skeleton. I turned to Charles and told him he better get on the phone to the St. Christopher's police or, better yet, the sheriff's office. The island was in the county but not the city, so it would be in Larrabee's jurisdiction. Charles was obviously shaken by our discoveries, but he didn't seem able to tear himself away from the edge of the pit, where he continued to watch the cleaning of the bones with a morbid fascination.

Both Calvert and Chandler were now working up at the head end of the skeleton. The latter observed, "This fellow's arms were stretched out above his head." Followed by: "Hey, what's this?" He held up something and then brought it over to show to me. It was a phalange or finger bone, and there was a gold ring around it.

I think I knew then what it was—and who it was. I knew I was going to have to sit down someplace, so I sat down on the ground where I was. Charles bent over beside me. I took the ring off the finger bone. It was a heavy gold signet ring with the initials *JVR* on its head. I handed it to Charles, who took it, looked at it, and then cried out, "Oh, my God! Oh, my God! Dad's ring! It's Dad's ring! This is Dad! We thought he had gone off somewhere, God knows where, but he hadn't. He's been here all the time. Oh, Christ, he was murdered by somebody, and they put him in a hole over here and left him here all these years!" He slumped to the ground beside me and sat there with his face in his hands. Fawnley came up to comfort him, but he shook him off.

I told Chandler and Calvert about James Randall and his disappearance back in 1939. As I did, the macabre realization came over me that Uncle James's body had been buried here all the while I had been digging on the other half of the mound only the next year. If I had been more thorough in my excavation, I would have made this grim discovery very much earlier. I couldn't help being glad that I hadn't, although I supposed if I had done so the authorities might have made more progress on what happened to James Randall than they did. Now it would be a cold trail for Sheriff Larrabee or anyone else to follow—forty-five years cold.

Who, I wondered, was the other skeleton, the one lying on James Randall's left? Was this just an Indian burial that had been intruded upon when whoever it was had buried James? I didn't think so. The dolichocephalic cranium, the length of the skeleton, and the position of the body all argued against it being an aboriginal burial. I think then I guessed who it was. It was Jackson, the Jackson whom I had last seen some dozen years before his death, on that day when Selena and I came over to the island. The Jackson who had disappeared about the same time James Randall had disappeared. Good, decent, kindly Jackson. Whoever it was had murdered him, too.

I held a consultation with Calvert and Chandler. I thought it would be quicker and better if we telephoned and had the authorities come over in their own boat. Meanwhile, maybe the two of them would be willing to continue uncovering and cleaning up the burials. The tools we had at hand—the single garden trowel and the pocketknife—were not ideal to the purpose, but they could make some headway on the job. There would be at least some cooking spoons in the Bull cottage that could supplement what they had. When I telephoned, I could ask the sheriff to go past a hardware store and buy some suitable trowels and some soft paintbrushes.

Before I set off to use the phone, I asked Charles about McGovern. Was he here on the island? Charles said no, that on Wednesday morning McGovern had brought the island's boat over to him, but that McGovern had stayed in St. Christopher's to be picked up, "probably by those fellows in the cabin cruiser" was the way he put it, and that he hadn't come back yet.

When I went up to the Bull cottage, I looked at my watch

and saw that it was late, after one-thirty. We'd let the time get away from us. It was the first time I'd been in the Bull cottage in years. The phone was in the front room, on a table that apparently served as a desk. The sheriff's office answered on the first ring, but it was a deputy. I learned from him that the sheriff had gone out for lunch; however, the deputy thought that by now he was probably on his way back. I impressed on the deputy that what I was about to tell him was serious and that it needed the sheriff's attention just as soon as possible. After that, I filled him in on the details. He wrote down what I'd told him and read it back to me. He'd covered the essentials, and we broke off the connection.

I hoped that he or the sheriff wouldn't forget the trowels and paintbrushes. I went out into the kitchen, rummaged around, and came away with two big cooking spoons and a spatula. After that, I went back down to the mound and suggested that we all take a break and have some of the lunch we'd brought over. Charles, who was looking pretty rocky, said he couldn't eat anything, and Fawnley, who declined, too, helped Charles to his feet and gave him an arm to lean on as they started up toward the cottage. Charles told us that he wanted to lie down for a while.

During lunch, I mulled over what had been found. Had the pressure that had been put on Charles, as well as on me, to keep him from digging in the mound—had the pressure been related to someone's foreknowledge of what would be found there? Webbie, Crawford, Hedrickson, and Selena— all of them had been opposed to Charles's digging in the mound. According to Lydia, Selena had asked both Webbie and Hedrickson to keep Charles from making any excavations, and Selena also had wanted me to dissuade Charles, as well as the state's archaeologists, from working there. I didn't like the sound and looks of it. Had Selena been implicated in the murder of her father? For murder it certainly must have been. It seemed most likely that the murder had occurred in that Christmas-to–New Year's week of 1939.

James Randall had been seen last in New Orleans two days after Christmas. It seemed likely that the bodies had been put in the mound at about that time. Had James been killed on the island? And had Jackson—if my guess about the other skeleton was right—been murdered here at the same time?

After we finished our sandwiches, we went back over to the excavation. Chandler and Calvert got back down in the pit and continued their cleaning of the burials. It was getting along toward three o'clock, but it was still too early, I supposed, to expect the sheriff to arrive, although I wished he'd hurry up. I went back to puzzling over things. Where were Charles and Selena that Christmas week of 1939? Were they here in St. Christopher's? Selena had been engaged to John by then, and the latter was living in New Orleans. But was he over there then—or had he returned to St. Christopher's, to be with his family and near Selena for the holidays? Then it came back to me that someone—probably Charles—had told me that Crawford had been at the Antoine's lunch with Calhoun Lockwood and James on that last day anyone had seen James.

I decided to walk back up to the Bull cottage and see how Charles was doing. McGovern's dog came out to greet me again, nuzzling my hand and whining. He didn't impress me as a very ferocious watchdog. I wondered about his owner. Where was he now? He could hardly be a suspect in the apparent crime that had just been discovered in the mound. I didn't know McGovern's exact age, but I doubted if he had been born by 1939.

I went into the Bull cottage. Fawnley was asleep on a davenport in the front room, with the dregs of a drink and the remains of a plate of food on a coffee table beside him. He didn't wake up, and I didn't disturb him but went on back to the bedrooms. The Bull cottage was smaller than the one belonging to the Randalls; all the rooms here were on a single floor. I peered into one messy-looking bedroom, with an unmade bed, quite probably McGovern's. Several others were empty and looked like they hadn't been used for some time, but there was one with the door closed, and I rapped on it. Charles told me to come in. He was lying on the bed. He still looked unwell, pale and exhausted, with dark circles under his eyes. I sat down in a chair on the other side of the room, facing him.

He said to me, "Colin, I'm sorry. I shouldn't have done what I did—although it all seems beside the point now." He put his hand in a trouser pocket and brought out something, James Randall's signet ring. He held it out to me. "Here, you'll want to show this to the sheriff when he gets here." I got up and took it. I saw that there were tears in his eyes again.

"Look, Colin," he said, "I don't know what to think anymore. It must have struck you, as it has me, that a number of people who were so anxious to keep me from digging over here—and I'm not referring to you—might have had some idea of what I might find."

"Yes, Charles, it has crossed my mind."

"Well, I don't know what to do or say about it. What would you advise?"

"I don't know for sure, Charles, but I don't think you ought to make any statements that could be considered accusatory of anyone until we know a little bit more about it all."

"And when will that be, my good Colin? When will that be when we know 'a little bit more about it all'?"

I had no answer for him, and we fell silent. After a while, I heard the dog barking outside, and then there was a pounding on the front door. Fawnley must have been roused from his sleep. I heard him talking with someone, and then he came back, rapped on the door, and told us the sheriff and some others were here.

I got up from my chair and went out, with Charles and Fawnley following me. Sheriff Larrabee was accompanied by a deputy and Agent Clancy. Larrabee explained that he had brought some others along, too, but that he'd left them down at the Indian mound.

The sheriff addressed himself to Charles: "Mr. Randall,

I'm afraid we've got more than one thing on our minds with this trip. Mr. Clancy here would like to search this house and also the other house and the smaller buildings on the island. There have been some . . . some developments. To be brief about it, Mr. Clancy will be looking for evidence of cocaine smuggling. He has a warrant to do so."

At that point, Clancy took a document out of his pocket and handed it to poor Charles. Charles took it in a bewildered sort of way, then handed it back without looking at it, simply nodding his assent.

Clancy stated briskly, "The sheriff has made one of his deputies available to aid me in this search. If you don't mind, we'll proceed immediately."

Charles, in a daze, nodded again. I must have looked pretty dazed myself. Fawnley, I thought, looked frightened.

After Clancy and the deputy went into the house to begin their search, the sheriff said, "Well, let's get on with this other business," and he started back down the path toward the mound, with the rest of us following him.

When we got there we found another deputy and a middle-aged man in a dark business suit talking with Joel Chandler. The man in the dark suit was introduced to us as Dr. Walker, the county coroner. There was also a photographer with a camera, standing on one of the back dirt piles by the excavation, carrying on a conversation with Bill Calvert, who was down in the pit. The coroner walked over to the edge of the pit, looked in, then climbed down into it. He went over to the skeleton that I thought might be Jackson, bent down, and tried to lift the skull. As it was still heavy with sand, it fell apart, with the mandible and some upper facial portions dividing from the calvarium and dropping to the ground. Perhaps unnerved by this mishap, Dr. Walker stepped back onto the lower leg bones of the late James Randall, breaking them in several places.

I could see that Calvert was fit to be tied at this point, but he politely took charge of the situation by telling the sheriff that he thought the bones should remain in position now until a forensic anthropologist could take charge of their removal. He recommended a Dr. Bob Klein, a colleague at Florida State and a physical anthropologist. Klein, he explained, had done previous skeletal identifications and other forensic work for the state police. Calvert was sure that the state police could arrange for him to come down from Tallahassee, and, with his and Chandler's help, the bone materials could be properly removed and boxed and taken back to Tallahassee for close study and identification.

After he mentioned identification, he turned to Charles and to me, and said, "These gentlemen have something which was found associated with one of the burials, the one on the right side of the pit, and they feel that it identifies that skeleton. I'll let them tell you about it."

Charles didn't seem willing to say anything, so I produced the signet ring and handed it over to the sheriff. "This ring," I explained, "has been identified by Mr. Charles Randall as having been the ring always worn by his father, Mr. James Randall, who disappeared under mysterious circumstances back in 1939. Mr. Chandler, here, found it around a phalange—a finger bone—of the burial on the right. It may very well identify that burial as the remains of James Randall; however, as the teeth of that burial show extensive dental work, and as I would assume that dental records are available somewhere, a positive identification should be forthcoming."

The sheriff nodded and told us that he had heard of the disappearance of James Randall, that it was something that had happened back when he had been a boy. He'd look up the records on the case. Now, if we would let him use the phone, he would get in touch with the state police in Tallahassee about bringing in Dr. Klein.

At that point, I told him about my theory that the other skeleton might be that of Jackson. Larrabee hadn't heard of Jackson and knew nothing of his disappearance. He didn't know whether he'd find it in the missing persons files or not; he rather doubted it. Chandler made the observation then that the burial on the left side of the pit was that of a very old man, and that I had told him that Jackson was old at the time of his disappearance. Unfortunately, the teeth, or what remained of them, revealed no dental work that might aid in identification.

I was relieved that through all this the sheriff had not asked why Charles Randall had been digging in the mound. Maybe he thought Charles had a perfect right to; after all, it was his property.

As it was now after four o'clock, and the photographer had completed his pictures of the burials, Calvert suggested that we cover the bones with tarpaulins or canvas, or whatever we could find for that purpose, and wait until tomorrow and the arrival of Bob Klein before doing any more. The sheriff agreed, and he turned to his deputy and said that he'd better spend the night here on the island and see to it that nothing was disturbed. The deputy didn't seem thrilled with this solitary assignment but glumly replied, "Yes, sir."

I explained that a bed would be available in the Bull cottage, but I thought I'd better make it clear to the sheriff that McGovern, the island caretaker, lived in the Bull cottage, that he might return sometime this evening, and that the deputy should know this. I added, "I don't know where McGovern is now, but he seems to come and go at irregular hours."

We were walking slowly away from the mound up toward the cottages when I said this. The sheriff stopped, turned in his tracks, and told me in a flat voice, "McGovern is dead. Mr. McGovern, Hebert, Tiger Westcott, and Mr. John Crawford were all intercepted by a U.S. Coast Guard boat down off Pensacola. This was last night. They were ordered to stop, but, instead, they were foolish enough to open fire on the Coast Guard cruiser." I conjured up a picture of the criminal-looking McGovern being overzealous with his AK-47.

"McGovern and Hebert were killed by return fire, and Westcott and Crawford were wounded. They are both in a hospital in Pensacola now, where Crawford is on the critical list. Mr. Clancy informed me of this when he arrived in St. Christopher's, not long after your call came in to one of my deputies this afternoon, Mr. Edwards. When he learned that I was planning to come over here, he asked to accompany me to search the houses on the island. It looks like Mc-Govern and the others had been using the island as a base for the transshipment of cocaine for some time. They think it was run in here at night from New Orleans, then redistributed from here in smaller amounts to cities like Gulfport, Mobile, Pensacola, and Panama City." After a pause, the sheriff looked at Charles and said, "I'm sorry to tell you this, Mr. Randall, but I've been given to understand that your kinsman Mr. Crawford has been involved in it all from the start."

I asked the sheriff, "Exactly when did all this happen? The shooting, I mean?"

"Just a little after midnight, last night," the sheriff told me.

I got the keys to the Randall cottage and sheds from Charles and went with Chandler and Calvert to look for something to cover the burials. The sheriff and the others stayed with Charles at the Bull place. We found a piece of tarpaulin and some old burlap bags in one of the Randall sheds.

We took these down to the mound. I helped arrange the covers for the burials. Calvert was still incensed over their desecration by the coroner. "Some of these M.D.'s act like they've never seen a damned skeleton before," he groused.

"I suppose the ones they saw in medical school were in a better condition of preservation than poor old Jackson's" was my reply.

As we were covering the remains with burlap, I noticed some little black disks down by the pelvic area of the skeleton that I thought was Jackson's. I gathered them up and rubbed them. They were very tarnished silver—two dimes and a quarter, poor Jackson's hoard, his "walking around money" that he never got over to the mainland to spend. I showed the coins to Calvert and Chandler, and then we put them back where I had found them and finished covering everything up.

We got back to the Bull cottage, Clancy and the deputy

helping him had found a breadboard, which they had wrapped in plastic and which, they told us, showed traces of cocaine. Apparently, it had been used to separate out portions of the substance for small packaging. As we were getting ready to leave the cottage, the telephone rang and the sheriff answered it. He listened for quite a while and then said, "Yes, I'll take care of it." After he came out onto the porch, he went over to where Charles was sitting and asked for a private word with him. They walked off the porch, out of easy hearing of the rest of us. From the alarmed expression on Charles's face while the sheriff talked, I took it to be something serious. During all this, I noticed that Fawnley was watching with some anxiety. Then Charles raised his voice in some indignation and said to the sheriff, "That seems quite unnecessary! I'll be responsible for my guest!"

But Sheriff Larrabee only shook his head, came up to Fawnley, and told him in a deep, official voice, "Mr. Thomas Fawnley, it is my duty to place you under arrest. The charges are illegal possession, transport, and sale of narcotics. I must detain you now and advise you of your rights. You may communicate with a lawyer just as soon as we get back to St. Christopher's." Having said this, the sheriff unhooked a pair of handcuffs, which he was carrying attached to his belt, and manacled Fawnley's hands behind his back.

Fawnley screamed at him, "You have no right to do this! I am innocent of any crime like that! Charles, Charles," Fawnley pleaded, "tell them that they can't do this to me!"

To save Fawnley and all of us the embarrassment of him sitting there before us in handcuffs, Charles asked if he couldn't take him inside the cottage to wait, but the sheriff refused the request, saying, "I think it would be better if Mr. Fawnley just rested himself here in a chair on the porch until it's time to go." So we sat there in uncomfortable silence for the next ten minutes, until Clancy and the other deputy came down the path from the Randall cottage, where nothing had been found in the narcotics line.

Sheriff Larrabee got up to meet them and explained, "Mr.

Clancy, while you were up there at that other place, a telephone call came through for you. It was from Pensacola.
Apparently Crawford made an extensive statement, impli-
cating Mr. Fawnley here, and that's why I have him under
arrest."

The sheriff paused and turned back to address Charles.
"Mr. Randall, I'm sorry to have to break the news to you like
this, but . . . well, Mr. Crawford's statement was taken from
him just before he died. In it, he also had things to say about
matters other than the drug running, things pertaining,
well, to what happened down there at the Indian mound a
long time ago."

Charles was white faced, trembling. "What did John say?"

The sheriff told him, "We'll have the full report, a copy of
it, later this evening, probably, not long after we get back to
town. I think I better leave it at that for the time being. Now
I think we all better get going."

When we got back to St. Christopher's, the sheriff and
Clancy took Fawnley away to spend the night in the local
jail. I got the four of us a taxi, and we took Charles home
first. I walked up to the front door with him. There was no
sign of Selena as he let himself in. Chandler, Calvert, and I
then went back to the hotel, where I had time for a shower
and a short rest before I joined them for dinner. After that,
I left them in the bar. I no longer had the energy and resilience
of youth, and I certainly hadn't bounced back after the
events and revelations of the day. I turned in.

$\triangledown$

9

IT WAS BEGINNING TO GET LIGHT. We were at Friday, the seventh. I wondered what this long June day would bring. Yesterday had certainly brought plenty. I thought about the burials in the mound and then about Uncles James, as I had known him. He had been nice, I always thought, nicer than Great-uncle Charles, who had been as I realized now, a rather arrogant and conceited old man. It also came to me now that James, the father, was also nicer than young Charles. My friend had a cold streak. There were times, I reflected, when he behaved as arrogantly as his grandfather. There had been a modesty about James, in spite of his extraordinary handsomeness, even more than a modesty, a kind of desperate quality, as though he was appealing for approval, even from us children. Well, I thought, whatever had been his personal demons, he was free from them now, had been free from them for a long time. Who had killed him and why?

I thought about old Jackson, too. That other skeleton had to be his, although they might have trouble proving it. I continued like that, off and on, going over one thing and another. The discoveries on the island had almost knocked Lydia's disappearance out of my mind, but I wondered then if she had shown up or if anything had been found out about her. I finally looked at my watch, saw it was just short of seven o'clock, and got up and dressed.

Down in the dining room I found Chandler and Calvert at a table with a newcomer. I joined them and was introduced to the new man. Bob Klein, baldish, somewhat older than his colleagues, said he had received word yesterday evening from the state police and had driven down from Tallahassee after dark to be on hand early today. The others had been in the bar last night when he pulled in, so they had filled him in on the horrors of St. James's Island.

They wanted to know if I wanted to go back over to the island with them. I was somewhat undecided. Yesterday had left me more tired than I liked, although I hadn't exerted myself all that much, not physically anyway. I told them that I would think it over and that maybe I'd join them later. I'd see what Charles wanted to do. Perhaps he and I would come over this afternoon.

Calvert was seated facing me and the doorway to the dining room. I saw him glance up, turned around in my chair, and saw Sheriff Larrabee entering.

The sheriff came over, was introduced to Dr. Klein, and said, yes, he'd been informed by the state police that he was here. I asked the sheriff if he wouldn't join us, if not for breakfast, at least for a cup of coffee, and he assented, pulling a chair up to a corner of our table. Larrabee told my colleagues that as soon as they were ready to go one of his deputies, who was out in the lobby, would take them in the launch. "I won't be going over just yet," he explained, "but I'll be along just a little later this morning."

Calvert, Chandler, and Klein, who'd finished breakfast by that time, got up and went off to prepare for their day. The sheriff, though, seemed to want to linger on, and this was all right with me. I was at the toast and marmalade and second cup of coffee stage, and, needless to say, I was curious.

The sheriff asked if I minded if he lit a cigar, and I told him to go right ahead. He did this with slow deliberation, and after a couple of good, hearty puffs, he posed the question: "Well, Mr. Edwards, what do you make of all that was found over there on the island yesterday?"

I replied that I didn't know what to make of it, except that one body appeared to be that of Mr. James Randall and that

I thought the other was a colored man named Jackson who had been the island's caretaker and had disappeared just about the time that Randall had vanished. Beyond that, I really didn't have any idea. I added that I couldn't see how the burials could have any connection to the very recent affair of the drug running and the toughs who had been using the island as their base. None of them had been old enough to provide a connection. And I added further—maybe just to see what the sheriff would say—that I didn't see how the burials or the drug running had anything to do with Webster Bull's death.

Larrabee looked at me rather critically and addressed the first part of my statement by saying, "Well, yes and no. I suppose it depends on who you call 'toughs.' Certainly, McGovern and Westcott wouldn't have been old enough, and I guess even Hebert would have been about ten years old in 1939. But Mr. Crawford, who I believe is a kin of yours, Mr. Edwards, would be old enough to provide a link back to 1939, and he did just that in the statement he made to the police in Pensacola before he died."

The sheriff paused then, and I thought he might be going to address the second part of my remarks, my statement about how any of it might relate back to Webbie's murder, but he didn't.

Instead, he went on about John Crawford: "I should tell you that after Crawford was wounded, he did not appear to be in *extreme* danger. He was fully conscious, and after a few hours' sleep he told the doctors that he wanted to give a statement to the authorities. Although the doctors advised against it, Crawford insisted, so a federal agent and a stenographer were brought in."

"When was this?"

"Late on Thursday morning. They thought that he probably wanted to establish himself as a government witness, to give himself a basis for a lighter sentence. And what he said certainly blew the cover on the drug operation. It had been set up about three years ago, when this fellow Mc-

Govern came over to the island as its caretaker. Mr. Crawford had been instrumental in getting him the job. He had been employed previously by the Lockwood Galleries in New Orleans, where Crawford himself had a job. Crawford did this with the connivance of Mr. Fawnley, who was his boss. It was arranged through Mr. Bull, and Mr. Bull and Mr. Randall were McGovern's employers, but Mr. Crawford was very clear in his statement that neither of these gentlemen knew anything about the drug running or McGovern's real purpose in being here. McGovern asked for only a very small salary, one hundred dollars a month, fifty each from Mr. Bull and Mr. Randall."

That, I thought, would have won his way into the heart of good old Webbie, and Charles—Charles with his mind on something else—just didn't pay any attention to what was going on around him. What a setup for someone like the late Mr. McGovern.

"Well, Mr. Edwards, a few months ago, the federal agents began to get suspicious. Cocaine was being retailed, in relatively small lots, all along the northern gulf here. I don't think they connected these deliveries with the island until these other fellows in the cabin cruiser began to show up regularly at the little dock at Cape Sands, just across the narrows from the island.

"What the Feds needed, though," continued Larrabee, "was to catch them red-handed, in the act of unloading some stuff, and they did just that late on Wednesday, or early Thursday morning, at Pensacola. The federal agents grabbed their onshore contacts with the goods on them just after McGovern, Crawford, and company dropped off a shipment. They'd been tipped off by an anonymous telephone call, which came in earlier in the evening, and they were ready for them. McGovern and his crowd made a run for open water and thought they could discourage a Coast Guard chase by opening up with machine guns or automatic rifles, but it didn't work. He really had gall, though, this guy McGovern, putting in to a harbor where Coast Guard craft were based. It's a good thing they got him. He'd have gone far in organized crime."

"John Crawford wasn't the boss then?"

"We don't really know. Maybe he was or thought he was, but they think McGovern made the important decisions—such as firing on the Coast Guard." Larrabee paused for a moment, then added, "They may find out more about the whole organization when they grill this bird Fawnley."

"I see. And, I take it, John died shortly after making the statement?"

"That's right. The doctors were surprised, but maybe Crawford himself wasn't. He may have felt that his time was up, and that was why he wanted to make the statement—to clear his conscience. You see, some other things that he told them had been on his mind for a very long time, and they weren't at all pretty things."

"And they," I asked, "had something to do with, with what was found over there in the mound?"

"That's right."

"Well, Sheriff Larrabee," I prompted, "don't keep me in suspense. What's the story?"

The sheriff patted the inside pocket of his jacket and said, "It's all right here in the copy of his statement. I'll tell you shortly, but I would prefer to wait until Mr. Randall gets here. After all, he's the next of kin to the deceased, and he should be the principal one to hear it."

"Is Charles coming over to the hotel?"

"Yes," the sheriff informed me, "I called him this morning and asked him to come over here to pack up and check out for his friend, Mr. Fawnley—a U.S. marshal is on his way over from New Orleans to pick him up. He'll be indicted there, where the headquarters of his cocaine operation was. But just as soon as Mr. Randall gets here and takes care of that, we can go into this other matter."

Shortly after that, as the sheriff and I were finishing the last of our coffee, Charles appeared in the dining-room doorway. I thought he looked much better than he did yesterday.

His night's sleep must have done him some good. We got up and joined him, and he and the sheriff went out to the desk to get the key to Fawnley's room. They went upstairs and were gone for about fifteen minutes, during which time I read some of the lurid details of the Pensacola drug shoot-out in the paper.

After Charles and the sheriff had finished packing Fawnley's things and settling his bill, the sheriff asked if we were planning to go over to the island today. I said, maybe, but I was waiting to see what Charles wanted to do. Before Charles had a chance to express any wishes or preferences on this, the sheriff, putting on his Texas hat, said that he wanted to tell us about the full text of John Crawford's statement but that it might take a while to do so. He also wanted to get on over to St. James's before much longer. Would Charles be willing to run him over in the island's boat? Then we could talk over there, where we wouldn't be disturbed. Charles said, yes, he'd be glad to oblige.

Charles took the wheel on our trip over. It was a sparkling, clear morning. When we got to the island dock, I noticed the metal detector was gone from where it had been left yesterday. The boys must have taken it up to give it a try.

We plodded our way up the path and turned off to the mound. Klein was down in the excavation, removing and tagging some of the bones, and Chandler was shoveling sand and earth out into a screen that was set up alongside the pit while Calvert worked the screen, raking a trowel back and forth in the sifting. He showed me a few more black-tarnished coins, a rusty belt buckle, and what looked like the remains of a metal-sheathed pen or pencil. He told me that they had run the metal detector over the unexcavated portions of the mound with no indications of any buried metals. I looked at Charles when he said this, and Charles simply shrugged; I guess his treasure-hunting aspirations had been quenched. The two deputies were helping move back dirt a little farther from the edges of the excavation. The deputy who had spent the night on the island reported no ghosts, but I think he hoped that he wouldn't have to pull nighttime duty there again.

The sheriff wanted to know if Klein could tell him anything about how the two men had been killed. Klein said he couldn't be definite, although a rib that would have been over the heart area of the individual tentatively identified as James Randall did show a nicking that might have been made by a bullet. So far, however, no bullet had come to light in the sifting. Chandler told us that, as soon as all of the bones were removed, they'd dig on deeper in the pit, just to be sure they hadn't missed anything.

The sheriff slapped at a sweat bee that buzzed around his face, readjusted his hat, and said, "Gentlemen, why don't we go on up to the first cottage, where it's a little more comfortable, and sit down, and I'll go into the matter I was talking about."

When we got to the Bull cottage, Charles examined the contents of the refrigerator and came back with three bottles of cold soda water. McGovern's supplies, I thought, but with the heat going up at ten o'clock, it tasted pretty good.

Sheriff Larrabee took off his hat and then his jacket. After hanging the latter over the back of his chair, he extracted a folded manuscript from its inside pocket. "This here," he told us, "is quite a statement. It looks like John Crawford had gone around for over forty years with something pretty bad on his conscience.

"But first let me ask you, Mr. Randall, what do you know or remember about Calhoun Lockwood? He owned an antiques business in New Orleans."

I could see that Charles was a little uneasy at this query. He closed his eyes for a moment and shook his head. Then he said, in a too-offhand manner, "Oh, he was someone who employed John Crawford when John got out of college, out of Tulane, back in the 1930s."

The sheriff didn't say anything but continued to wait, studying Charles more intently.

"Well," said Charles, a little irritably, "I met him a few

times, on those occasions when I went over to New Orleans. Selena, my sister, was engaged to John Crawford then, and I'd go to New Orleans with her when she went to visit him. This was back in the late thirties, shortly before she and John were married."

"You never saw him after that, Mr. Randall?"

"Oh, yes, I suppose I did. I liked the city, the French Quarter. I went over now and then, during and after the war."

"You knew, did you not, Mr. Randall, that your father had been to see this Lockwood on the day immediately preceding his death, that they had had lunch together, along with Mr. Crawford, on that very last day he was seen alive."

"Yes, of course, Sheriff. This is old history. What new things do you have to tell us?" Charles replied, rather testily.

"Well, I just thought I'd get everything laid out. I've been looking up the files on your father's disappearance, and I just wanted to be sure I had everything in order. It was a long time ago, long before my time, so to speak, and it gives me a better sense of things to hear it from someone who was around then."

I wondered about the sheriff. I was beginning to think he liked to play the big, old, dumb, slow boy. Charles scowled but didn't say anything. The sheriff was starting to get under his skin.

"Well, sir," the sheriff went on, holding the manuscript up in his hand but still not unfolding it, "this man Lockwood figures mighty prominently in this statement. He has what you might call a leading role in it, and what Mr. Crawford says about him makes him out to have been a pretty ruthless character. Would that have been your opinion of him, Mr. Randall?"

I thought the sheriff was giving Charles something close to what could be called a grilling.

"Ruthless? Why, I don't know. I think that would be a little strong. He was given to sharp practice sometimes in the sale of his wares, but then most antiques dealers behave about the same way."

"Mr. Randall," the sheriff snapped, "do you call murder no more than 'sharp practice'?"

"Murder?" exclaimed Charles.

"According to Mr. Crawford's statement, Calhoun Lockwood murdered your father right here on this island on the night of the twenty-seventh of December, 1939." The sheriff gave this out in very measured tones. He went on: "At the same time, he murdered the colored caretaker, one Thomas Jackson. The bodies of the two men were buried in the Indian mound, where you found them. There was an excavation there, which was already open and ready for such a purpose. The excavation had been made by Crawford, Jackson, and your father that night."

Charles shook his head, then put his hands up to his face. "Oh, God, oh, God," he moaned.

I asked then, "What do you mean, Sheriff Larrabee, when you say that they had made an excavation in the mound that night?"

Larrabee waved the folded document at me. "Mr. Crawford says that Calhoun Lockwood had surprised them all just as they were clearing away the dirt from what had been a lead-lined, wooden chest down in the bottom of the hole they had dug into the mound. This chest, according to what Mr. Crawford says in his statement, was filled with little gold figurines, pre-Columbian figurines, he called them. He says there were almost five hundred of them. They had come from down in Colombia, South America. They had belonged to a family called Gomez, who lived in a place called . . ."

The sheriff opened up the document, took out his glasses and put them on, consulted the document, and told us, "They lived in Cartagena." (The sheriff pronounced it "Carta-jeena.") "That's a seaport town down there in Colombia."

"My God," Charles whispered. "Dad did find it then."

Ignoring this the sheriff said, "According to this statement, James Randall had found some sort of diary that had been left by Alexander Randall, which led him to the discovery. Apparently, the treasure had been hidden because Alexander Randall had taken it from a Peter Lockwood, who had been the captain of one of Alexander's sailing ships back in the 1870s. Peter had married a lady from Cartagena named Alicia Gomez, whose family originally assembled the collection. Calhoun was their son."

I recalled what Tommy Fawnley had been rattling on about the other night, about Calhoun being the son of a Colombian woman named Gomez.

The sheriff continued. "Calhoun Lockwood told Crawford that his father, Peter, had been murdered by Alexander Randall, murdered for the gold."

"How did Calhoun Lockwood come to meet up with James Randall and the others out here on the island, in the middle of night?" I asked.

"Because Crawford betrayed Randall to Lockwood," the sheriff explained. "James Randall had told Crawford, his prospective son-in-law, that he thought he had discovered where the gold was hidden and that he wanted his help in digging it up and arranging to sell it to Lockwood. He had gone to New Orleans that day after Christmas to discuss the deal with Lockwood and also to bring Crawford back to help him. Crawford agreed to help, but before he did he told Lockwood what they were going to do. Lockwood then followed them back to the island the next afternoon and surprised them that night just as they found the gold."

I visualized the nightmarish scene. Digging by lantern light under the trees. The figure of Calhoun Lockwood emerging from the shadows, gun in hand.

"Damn his soul," shouted Charles. "I don't see how anyone could have been so foul as John—to conspire in murdering his own father-in-law."

The sheriff shook his head and told Charles, "I don't think we can quite say that. At least Crawford had no such intentions, or so he says in here." He tapped the papers, refolded them, and put them back in the pocket of his jacket. "He says that he didn't know Lockwood was going to do what he did, that he thought Lockwood was just going to 'hijack' the gold."

The sheriff reached around and took the cigar case out of his jacket pocket, put a cigar in his mouth, and lit it. "You see," he went on, "Lockwood had hired Crawford at his gallery, just after the latter got out of college, because he learned that Crawford was from St. Christopher's and knew the Randalls, was, in fact, engaged to James Randall's daughter, Selena. This seemed an opening to recover the gold, as well as get back at the Randalls for murdering his father. He established a contact with James Randall through Crawford and Selena and even engaged him to do some legal work for the gallery. Then luck came his way when James advised him that he thought he could bring him an amazing collection of pre-Columbian gold."

"Why did John betray Dad?"

"Money," the sheriff said. "Calhoun Lockwood promised Crawford a larger sum, or a larger share of the value of the gold, than James Randall promised him. Money, or the want of it, was Crawford's weakness. When Lockwood shot Randall, Crawford was horror-struck . . . and he was also terrified. Lockwood had the gun; he, Crawford, didn't. He said in his statement that Lockwood then offered him half the value of the gold—or, at that time, about twenty thousand dollars—if he would keep silent about the murder and the theft; but, from Crawford's point of view, it was either accept the offer or probably be shot himself and dumped into the excavation along with Randall and Jackson. Lockwood shot Jackson right after he shot Randall. He didn't want any witnesses, beyond Crawford, that is, and he had Crawford's mouth sealed by a generous share of the spoils and Crawford's complicity in the crime."

"The gold," I asked, "it was all removed by Lockwood and Crawford that night?"

"That's right," said the sheriff, "and then they dumped the two bodies into the hole, and Crawford and Lockwood covered them up and carried the gold away. From what Mr.

Crawford has said, they took it over to the mainland in a rowboat that night. Lockwood drove back to New Orleans. Crawford had taken Mr. Randall's car keys from his body, and he drove that car partway back, ditching it in Pensacola before going on with Lockwood."

It was a hell of a grisly story, I thought. This topped everything I had ever heard about Lockwood. John had moved into it step by step. He had gone along, on that horrible night, with a gun pointed at him. But why didn't he, afterward, go to the police and expose Lockwood for what he had done? I supposed the answer to that was greed. John had come into some money right after he married Selena, and this inheritance must have been his share of the gold, of the blood money. He had lost most of it a short time later and was back to being the same greedy, weak man he had always been.

It was noon. I brought out the lunches the hotel had fixed for us. The sheriff tucked in, and I nibbled a little bit. Charles, refusing to eat, sat staring out at the woods surrounding the cottage. McGovern's mongrel dog came up to us on the porch and sniffed around. I fed him one of my sandwiches and wondered, from the way he gulped it down, if the poor beast had been fed since his master's disappearance. The dog's appearance led me to think of Charles's single gold alligator. I said to Charles that I imagined it had been dropped when Lockwood and John had gathered up all the other items in the lead-lined chest before filling in the hole to cover their crimes. But Charles seemed uninterested in my comment.

I speculated inwardly upon what kind of a file our discoveries in the mound would produce in the sheriff's archives. Presumably, one of case closed, for with Calhoun Lockwood and now John both dead, there were no criminals extant to indict and convict. But I stopped just after I said this to myself. Had John told Selena of what he had done, or of what Lockwood had done? Was this why Selena had been so opposed to digging in the mound? Did she know about the death of her own father? Was she—what do they call it?—an accessory after the fact, liable to criminal charges for not divulging what she knew, if indeed she knew it, at the time of the crime?

"Sheriff Larrabee," I asked, "does John Crawford's statement implicate anyone else in James Randall's death?"

The sheriff turned and looked at me in a pretty narrow-eyed way. "No one else was mentioned in the statement, Mr. Edwards." But after he said that he continued to look at me until I self-consciously averted my eyes. Then he asked me, "Do you think there might have been someone else, Mr. Edwards?"

"No, no, I was just wondering" was my embarrassed reply. Charles had looked the other way during this exchange, avoiding getting into the discussion.

After lunch we went down to the mound. Chandler and Calvert had come across the remains of the original treasure chest, some sheets of the lead lining and rusted hinge and binding bits. Klein told the sheriff that he would take all the skeletal remains and the other materials to the State Police Lab in Tallahassee and that he would send back a report on them just as soon as possible. Calvert asked the sheriff if he wanted the excavation left open or refilled. I think Larrabee was uncertain, but Calvert made the decision for him by saying that he knew it would be all right with the State Parks people to leave the hole as it was until they took over and made their plans for future archeology in the mound, if any. The sheriff then announced that he would see to it that sightseers and other trespassers would be kept off the island until the state took over.

We had just started down the path to the landing when one of the deputies came running after us and told the sheriff that he was wanted on the phone back at the Bull cottage and that it sounded like it was important. The call was from a Deputy Collins, who was at the Cape Sands Motel. The sheriff went back to take the call. The rest of us, sharing the burdens of the metal detector and the cardboard boxes of bones and other materials from the excavation, continued on down the path. When we got to the landing dock, we waited for the sheriff while Chandler and Calvert helped the other deputy load the boxes and the metal detector in the launch. In about five minutes Larrabee and the first deputy came down the path, walking fast.

The sheriff looked grim. Turning to Charles, he asked, "Mr. Randall, I wonder if you would let one of the deputies take me over to Cape Sands in your smaller boat? Something's come up, and I'm needed over there in a hurry. He can then run your boat back to the Riverfront Dock in town. The rest of you can go on back now in the launch, although maybe Mr. Randall and Mr. Edwards would like to go with me. Deputy Collins is there at the Cape Sands now, with a car, and he can drive us back to town in it—just as soon as I take care of some business over there."

Both Charles and I agreed to ride over to Cape Sands with the sheriff and his deputy. The rest of the group, with everything packed aboard, took off for St. Christopher's in the sheriff's launch.

Then, before Charles and I got into the smaller boat, the sheriff said, "Gentlemen, I've got some more bad news. The body of Mrs. Hedrickson was found over near the Cape Sands Motel about an hour ago. She'd been shot, shot through the head. She was found in Mr. Crawford's car."

While Charles and I were getting into the boat and absorbing this new horror, the deputy started up the motor, cast off, and headed for the mainland dock at Cape Sands. My God, I thought, things are going crazy, or certainly somebody is. Lydia, poor old Lydia! Shot through the head! What was she doing in John Crawford's car? Where and when had I last seen it, that beat-up, green rattletrap? It was in the Cape Sands Motel parking lot the day—Tuesday—Selena and I had lunch after Webbie's funeral. John had come into the bar to consult with Tiger, and then they'd gone off together in the cabin cruiser. Presumably, John had left his car there then.

I was with the deputy in the front seat of the boat, and the sheriff and Charles were in the back. As the mainland rapidly grew nearer, the sheriff said, "It's right close to the mainland down here, isn't it? Not much more than five minutes in a fast little boat like this." I agreed that it was close, that in the old days there would be times when you could attract Jackson's, or Thompson's, attention by standing on the mainland and waving your shirt.

As we came up to the Cape Sands pier, Charles told the sheriff, "They didn't have much of a dock here in the old days. Of course, that was before the motel was built. Now, with tourists around who want to go out to fish, they've built a good pier."

We were going along at half speed, looking for a place to tie up. There were at least a half dozen small boats docked there, and Charles complained, "Damn all these little boats. At night, there are not so many, but then you have a hard time finding the rings on the pier to tie to."

There was a boat rental place near the pier, and beside it was a little convenience store. After we docked, the sheriff led us over to the store and got into conversation with the owner. After talking about the number of tourists and kindred matters, the sheriff asked the proprietor how late he was open at night. The proprietor informed him that this time of year he usually closed up about seven or so, so he could drive back to St. Christopher's before dark. The sheriff wanted to know about the boat rental establishment, and the man explained that it was run by the motel people but that they never rented any boats after 6:00 P.M.

After this exchange, we started up the path to the motel and saw Deputy Collins, identifiable by his badge, coming to meet us. He had a man with him who turned out to be the one who had greeted Selena and me in the lobby of the motel on the day we came for lunch. The sheriff introduced him as Jerry Reed, the manager. Collins told the sheriff that it was Mr. Reed who had found the body.

Reed explained, "You see, this car had been here since

sometime Tuesday. I knew it was Crawford's car. He often
left it here when he'd go off with the others in that cruiser,
so I didn't think much about it at first. Then, this morning,
I heard the news that he had died yesterday as a result of that
fracas over at Pensacola. So I thought maybe I'd better let the
authorities know his car was still here. They'd probably have
to come and pick it up or maybe tell his family. Well, I went
out and looked in it, and, when I got close up to it, I could
see there was somebody lying down in the front seat. You
couldn't see them until you got right up to the window. At
first, I thought it was just some bum, sleeping in the car. I
opened the door. The doors were unlocked. Crawford always
left it like that; I don't think the door locks work. She must
have slumped over sideways in the seat after she'd been shot."

"The keys weren't in the ignition, were they?" asked the
sheriff.

"No, sir. He'd locked that part of the car, all right."

"Well, what did you do then?"

"I tried to see who the person was," Reed said. "It was no
one I recognized. It was pretty obvious that she was dead.
When I looked at her face, it was awful. Her whole forehead
was blown away."

Collins told the sheriff, "It looks as though whoever did
it shot her through the back of the head. There's a bullet
entry hole there, with the big wound in front, and we found
the spent bullet on the shelf over the dashboard, where it
had dropped when it barely nicked the inside of the wind-
shield. Looks like a thirty-eight-caliber revolver."

"Anything else in the car?" the sheriff wanted to know.

"Nothing except some tools in the trunk. I've tried to be
careful, and maybe the boys can get some prints. I've called
the state police, like you said, and also the ambulance and
the coroner. They're up there by the car now. I've left everything like it was, except for picking up the thirty-eight slug,
so you can see the whole thing for yourself."

"That's good, Collins." We all walked around one end of
the motel and came out into the parking lot where Selena

and I had parked when we were there. As well as I could remember, Crawford's old green sedan was where it had been when we left the restaurant that day. There were several other cars, including a state police vehicle and an ambulance, pulled up near John's car. I recognized the coroner, who was talking with two men who looked like the medical attendant and the driver of the ambulance. A state police lieutenant was standing by. The sheriff went up and shook hands with the lieutenant and then talked for some time with the coroner. Afterward, they all three went over and looked in the open front door of the green sedan.

I kept my distance, as did Charles. I had no wish to see poor Lydia in the condition that Reed and the deputy had described. After a while, the two ambulance men went over and eased Lydia's body out of the car, put it on a stretcher, covered it with a sheet, and slid it into the back of the ambulance. The sheriff, the lieutenant, and the deputy then opened all the doors of the sedan and inspected it on the inside. When they had finished, they shut the doors, and the lieutenant sealed them all on the outside with some kind of tape. I heard the sheriff tell the deputy to call into St. Christopher's for a wrecker to come and tow the car away.

It was only two in the afternoon, but I needed a drink. Charles agreed, and we left the forces of the law talking with one another while we went into the bar and seated ourselves at a table. The bartender came over to take our order and commiserated with us on the event outside, telling us that he'd seen that car out there for almost three whole days and that for much of that time "this poor lady's body had been right in there on the seat. Terrible!" There was no gainsaying him.

"What do you think?" I asked Charles.

"What can I possibly think?" Then he surprised me by asking if I had seen anything of Harry Hedrickson since I had been here in St. Christopher's.

"I had a run-in with him, Charles, at the St. Christopher House. It was last Sunday night. It was about digging in the mound on the island. Didn't I tell you?"

He ignored my question but went on to say that Harry, as far as he was concerned, was a pretty nasty character.

"You mean nasty enough to do his wife in? Is that what you're trying to say?"

Charles shrugged and looked away when I asked this, and we devoted the next few minutes to our gin-tonics.

Sheriff Larrabee came in during this pause in our conversation and sat down at the table with us. I asked if he would have a drink, and he told the bartender that all he wanted was a glass of ice water. He fanned his face with his cowboy hat and said, "Mrs. Hedrickson has been dead for anywhere from twenty-four to forty-eight hours. As I told you the other day, Mr. Edwards, the last person to see her, as far as we know, was the taxicab driver who left her here on Wednesday night. Whether she came into any part of the motel, we don't know, but at least she never came into the restaurant and bar."

I asked if anyone had heard the shot that had killed her.

"We're looking into that, Mr. Edwards. It's confusing, though, because our dance band could have covered up the sound of the shot. Besides, it's likely that the shot was fired in a closed car."

After the sheriff had delivered himself of this opinion, he said, "Just as soon as you gentlemen finish your drinks, Deputy Collins will drive you into St. Christopher's. I'm going to stay around for a while and ask some questions."

$\triangledown$

10

SATURDAY MORNING. LAST NIGHT, I'd had dinner with my archaeological colleagues at the hotel. I'd asked Charles to join us, but he begged off when we got back to town from the Cape Sands. Lying there in bed, I thought about poor Lydia. I may have been the last friend she spoke with before her death; Colin, remembered for his politeness. Or was the last friend the one who had fired the bullet through her brain as she sat in John Crawford's automobile? And what was Lydia Hedrickson doing in John's car in the parking lot of a place like the Cape Sands?

Did John have anything to do with Lydia's death? After her talk with me Wednesday night, Lydia had left the St. Christopher House at a little after nine. The taxi driver had told the sheriff that they arrived out at the Cape Sands in about a half hour, so a little after nine-thirty, perhaps nine-forty-five, would have been the very earliest she could have been killed. It seemed highly unlikely that John could have done it. He would have to have rushed back from the Cape Sands to Pensacola, or some point near there, to get aboard the cruiser and participate with his companions in their drug running, which had ended in their fatal clash with the Coast Guard at a little after midnight. This would have meant fast transportation—an automobile—and John's car had been left there at the Cape Sands. But John in the role of the killer seemed stretching it. What would have been his motive? Besides, he had said nothing about Lydia in his somewhat detailed deathbed confession.

Indeed, who had a motive? This question was the same as it was in Webbie's death. I suppose it took us back to the St. James's Island Trust again. Lydia had been a full participant in the trust. After Webbie's death her share had gone up to five million dollars. So now, with Lydia gone, Charles and Selena had it all, five million apiece. Had one of them done Lydia in? If so, which one? Or had they operated as a team, and, if so, how?

As I got up to begin the day, I thought of Lydia's last concerns in her conversation with me. They weren't about anything that had to do with the Island Trust or about money. They were, shall we say, matters of the heart. Her thoughts were of her husband, the unattractive Harry Hedrickson, and his liaison with the attractive Selena. Selena had gone out to dinner that night with Harry. Where had they gone? To the Cape Sands? Had Lydia confronted them there, and had Harry or Selena killed her, or conspired to kill her?

My morning worrying also ranged over the discoveries on the island. I reflected on the drama and tragedy surrounding them. Calhoun Lockwood had not only had greed but revenge as a motive. He had carried that hatred across generations to avenge his father's death, as well as to recover a family treasure. It was bizarre. But was Lockwood's behavior any more bizarre than that of the Randalls? Or were they any better than he? After all, Alexander Randall's crime of murder and theft, back in the 1880s, had begun it all; old Charles and James had been treasure mad; for that matter, so was the present Charles.

And what of the drug runners? They were all dead now, except Tiger. Did they let you wear silvered sunglasses in the federal penitentiary, where it seemed likely he would now take up residence? And now there was Tommy Fawnley. He was in it, too. He'd undoubtedly be tried as a coconspirator. Maybe he'd get off lightly. After all, he hadn't participated in the naval battle with the Coast Guard. I wondered if Charles had had any suspicions of Fawnley's drug activities. Apparently he saw a lot of him in New Orleans. And whenever I'd asked or talked about McGovern, Tiger, or Fawnley, Charles had always seemed anxious to change the subject.

I tried to stop thinking about it all, dressed, and went downstairs, where I joined my three colleagues for breakfast. They told me they were leaving for Tallahassee as soon as they finished. "Gentlemen," I said, "I'm afraid I owe you all an apology. When I invited Joel and Bill down here, I had no idea I'd be dragging them into something like this. What was found over there on the island was certainly not anticipated by me."

"Think nothing of it," said Chandler, with a grin. "I wouldn't have missed it for anything. Besides, as you know, I'm something of a specialist in European Contact Period archaeology, so I took to it naturally."

"Well," I appealed to Calvert, "I hope it hasn't screwed things up with the Park Service for the sale of the island?"

"I don't think so," he replied. "It could have been a little embarrassing, what with Mr. Randall and his friend going over there and digging a big hole in the mound, but in view of all the newspaper publicity connected with the solving of a forty-five-year-old murder, I don't think the Park Service will raise any fuss. The digging has been lost in the shuffle. I suppose one of the main things now will be to keep the curious away from the island until all the publicity dies down. The sheriff seems to be willing to take responsibility for that, at least until State Parks take over."

I was interested to know how much any of my breakfast table companions knew of the background of the "crime in the mound." They hadn't been with us when the sheriff had detailed John's statement to Charles and me yesterday. They indicated that they knew the gist of what had happened. The deputies had briefed them on at least some of it when they were working at the mound.

"Real macabre, Faulknerian stuff, isn't it?" said Klein.

But Chandler and Calvert, who were both southerners, came back at him with statements to the effect that it was the kind of thing that had happened in other places in the United States, too.

When they were ready to leave, I walked out to the parking lot with them. When they drove away, I felt abandoned. I realized that I hadn't felt so *alone* here in St. Christopher's while they were around. I knew then that it wouldn't do for me to live here. I no longer "belonged." I had, as Charles and others had told me, become a Yankee. But it was more than that. Like many an academic, I was not quite comfortable unless I was around my own kind, those who spoke my language. My various collateral relatives, including even Charles and Selena, were not my own kind anymore and hadn't been, I suppose, for over forty years. It was no reflection upon me or upon them; we had lived different lives.

The morning mail delivery came to the hotel, with a letter and a postcard for me. The letter was from my youngest daughter, whom I had not yet heard from on this trip. Reading about her doings, and those of her husband and children, brightened me up a bit. The postcard was from a seven-year-old granddaughter, written from a summer camp: "Dear Grandfather," it began, "How are you? I am fine." On quick reflection, I didn't think I was fine.

I wandered around the lobby and realized I was feeling lower than usual this morning. Perhaps that wasn't so surprising. The events of the last few days were beginning to have their cumulative effect upon a seventy-two-year-old grandfather. What would I do with myself today? Maybe I was missing my daily visit from the sheriff? I even considered strolling downtown and just happening to stop by his office. How would I explain my presence? Could I just start out by saying, "Sheriff Larrabee, when we left you out at the Cape Sands yesterday afternoon, you told us you were going to ask some questions. What did you find out that would throw any more light on Mrs. Hedrickson's death?" What would be the sheriff's reaction if I came out with that? Would he tell me to go to hell? No, more likely he would give me one of those apparently casual, but secretly crafted, circumlocutory answers: "Now, Mr. Edwards, as you must realize, this is a very complicated case. We still don't know a lot of things, but when we do we'll be the first to let you and the good citizens of St. Christopher's know." I decided against going down to see him, and I didn't even go out for a morning walk. Instead, I went upstairs to my room.

When I got there, my phone rang. It was Charles. "Colin," he said, "I have to drive over to New Orleans today to help Tommy. Among other things, I must arrange bail for him, and I'll probably be needed to look after some matters in the galleries. But before I go, I'd like to stop by the hotel and talk with you. There are some things I want to tell you, but I don't want to do it over the phone. If it's all right, I'll come over now on my way out of town." I assured him that it would be all right, and he said he'd be there in five minutes.

I went downstairs and met Charles, but he said he'd prefer it if we talked in my room, so we went back up. I gave him the only comfortable chair and propped myself up at the head of the bed. Charles seemed more nervous and tense than usual. He got right to it. "Colin, I'm afraid Selena's in a hell of a mess. You see, the sheriff found out yesterday, by inquiring around at the Cape Sands, that she and Harry Hedrickson had been out there together on Wednesday night, the night Lydia disappeared."

So, I thought, this was Selena's date with Harry, the one Mildred had referred to when she had said that "Miss Selena had gone out to dinner with Mr. Harry Hedrickson." I wasn't too surprised that they had ended up at the Cape Sands.

"It seems," Charles continued, "that she and Harry had been out there before and been seen there together by the help. I hate to see Selena cheapened like this, and in this case it's even worse. You see, the sheriff took both Sel and Harry down to his office for questioning this morning. To make it short, they're suspects in Lydia's death."

"Charles, I don't know all the facts the sheriff has, but certainly they aren't being charged with murder just because they were out at the motel at the same time that Lydia was. That doesn't prove anything."

Charles shook his head. "No, it's a little more than that.

There's been gossip around town for some time now about Selena and Harry. Lydia had talked to others, to Mabel Bull for one, about Harry's running around with Sel. You see, Sel had been dating Webbie for out-of-town dinners and late nights at the same time she had Harry on the string, playing along with both of them. The sheriff has picked up on all this."

"Even so," I told Charles, "adultery is not necessarily linked to murder. I'm sure Sheriff Larrabee is aware of that. Was there anything specific in the Cape Sands people's statements about Harry, or Harry and Selena, other than the fac of being out there on Wednesday night?"

"I don't know all the facts, Colin, and I haven't ha$\c$ a chance to talk much with Sel since the questioning," Charles replied. "Naturally, she's pretty upset. All I know is that she and Harry had dinner there at the Cape Sands Restaurant and afterward went to their room at about ten o'clock. Then there was some sort of row, because people in the room next to theirs said that there was quite a ruckus. These neighbors couldn't be sure whether there were just two people in the room or more than that, but it was quite a quarrel. They said they could hear both a man's and a woman's voice."

It did sound bad, but I still wasn't ready to accuse Selena of murder.

Charles continued. "I guess Sel and Harry left there about midnight, and she came on home, and so did Harry. When Harry got to his house, Lydia wasn't there."

I asked him, "When Harry and Selena left the Cape Sands, did they see anything of Lydia? I presume they had their car parked in the parking lot out there, the lot where John's car was found."

Charles said he didn't know.

I wasn't quite sure what Charles wanted me to do. Nothing, I guessed. I supposed he just wanted someone to talk it all over with.

Charles, after saying nothing for several minutes, resumed. "You remember, Colin, what I told you on that first night you came down to St. Christopher's and came over to see us? I said then that I was in danger, and I think I still am. I thought then it was Webbie, but he was an intended victim, too. Now I think Harry Hedrickson is the devil in the piece. I think he killed Webbie, and now he's killed his wife. He probably tried before when he shot at her in their house. He wants to get his cracker hands on the money for the sale of the island."

"But, Charles, as I understand it, he can't. The Island Trust, as you've explained it to me, belonged to only four heirs. Two of those, the two Bulls, are now dead; you and Selena are the inheritors."

"No, Colin. Harry, damn him, has said for a long time that he was going to challenge the trust and the way that it was set up. He felt that, as Lydia's husband, he should get her share if she should predecease him."

"I shouldn't think he'd be in a very good position to do that, especially now, if he is about to be formally charged with her murder. And, if he were convicted of it, he'd be completely out of luck."

Charles seemed to ignore this. He got up and stared out the window. Then he shook his head in a worried way and said, "Colin, it's Harry—Harry Hedrickson. He's been behind this all along, and I'm afraid I'm the next victim."

"Nonsense," I told him. It was the only thing I could say. I didn't want to feed his paranoia now any more than I had wanted to on that first night I saw him here, but I probably wasn't as confident now as I had been then. Charles then said that he'd better get going, and he thanked me for listening to him. But as he started toward the door, he turned and said, "Colin, I'm concerned about Sel. I think she's been taken in by Hedrickson. If she was with him when he shot Lydia out at the Cape Sands, I don't think she had anything to do with the shooting. I don't think she would have become involved in anything like murder. I hate to go off and leave her alone now, but I have to. Won't you, well, look after her when I'm in New Orleans, especially tonight? It would mean

a lot to her if you could go over and see her. It's Mildred's
day off, and she'll be there in the house alone. As we both
know"—and he smiled a little ruefully at this—"she's always felt very close to you."

I didn't know whether to laugh or cry at this last statement, but I promised I would look in on Selena.

Downstairs, as I as walking out to his car with him,
Charles told me, "Thanks, again, for letting me unload on
you, old man, but I had to tell someone. It's damn worrying."
And, as he was leaving: "Thanks, too, for promising to go
over and see Selena."

After Charles's departure, I read the Tallahassee paper,
which was full of both the Lydia Bull murder and the discovery of the skeletons on the island.

At eleven o'clock, with an hour to go before lunch, I went
for a walk. How much longer, I asked myself, was I going to
hang around down here? Did I owe it to Charles to stay until
things got settled—whatever that might mean? Did I feel
that I owed it to Selena to stay? I was sure she wouldn't care
one way or the other. Had I, for a time, for a very brief time
a few days ago, had the romantic notion that Selena and I
might . . . might what?

When I got back to the St. Christopher House there was
only a single patron in the dining room, seated at a table for
two over by a window. It was Sheriff Jess Larrabee. He nodded
to me and gestured a silent invitation to join him. I went
over and sat down, greeting him by saying that I was surprised but pleased to see him and that I didn't realize he
came here often for lunch.

"I don't; only now and then. I remember it from Aunt
Connie's time, though. The food's still good."

I agreed with him on that. He had just placed his order,
so I gave mine to the waitress, and when she had gone I
waited for him to tell me what was on his mind. I didn't
think the St. Christopher House cuisine, good as it was, had
been Sheriff Larrabee's only purpose in coming here for
lunch. I hoped he'd let me know about his questioning of

Selena and Harry, but he didn't, or at least he didn't begin
that way. Instead, he took a little slip of paper from his shirt
pocket, looked at it, and asked me, "Mr. Edwards, can you
remember if Charles Randall made a telephone call to you
on the evening or night of Wednesday, June fifth, here at the
hotel, a telephone call that originated from the phone on St.
James's Island?"

I thought back. Wednesday. That was the evening I came in
rather late from Tallahassee. I had tried to call Charles on the
island more than once that night, but had had no response.

The sheriff looked at the slip of paper again and explained,
"The telephone calls made from the island phone to the
town of St. Christopher's aren't local calls; they're registered
as long-distance calls. So we've got a record of them. Mr.
Randall made several calls that night, and one of them was
taken here at the hotel. The man at the desk can't remember
if the call was for you or not."

It came to me then. "No, Sheriff, I didn't receive any call
from Charles last Wednesday evening, but I think Tommy
Fawnley did. He was here at the hotel. I talked with him at
dinner. It was the first time I'd met him. He told me that
Charles Randall had called him here at the hotel, from the
island, shortly after he arrived. I believe Fawnley said he got
in here at about five P.M."

The sheriff checked his slip of paper again, and said,
"That fits. The call came in here at five-twenty-one." He
chewed on his luncheon chop for a while, then said, "Tell
me, Mr. Edwards, do you consider Mr. Randall to be a good
friend of Fawnley?"

I wasn't quite sure what to make of this question. I didn't
know if the sheriff was probing into Charles's personal life
or not. I played it pretty straight. "Well, I understand that
they are associated in a business way in the Lockwood Galleries in New Orleans. I believe Charles has a financial interest in the business there. Why do you ask?"

The sheriff kept his eyes on his plate. "It's just that one
of the calls Mr. Randall made from the island, a call at a little

after five P.M. on Wednesday, was to an emergency number at the Drug Enforcement Administration in Pensacola."

I was shocked. "You mean the call that tipped off the—"

"Mm-m." The sheriff, with his mouth full, interrupted with a nod before I could finish.

So Charles had been the one responsible for the bloody interception of McGovern's, and John's—and Fawnley's—drug business. I was stunned.

The sheriff went back to his list of phone calls, and said, "There's another call here that he made to his own residence at six-forty-seven P.M. that Wednesday."

I remembered that, when I had tried to call Charles at home, Mildred had told me that he'd just telephoned from the island, asking if Selena was there.

"And there's one other call that Mr. Randall made to St. Christopher's that night, at a little after eight P.M., but—well—I think I'll keep that to myself for a while. With that, the sheriff sat back in his chair and let our waitress clear away his plate.

I assumed he'd gone back into his laconic, close-to-the-vest lawman act, but I pressed him anyway. "Have there been any new developments with regard to the shooting of Mrs. Hedrickson?"

Rather casually, the sheriff avoided my question by asking another: "I understand that Mr. Charles Randall came over here to see you this morning. Is that right, Mr. Edwards?"

I silently chalked up another point for the Larrabee intelligence system. This one, almost certainly, would have to be laid at the desk of the hotel's clerk. I admitted that, yes, Charles Randall had been here this morning and we'd talked.

"Well, then, you know about some of the developments. Mr. Hedrickson and Mrs. Crawford were interviewed down at my office this morning. They were both at the Cape Sands Motel on Wednesday evening last, the night Mrs. Hedrickson was killed there. They have both given testimony that Mrs. Hedrickson came to the room they had engaged at the motel and that a long and acrimonious argument ensued.

This would have been a little after ten o'clock. Mrs. Hedrickson left them, and it was some time after that, I suppose around ten-thirty or so, that she was shot. One of the cooks in the kitchen, which is on the parking lot side of the building, said he thought he heard something that sounded like a shot at about that time. Mr. Hedrickson and Mrs. Crawford claim to have remained in their room until about midnight, when they left the motel and returned to St. Christopher's. They also claim they did not see Mrs. Hedrickson again."

It sounded a little worse, a little more incriminating, for Selena than what Charles had told me this morning. Lydia had confronted her husband and Selena in the motel bedroom, and the loud argument that the neighbors had heard must have been the result of this confrontation. Had Harry then pursued his wife, shot her in John Crawford's car, and left her body there? One might make a case for this. But it seemed a little strange for Harry to have gone back to the motel room after the shooting and to have stayed there for another hour and a half. Assuming, that is, that the murder did take place at ten-thirty, per the motel cook's testimony. Did this element of doubt make Larrabee hesitant to bring an indictment against Harry? I would have liked to ask the sheriff some more questions along these lines, but I didn't.

"And now that you're asking me about developments, sir," continued the sheriff, "perhaps I should tell you that I got a report just a little while ago from Tallahassee on the bullet that killed Mrs. Hedrickson. It was a thirty-eight caliber, and it was fired from the same revolver that fired the bullet that killed Mr. Bull and that was fired into the wall of the Randall library and into the other houses in that part of town."

I thought the sheriff almost smiled at me when he told me this. Was he teasing me? Did he suspect my fantasized role as the amateur sleuth, the one who breaks the case for the professionals? Was he saying to me, You're always complaining that we don't tell you anything. Now take this and see what you can do with it!

All I could do was to say, "I see." Though, I added, "I suppose there's been no sign of the gun."

"No, Mr. Edwards, there hasn't" was his flat reply.

We both skipped dessert, and shortly after that the sheriff said he had to get back. I wondered where he was going, and what he was going to do after he got back.

I spent a couple of hours in an afternoon nap. I dreamed about Lydia. It was not an unpleasant or frightening dream. We were somewhere out around the Cape Sands Motel, but it was a warm, sunny afternoon rather than at night. I thought she was a nice, pleasant woman, and she was telling me that everything was going to be all right now, and that in some unexpressed way this satisfactory resolution of our problems was the result of my politeness. I felt relaxed and comforted by her reassurance. Then I came awake suddenly. My phone was ringing. I collected myself out of my foggy pool of midafternoon sleep and answered it.

"Colin," said Selena.

"Yes."

"Colin, I, I need someone to talk to. Charles has gone off, I think to New Orleans. I—we've—had a horrible morning. I feel like I'm losing my mind."

"Yes, I know, I've heard something about it, from Charles." For some reason, I hesitated to say anything about the sheriff. I added "Of course we can talk, my dear." One part of me said she was someone for me to avoid, but another part—the stronger part, I guess—wanted to reach out to her.

"Oh, Colin, Colin."

"Look Selena, why don't you have dinner with me tonight here at the hotel? I'll come by and pick you up at, say, six-thirty. We can have dinner and then talk here or drive somewhere."

"Colin, I'd love to, but, frankly, I prefer not to be seen in public after . . . after all that's been happening. Won't you, instead, come here for a bite of dinner with me? If you can put up with what I'll fix? This is Mildred's evening off, but I'll give you something."

I told her that I would, and she said to come at six-thirty. Afterward, I had feelings of guilt. Was I too ready to run at Selena's beck and call? Wouldn't I have done better to avoid her? But I couldn't. She needed me. Just like the time back in the sandbox days when she had cut her toe on a piece of broken glass and I'd helped her up to her back door, bleeding and crying, to the maternal ministrations of Georgia, while Charles had gone on with whatever he was doing without paying any attention to her wailings.

My watch said it was only three-ten, much to early to get ready. I lay there on the bed and let my thoughts go far away, to archaeology, to a book I was trying to write back home; I began revising the outline of it in my mind. I was quite successful in getting through the time this way. Before I realized it, it was after six.

I got up, showered, and dressed. I was doing those things, I reflected, at just the same time that I had done them a week ago, on the Saturday of my arrival in St. Christopher's. That was when all this nightmare really began, with my talk with Charles that night. Or had it begun even earlier, with what Webbie had told me back in Boston? Or, God knows, had it begun much longer ago than that?

I decided to drive over the Randalls'. Selena came out on the porch to meet me as I parked the car. She was demure in a white linen dress with a circlet of heavy green beads at her throat. Her ordeal with the law had not seemed to have taken much out of her, or if it had, it didn't show. She greeted me with a cheek-to-cheek kiss and closed the door after us, leading me back to the study, which was cool and dark.

"What would you like to drink?" she asked. I told her that a gin and tonic seemed called for, with a slice of green lime in it. I explained that it would conform to the color scheme of the white dress and the green beads. She laughed and said that sounded fine—and it also sounded like me. She excused herself and went to the kitchen to fix the drinks.

There was a lamp lighted near the sofa, and I sat down by it. As I leaned back, I noticed a little picture in a gold frame on an end table in the circle of light. It was an old hand-tinted photo of the kind done before color photography. It showed the lovely Selena as a child in a Red Cross nurse's uniform, with the little red cross on the white cap and her very pretty face framed by her dark bangs. While I was looking at the picture, Selena came back with the drinks.

"Oh, that. Me as a child. I must have been about five then," she told me.

"Yes," I said, "I know. I remember the day very well."

She seemed slightly puzzled. "What day?" she asked me.

"Armistice Day, in 1918. Don't you remember when you raised a fuss because you wanted to sit in the middle at the back of the car when we were going to be in the parade—you, Charles, and me, with Great-uncle Charles riding up in the front seat?"

She shook her head in amusement. "No, I don't Colin. Colin, you have the most, the most fantastic memory of anyone I've ever known. No wonder you're an archaeologist. You're obsessed with the past!"

"Yes," I said, "I'm obsessed with the past."

We went in to dinner, a cold collation. It was nice, I think, although I don't remember much about it. During the meal we began to talk about what had happened. She was the one who brought it up.

"Colin, I know I'm to blame for a lot of things in my life, but I didn't have anything to do with Lydia's death. I swear it. It was awful last Wednesday night. I shouldn't have gone with Harry. I went to tell him I wanted to break things off, that I didn't want to see him anymore."

We were eating dessert by then. She put down her spoon and blinked back the tears. Selena, I thought, cried easily—for a tough woman, and she was a tough woman. Was this a show, for my benefit?

"Harry and I had dinner at the Cape Sands, and we quarreled during dinner. I wanted him to take me home, but he wouldn't let go of our quarrel. He didn't want me to stop seeing him. We went to the room he had reserved. We were

no more than there when someone rapped on the door. Poor
Lydia, she was angry and in tears. She told Harry that this—
with me—would have to stop, that she wouldn't put up with
it any longer. I tried to make things better. I told her I was
sorry. I really was. Oh, Colin, I do such stupid things, get
myself into such messes. I said that I was the one to blame,
that she should take Harry back and forget about it all. That
it hadn't meant anything. But Harry, Harry has a temper,
and he was drunk, too. He started shouting at Lydia; he
called her a dull, conceited woman who thought she was too
good for him. It was awful. It got so bad the people in the
next room pounded on the wall and threatened to call the
management."

"It sounds awful."

"Finally, Lydia told Harry that she didn't want to see him
anymore and left."

"When was this? What time, I mean?"

Selena turned on me fiercely. "Stop it, Colin! You sound
exactly like the sheriff!" And then, "Oh, I don't know exactly
what time it was, sometime after ten o'clock, I suppose."

"And when did you leave?" I asked her.

"I don't know, really. Harry had a bottle with him and he
began to drink some more. I was afraid he might pass out. I
had an awful time getting him out to the car, and we went
home. I did the driving, not him. I left him and his car at
his house and walked over here. I guess then it was after
midnight.

"Oh, damnit," she said with a sigh, "I've been over and
over this with that man Larrabee until I can't stand it!" She
ended putting her face in her hands and sobbing.

I'm afraid I wasn't very pitying. "Selena, tell me. Did you
see anything again of Lydia after she left you and Harry in
the room?"

She looked up, eyes misted, and shook her head. "No, I
didn't, and Harry didn't either. He was with me all the time.
I thought she must have gotten into her car and driven away,
but Harry said they didn't have a second car, that Lydia didn't

drive, so we didn't know how she'd gone back to town."

"As it turned out, she didn't," I said.

"I know," sobbed Selena. She dried her eyes then, and after a pause she told me that she'd been a terrible hostess. I asked her if she wanted me to leave, but she said no, please don't. She couldn't stand being alone just now.

We left the dinner table. Selena said that Mildred would clear it up when she came in tomorrow morning. Charles had given her most of the day off, and she was spending the night with her sister.

I went back to the library while Selena prepared us some coffee and brought it in, along with a bottle of brandy and two glasses. We sat on the sofa together, and she served us on a coffee table. While she was doing this, she looked up and smiled wistfully at me, then passed me my cup and saucer. I couldn't harden my heart against this woman even though I knew I should.

A big mantel clock ticked, the same one that had ticked back when she and Charles and I used to read those fabulous books here on the library floor. Selena and I must have sat for some time in silence, listening to the ticking. At last I reached over and touched her arm.

"Selena, my dear, tell me, why did you take up with someone like Harry, or, for that matter, with Webbie?"

She didn't answer me but stared at the floor.

I asked her then, "Selena, did you know your father had been buried over there in the mound on St. James's Island, that he had been murdered and put away there for all that long time?"

When she looked at me then, she looked her full age and more. She looked ravaged by grief. I didn't think she was going to answer this question, either, but she finally said, "I . . . I didn't know it at first. John never told me until two years later, well after we were married. I didn't know what to do then. He told me that if I said anything he'd claim that I had known from the beginning, that I would be an accessory after the fact. He said I'd benefited from the money he'd received from the sale of the gold just as much as he had. We'd bought a house in New Orleans with some of it. Before, he had told me that he had received the money as an inheritance of some kind."

"When you found out—was this why you left John?"

She nodded but then added, "In part, yes, but other things between us began to go bad. You see, our daughter—she isn't dead—she was born brain damaged. John couldn't take it. After the war, he refused to contribute decently to her support. I got a job and carried all the expenses until we were divorced. I still have her to look after. Now, with the sale of the island coming up, I'll be able to leave a trust for her, thank God, after I'm gone."

She faced me directly now and said, "Colin, the reason I came over here at Christmastime was because I had learned about the forthcoming sale of the island, and I wanted to talk with Charles about his plans after the sale. He had written me that he wanted to restore this place—at great cost. Money was not to be spared. He wanted to maintain an establishment, he said, like Great-grandfather Alexander, like Grandfather Charles. We owed it to ourselves and to our southern heritage, he said. He wanted me to contribute from my share of the island sale to this, this vanity of his. I told him no, that I wouldn't, that if he wanted to continue to live here there was no reason he shouldn't, but that I wouldn't contribute financially to his plans. Ever since then he has persecuted me."

"Persecuted? How?" I asked her.

"With this business about digging up the mound on the island," she answered. "Somehow, some way, Charles found out, or suspected, that our father was murdered over there. He knew he could torment me, and he also thought that if the evidence of Father's death was unearthed, he could claim that I was involved in the crime. As a convicted felon, I would have had to forfeit my share from the sale of the island. He would have all of the Randall share then."

"And you thought that Webbie, and then Harry, could help

you stop Charles from doing this?" With some anger, I added, "And you thought that maybe I could, too? And that you would, shall we say, bind Webbie and Harry to your cause? And then you could bind me in the same way?"

"That's an ugly thing to say, Colin. It isn't like you."

"It was an ugly thing to do, Selena."

"Colin, it wasn't like that. I would never do that to you."

She was interrupted by a sound in the hallway. We had left the library door open. We heard footsteps, familiar-sounding footsteps. Charles walked in. He was looking unusually bright eyed.

"Well, well, if it isn't the professor," he exclaimed. "I'm so glad you came over, my dear fellow. My lovely sister needed cheering up and support, and there is no one to whom she would rather turn than Colin Edwards. Is that not right, Selena? Doesn't she look lovely, Colin? All in white, so virginal."

It was obvious that Selena was surprised, as was I. "Charles," she asked, "weren't you going to New Orleans? What happened? Are you all right?"

"Of course, I'm all right, my delightful sister. I am as right, as they say, as rain. In fact, I have rarely been 'righter' in my life—given my advanced years. What happened is that I stopped at no great distance from here, at the Cape Sands Motel on the coast highway. You know it well, do you not, Selena, darling? It is a favorite watering place of yours. You should introduce Colin there sometime."

Selena cut him off. "But I thought you had to get over to New Orleans to look after Tommy."

"Tommy? Thomas Fawnley? That stupid little beast. A few days in the slammer will be a riotous time for him. He'll be very popular there. No, I had other and more important things to do back here, so back here I came—after a spot of refreshment and a nice lie-down out there."

Was Charles drunk? Or, to my mind worse yet, was he coked up, enjoying some of McGovern's wares? I wasn't sure of the symptoms of the latter. Whatever it was, I hadn't seen him like this since I'd been in St. Christopher's; for that matter, I'd never seen him like this.

"No, my pretties," continued Charles, "what I have come back for is to resolve these horrible crimes we good citizens of this fair city have been so plagued with in recent days. The slaying of one Webster Bull, at the doorway of his mansion, not far from this very house, and the equally heinous dispatch of the virtuous Lydia Bull Hedrickson, whose only sin in life had been to take as husband that low fellow Harry Hedrickson. Those are not things to pass unnoticed."

Selena snapped, "Oh, Charles, stop it!"

"To say nothing, of course, of the random shots that were fired in the dead of night through the windows of the residences of a peaceful and law-abiding citizenry." Charles shook his finger at me and went on. "But where, where my good professor, is the murder weapon, the weapon of terror? The lean sheriff of St. Christopher's, Squire Larrabee, cannot find it, can he? He and his minions are completely at sea."

Selena was looking worried. I wondered if she had seen Charles like this before.

Charles's volubility was unstoppable. "What we need now—and I would tell the sheriff this if he were here in our circle—is a systematic search for the weapon with which those crimes were committed. Such a search will take diligence and imagination, and whereas the worthy Larrabee is an exemplar of the former, he is sadly lacking in the latter quality. Now where would you, Colin, where would you look if you were searching for a revolver, a revolver, we are told, of caliber thirty-eight, a dangerous, a lethal weapon?"

"Calm down, Charles," I said.

"The professor beseeches me to calm down, but this will get us no further in our researches into the criminal mind. Calmness is not called for. What we need is action."

This was all both boring and intolerable. I looked at Selena questioningly, as if to say Should I do something about this, although I wasn't quite sure just what it would have been. I thought she avoided my eye.

Charles went on with his tirade. "Should we search the desk first?" He went over to the desk and began opening the drawers in a mock search. "No, no, it is not in the desk. Our criminal is not so obvious as that, is he? Where, then? Could the murder weapon be hidden behind books? Maybe." He walked over to the bookcase and suddenly pulled a dozen books out of shelf, letting them thud to the floor in a pile. "But there are so many books"—and he gestured around the room—"that it would be unconscionable to bring them all down. No, it is selective insight and imagination that we need. Think, Colin, where, if you were the murderer, would you hide the gun?"

"Charles," I said, "you're making a fool out of yourself. I don't know what's the matter with you, but whatever it is, stop it!"

He moved away from us toward a far corner of the room. "No, wait, Colin," Charles said, holding up a forefinger. "Let us consider this more carefully. Now where would you, as an archaeologist, search for a hiding place?" He went to the corner of the bookcase where the Marajó burial urn that had fascinated me so as a child was on the shelf. "Why not in this antique jar? Surely no one but an archaeologist would think of looking in it." He reached inside the urn. "Ah, just as I thought," he said, "here it is," and he drew a metallic blue revolver out of the urn. "Now what do you know?" he exclaimed with a wild grin. "I believe the caliber of this revolver is thirty-eight, the caliber of the infamous murder weapon we seek."

Charles brandished the revolver around and ended up pointing it at me. The muzzle, I thought, looked as big as a cannon barrel. "For God's sake, Charles, look out! Don't point that at me! It might be loaded!"

Charles continued to grin. "Why, my dear old boy," he said, "of course it's loaded. That's exactly why I'm pointing it at you. It's the logical preparatory step to pulling the trigger and shooting you, which is what I'm going to do, although perhaps I should ascertain first if it is, indeed loaded." He shifted the muzzle slightly to the left and fired. The detonation was shattering, and the bullet plowed through the back of the sofa between Selena and myself.

Selena screamed. I was too scared to make any kind of noise.

Charles backed to the desk and sat on the edge of it, still facing us. The revolver was again pointed at me. "Ah, that's better," he said. "I've had a hard day. I need to get off my feet. You know, I work so hard trying to make things come out right. If only people would cooperate. The other night now, last Wednesday, I had things all worked out. I called Lydia from the island and asked her to meet me at the Cape Sands Motel, in the parking lot, in John Crawford's car. Then I nipped over in the boat. You can get there in five minutes, and it was dark and no one saw me. I was going to take Lydia, poor stupid Lydia, to your motel room, Selena, to confront you and the obnoxious Harry, but after I met her there at the Cape Sands, she absolutely refused to let me go in with her. She said that it was something she must do herself and that she didn't want me there."

Charles was trembling now, but he continued. "You see, my plan was that I would shoot all three of you—Selena, Harry, and Lydia—and then place the gun in Lydia's pudgy little hand. It would have been the perfect tragic denouement of a love triangle. The jealous wife kills both the erring husband and the scarlet woman, then turns the gun on herself. But, as I say, I had no cooperation from Lydia. She insisted on going in to see Harry and Selena by herself. Then, after her talk with the guilty pair, she came back out and joined me in John's fetid sedan. It was there, as she was relating her story of tearful indignation, that I dispatched her. Now if she had cooperated, Selena, you and she would have been out of the way, and the only innocent bystander to suffer, if one can think of the repugnant Hedrickson as an innocent bystander, would have been the readily expendable Harry himself. Now, alas, the more aesthetically satisfactory Colin is forced into the role of the innocent victim."

"Charles, Charles, you're mad!" shouted Selena. "Why should you want to kill us?"

"Use your imagination, my ever delightful sister. I don't want to kill poor old Colin. He's not a bad sort at all, not like Webbie or Harry. In fact, I've always been rather fond of him, although he can get a little professorially tedious at times. No, Selena, it is you whom I must kill. I want all ten million dollars from the island sale. I've explained to you at great length why I need the money, and, if you had been a loyal Randall, you would have agreed to my simple requests for our restoration. I've already gone to considerable trouble killing Webbie and Lydia toward this end. You, in view of your intransigence, are the only one left to be eliminated."

Charles chuckled. "The projected scenario unfolds like this. The distinguished Harvard professor sitting by your side, Selena, is your much betrayed and often rejected lover, loyal to you all these years. Now enraged by your crowning infidelity with the vulgar Harry, he shoots you and then himself."

He turned to me. "Colin, old boy, afterwards I shall place the gun in your hand. It will look more suicidal if I shoot you in the head. I hope you don't mind, dear lad. Now Webbie, I shot him right through the heart. You know it was terribly simple last Saturday night. After you left here, I simply slipped out by the back door, cut through some neighboring backyards, walked around to the Bull front door, rang the bell, and, when he came to answer it, I let old Webbie have it. He looked so surprised and hurt when I did it. You should have seen his face, Colin."

Could I, I wondered, make any sort of a lunge at Charles, grab the gun, stop him? It didn't seem very likely. "Charles," I said, "you can't do this." But I doubt if my voice carried conviction. The trouble was, I knew he could do it. If he'd already murdered Webbie and Lydia in cold blood, what the hell would stop him now? He was crazy, crazy mad. Webbie and Selena had been right with their worries about him.

"I must, Colin," he told me, with anger now. "I'm sorry

in your case, but Selena deserves to die. She knew our father had been murdered and buried out there on the island, murdered by John Crawford and Calhoun Lockwood, a worthless bum and a degenerate, and she did nothing about it. Oh, yes, she knew all right. Tommy Fawnley found out from Lockwood, and he told me." Charles looked terrible now, the skin stretched tight over his skull, his eyes hollow and burning. Saliva was collecting around the corners of his mouth.

He paused only briefly in his ranting, then went on. "Yes, I like revenge, revenge on my bitch of a sister and on that scum Crawford. Why do you think the Coast Guard happened to intercept John and his riffraff crew? I'll tell you why. I called and told them. I knew their schedule. I found it out from Tommy. I'm glad they shot the hell out of them. They deserved it."

Charles was breathing hard. Looking directly at me, he said, "Well, I must get on with my task now. You first, Colin." He leveled the pistol at me.

I thought, I might as well do something. I'll get shot anyway. I'll try to jump him.

At that moment Selena, at the other end of the sofa, threw her brandy snifter at Charles. He tried to dodge it, but the brandy sloshed in his face before the glass hit the floor and shattered. I lunged at him as he wiped his eyes, grabbing him around the arms and waist and jamming him back hard against the desk. He held on to the revolver, but he couldn't get his hand free to point it at me. I was heavier and stronger than Charles, but he had a maniacal wildness in his struggles to break my grip.

Then Sheriff Larrabee was in the room reaching over me and taking the gun away from Charles.

"All right, Mr. Randall," he said, "I'm afraid that's about it." He stuck the revolver in his belt, pushed me aside, and handled Charles like a matchstick, twisting him around, bringing his clawing hands behind his back, and snapping the handcuffs on him, all in a matter of seconds.

I saw that Selena had slumped down in her corner of the

sofa. She looked deathly pale. The sheriff turned and called, "Mildred, you better get in here and look after Mrs. Crawford. Maybe you'd better call a doctor."

Mildred came in, sat down beside Selena, and put an arm around her.

The sheriff came over and gave me that sort of sizing-up look that he had given me every time he had seen me and said, "Well, Mr. Edwards, you wanted me to let you know when we found the murder weapon. I'll bet that's it," he concluded, pulling it out of his belt and showing it to me.

Charles, with his head down, was still sitting on the edge of the desk. He looked up at me in a very accusatory way, and said, "You've betrayed me. You and Sel have betrayed me." Then his eyes seemed to go vacant, and he stared at me like he didn't know me.

I went over, poured myself a brandy, gulped it down, and sank into a chair.

The sheriff looked down at me and inquired, "Are you feeling all right, Mr. Edwards?" When I nodded affirmatively, he said, "I'd rest there a bit if I were you. Maybe the doctor better have a look at you, too, when he gets here."

Mildred, who had gone out for a glass of water, was helping Selena drink it.

The sheriff told me, "You know, Mr. Edwards, I was right sorry not to be able to help you sooner, but Mildred gave me a telephone call just a little while ago, and I got over here as fast as I could. She said that she had just come in and that Mr. Randall was with you and Mrs. Crawford in the library, that he was talking loud and crazylike, and that he had a gun. I was there outside that door for some time"—he paused and nodded toward the doorway—"while Mr. Randall was talking. Sorry not to have come in sooner. I was all prepared to shoot him before he shot you, but I suppose it's better the way it is."

"Yes," I said, "I guess it's better."

▽

Epilogue

I AM BACK IN BOSTON NOW, and it is October, so we're at the peak of the fall foliage, with the red, the yellows, the russets—and the crispness in the air. It is so very different here from St. Christopher's. I feel like I belong here, even though I am, by old Boston standards, a newcomer. My separation—I almost said alienation—from the home of my birth is complete, but I suppose it had been that way for a long time. It was only made very clear to me by last summer's visit to St. Christopher's.

I pass my days now as a retired professor should. There is a spot of writing and library research—not too much, but enough to keep me at least somewhat current with what my younger colleagues are doing. I even publish a paper now and then. I go to an occasional conference or meeting, but not too many; I was never much of a *congresista*, so I don't miss them. I enjoy seeing my daughters, my sons-in-law, and my grandchildren. I go to my clubs and chat with my age-mates. I have pleasant times with the widow of a deceased colleague whom I see frequently. In general, I behave as a senior citizen of my background and position should. As I said at the beginning of this narrative, I now feel safe and secure from old dreams.

I stayed in St. Christopher's just another week after that second Saturday night with Charles and Selena. It was a week of funerals. Lydia's was held on Monday. There was an outpouring of St. Christopherians at St. Luke's to pay tribute to a woman and a wife beyond reproach, one not only betrayed by a husband's infidelities but foully murdered. The church was full that morning. Selena insisted on going, and I escorted her. I could not help but admire her, in her role as the scarlet woman who nevertheless held her head high. How little I knew her, really. The Selena I knew, or thought I knew, was a creature of, in her own words, my obsession with the past. The service went on for some time, the lessons, the prayers, eulogies from the minister, from Bull relatives, the latter being people whom I had forgotten, or, more likely, had never known. Harry was there, as chief mourner, with head hung low. He would be forgiven. Selena never would.

Selena and I didn't go to the reception afterward, although she spoke briefly with Harry at the church door, much, I think, to his embarrassment. I shook hands with him and gave him my sympathies. This was my Christian best. I cannot like the man. Perhaps he feels the same about me, for he seemed not to focus on me very well or to know who I was.

On Tuesday, the service was held for John Crawford. His sister, Mabel, was black veiled and weeping, and she was supported by some Crawford relatives. The church attendance was thin. St. Christopher's was showing its disapproval of an errant son, one who, although born into its high circles, had disgraced himself. I again escorted Selena, and we sat somewhat isolated and to the rear of the others in the church. Harry Hedrickson was prominent among the mourners and, I thought, especially attentive to Mabel. Again, Selena and I did not attend the reception.

The third funeral, held on Wednesday, was for James Randall, that service so long delayed after death. The attendance was even slimmer than it had been for John Crawford. James was too far in the past; he had been forgotten by all but a few. There was a sprinkling of older Randall kin. Notably, Mabel and Harry did not put in an appearance. I read the eulogy, one in which I remembered James's kindness, good humor, and handsomeness. As I have said, he was the best of the Randalls, my mother excepted. Selena had a reception for a handful of people who came to the house afterward. I was there, and later she and I had dinner at the St. Christopher House. I walked her home from the hotel and said good night at the door.

The fourth and last funeral, held on Thursday at St. Luke's, was for Thomas Jackson. It was my doing. I asked Selena to go, but she begged off. She had to go to New Orleans that day, something in connection with her daughter. She would be back Friday evening she told me. As it turned out, there were only two of us in attendance: Mildred, the Randall servant, and myself. I read a brief eulogy. I knew little of Jackson, but I spoke of faithfulness, that one quality that I knew could be associated with him. Mildred and I went to the cemetery with the casket after the church service. After it was lowered into the grave, the two of us walked back through the burying ground. I thanked Mildred for coming and asked her if she had known Jackson. She told me no, that she had been too little to remember him, but that her mother knew him. She went on to explain that her mother had been Georgia, the black maternal goddess who used to preside over the Randall kitchen, back door, and sandbox. I don't know why, but this surprised me.

"Mildred," I confessed to her, "I'm ashamed to admit it, but I don't believe I know your name, your last name, that is."

"Oh, Mr. Colin," she told me, "it's Randall, Mildred Randall."

Did her handsome café-au-lait face betray—what? A common heritage? But then, black servants had taken masters' family names in the slave days—back in buccaneering Alexander's days.

"Mr. Colin," Mildred said, "I'm glad you had this funeral for Thomas Jackson. I know it was a long time ago, so long ago, I suppose, that most folks have forgotten all about him, and now he's nothing but a few poor old bones. Still, it's fitting for him to have a proper burial." Then she continued to speak as we walked along. "My mama told me that your father, Mr. Robert, he always did the right thing, and I guess you are like he was. You want to do the right thing." Then after a little bit: "Mama said, too, that you were the politest little boy she ever knew. I guess your mama must have brought you up right, just like a little gentleman." Mildred chuckled.

Friday morning, Sheriff Larrabee called me and asked how much longer I was planning to stay in St. Christopher's. I told him that I would probably leave the coming Sunday. He explained, then, that he would much appreciate it if I would stop by his office and read over, amend if necessary, and sign the written version of the statement that I had given the police stenographer the past Saturday night, when Charles was taken into custody. I said I would be happy to oblige. Actually, I was glad of the opportunity. There were some things that I wanted to be enlightened on.

Charles, I knew, had been taken to Tallahassee for psychiatric observation, pending his trial for double murder; however, from what I had learned from Selena, it seemed unlikely that he would ever come to trial. It was much more probable that he would end his days in one of those places where they incarcerate the criminally insane. Now, four months after, I can report that poor Charles is so institutionalized. And insane he is, and was. While I am no authority in such matters, that remarkable interview he had with Selena and me, while he held us at gunpoint, was enough to convince me that my old friend was crazy. How could one not be crazy, after the sheriff had him in hand, to turn and denounce me for betraying him—betraying him by not letting him shoot me?

When had Charles started to go off the rails? I have wondered since. Was it in the last year or two, as Webbie had been trying to tell me up in Boston when I brushed off his remarks? And was his breakdown the result of his New Orleans connections, with Lockwood and Fawnley, with drugs? Charles had ingested cocaine that Saturday before he showed up at his house. This came out in the immediate medical examination. To some, perhaps, this is the preferred explanation for Charles's murderous behavior. It places the blame outside Charles, and outside St. Christopher's, as something done to Charles rather than something originating within him. Harry Hedrickson, I thought, would have approved of this explanation. But I don't believe it, and I don't think Selena does either. Was it when, after Princeton, he refused to go to law school and said he wanted only to return home to St. Christopher's and live the life of a southern gentleman of the old school? Or perhaps it was even longer ago than that. Generations-deep, inner evil.

I found Sheriff Larrabee his usual self. The Texas hat was on a hatstand in the corner of his office. He was seated at his desk in shirtsleeves, with his star of office pinned to his shirt pocket, his expression noncommittal, laconic. We went over my statement in some detail. He had some questions, and I had a few changes and additions. After we made these, he called in a secretary and asked her to type up a clean version, which I could sign. While we were waiting around for her to finish this, the sheriff leaned back in his chair and asked me, "Mr. Edwards, did you ever suspect your friend Charles in all of this?"

I told him that I had not, at least not up to the moment Charles had faced me with the revolver in the Randall library and regaled me with the story of his villainies and his intention to kill Selena and myself. No, I reiterated, I had not suspected him at all.

The sheriff continued to eye me with his steady gaze. I wondered to myself if it would be permissible now—in the denouement of the investigation, so to speak—to turn the tables on him and ask the same question. After a little hesitation, I did so.

For a full minute, I thought maybe this was going to be ruled out of bounds, but then the sheriff responded. "Mr. Edwards, I began to get mighty suspicious of Mr. Randall when I checked up on those telephone calls that were made from St. James's Island on that Wednesday, June the fifth. Some person, or persons, made four telephone calls from that number on the island in the late afternoon and early evening that day. One of these calls was to the Drug Enforcement Administration people in Pensacola, and another came in here to the hotel for that fellow Fawnley. The caller in both cases was a man, a man's voice, according to both Pensacola and the desk clerk here. A third call went to Mr. Randall's residence, and we know that that one was from Mr. Randall himself and that he wanted to speak with his sister. She was out, but Mildred took the call. That leaves one other call. It was the latest of the four. It was made to the residence of Mr. Harry Hedrickson at eight-thirty. Shortly after this, according to the Hedrickson maid, Mrs. Hedrickson made a telephone call herself."

"And that call, Lydia's call," I cut in, "was the one I received at the hotel just before she came over there to see me."

"Correct, Mr. Edwards."

"And then Lydia left here and went out to the Cape Sands?"

"Correct, again, Mr. Edwards. I think Mrs. Hedrickson went out there because Charles Randall had told her, when he called, that his sister and Harry Hedrickson would be found there together in one of the motel bedrooms."

"So Charles then crossed over the narrows from the island to the Cape Sands Motel, where he met Lydia and eventually killed her."

"That's right," the sheriff told me. "You see, Mr. Randall appears to have had some experience in crossing the narrows at night, and tying up at the Cape Sands boat dock. He referred to it last Friday, when we all went over from the island to the Cape Sands dock just after Mrs. Hedrickson's body had been found. He said that tying up there after dark presented some difficulties. Remember? Anyhow, it struck me as odd. How often did a seventy-year-old gentleman run his boat across the narrows after dark?"

"Yes, sir, Mr. Edwards," the sheriff went on, "Mr. Randall was careless in lots of ways—in things he said and in making those phone calls. And he was daring, too, when you think of it. Someone might have seen him over there in the parking lot at the Cape Sands, but I guess no one did, leastwise no one's come forth to say so. Then there was that walking over there to Mr. Bull's in the middle of the night, shooting him at his front door, and then just calmly walking back home."

"Sheriff, did he do all that other shooting, through his own library window, and through the Bull and Hedrickson windows?"

"Well, we don't know for sure. Mr. Randall hasn't really made any statements—rational statements, that is—since he's been taken into custody. But we think that he's the one who shot through those windows. He did that just to confuse us. He probably wanted us to think that there was some nut going around taking potshots at people in the neighborhood."

I thought that there had, indeed, been some nut going around.

The sheriff was silent for a moment; then he added, "You know, Mr. Edwards, all along it was just as though Mr. Randall thought he was smarter than anybody else, that he was above everybody else and the law, too, that nobody counted except himself."

Yes, that was it, I thought. Charles felt he was above the law. He was Charles Randall, the grand seigneur, the one who could trample other people's sand castles at will. He had had charm, and his conversation, so brilliantly egotistical, had always captivated me. In fact, his flamboyance had always made me feel rather humdrum, a bit of a grind, as he would have put it. But this flamboyance, I could see now, had been a facade for his arrogance, his willfulness, and, worse, his complete disregard of, and contempt for, others— as we found out in the end.

"Why?" I found myself saying aloud.

The sheriff, on a somewhat different line of thought, nevertheless gave me some sort of an answer. "For money, Mr. Edwards. He murdered Mr. Bull and Mrs. Hedrickson to eliminate them from their shares of the Island Trust. He was going to murder his own sister for the same reason. He'd have had the whole ten million then."

"I wonder if Selena ever suspected him?"

Larrabee gave me his quizzical look and said, "I'd think you'd know more about that than I would, Mr. Edwards." I sat in slightly embarrassed silence for a moment at this perceptive answer. He didn't miss much, did he, the sheriff?

As though to relieve my brief embarrassment, the sheriff commented, "That was a mighty quick-witted and spunky thing Mrs. Crawford did, wasn't it, when she threw that brandy in her brother's face?"

"Yes," I said, "she saved us."

"Oh, you did pretty well yourself, Mr. Edwards, tackling him like that. You did pretty well for an old . . . for a man of your years."

He got a cigar going satisfactorily, then said, "I hope you didn't think I was too slow in coming to your rescue then. You see, Mildred had come back to the Randalls' house early. She'd decided not to stay at her sister's; she said she was worried about Mrs. Crawford and thought she better be with her. It was a lucky thing she came back. She'd come into the house through the back door just a little bit after Mr. Randall got there, and she heard him talking in his crazy way in the library. So she telephoned me, at my house. I was just finishing supper, but I got there in about five minutes, and Mildred let me in the back door. I was out there in the hall, just out of view, while Mr. Randall was carrying on to the two of you. Then he fired that shot. I guess he was trying to scare you."

He did, indeed, scare me.

"I could have drilled him at any time then, but, well— that's dangerous. He might've contracted on the trigger and shot you before he dropped. Besides, I got to hear his whole confession. Anyway, as I told you then, I think it's better the way it came out. I've always hated shooting a man."

I couldn't think of anything to say to this, but the secretary brought in my statement, so I didn't need to reply. I read over the statement and signed it. There were two or three more things I was curious about, though, and I had to ask about them. "Tell me, Sheriff, why did Charles inform on the drug running?"

"We're not sure of all the answers to that, Mr. Edwards. For one thing, he wanted revenge on Mr. Crawford, like he said to you the other night. But also he probably wanted Mr. Fawnley eliminated from this antiques business that they owned together in New Orleans. His appetite for money seems to have been a big one. How much he knew about the drug racket is unclear, although he did use drugs himself."

"What about the little gold alligator that Charles said he found in the mound? Did he really find it there, or did he just claim to have found it there to give himself an excuse for wanting to dig in the mound?"

"I don't know, Mr. Edwards. I don't suppose we'll ever know that. What do you think? After all, this is kind of in your line of things, isn't it? Archaeology?"

I could only shake my head and refrain from attempting to explain to the sheriff the limits of archaeology.

There was one more thing, though, that I had to ask: "Sheriff Larrabee, was I ever a suspect in any of this business?"

The sheriff gave me a real smile then, probably the only one that I'd seen him come up with in the almost two weeks I'd known him. "Well, sir," he told me, "when everything's been pretty quiet in a place, and a stranger comes to town and suddenly all hell breaks loose, more or less right around where he's been, then you got some cause to be suspicious, don't you think?"

Put that way, I had to admit he had a case of sorts. I stood up then, and we shook hands. I asked him to give my farewells to Chief Ellis and the deputies, and the sheriff said he would. As I turned to go, he put a hand on my shoulder and said, "I'm mighty sorry your vacation down here has been spoiled for you, Mr. Edwards. Don't think too unkindly of us because of it. Come back and see us sometime." And then, as a parting remark: "These things happen, you know. I hope, by God, they don't happen very often, but they do happen." I raised a hand in a kind of parting gesture and took my leave.

Selena called me on Saturday morning. She had arrived back from New Orleans Friday evening, driving down from the Tallahassee airport. I told her that I would be leaving tomorrow, that I'd like to see her before I left, and wouldn't she join me for dinner at the hotel?

"No, Colin, it's my turn to be the host, especially on your last night in town. Won't you come over for a cold supper? Mildred's made us a shrimp salad, and I've brought an excellent bottle of wine from New Orleans to go with it. Come over about seven." I said that I would, and Selena added, "Incidentally, Mildred's quite an admirer of yours."

I walked over from the hotel to the Randalls' on the last night in St. Christopher's. The light of a long June day was still with us, and the children were playing and calling to each other on Palmetto Street. I rang the Randalls' bell and watched through one of the glass panels until Selena came out into the hall to let me in. She was wearing her green silk dress, the color in which I remember her best. She led me back to the library, where a tray with the fixings for drinks was set out on the desk, and asked if I would be the bartender. I asked her how about a martini, and she said that would be splendid, so I stirred them in a glass pitcher.

"How was the trip?" I wanted to know.

"Oh, it was all right," she told me. "Marie is doing well in the home there, but I'm hoping to be able to send her to a nicer place soon, now that I'll be able to afford it."

This was the first time I had heard the daughter's name— Marie—she was named for her grandmother. She would be forty-one years old now. I found it difficult to know just what kinds of questions to ask about her and didn't. We talked, instead, about Selena's plans for the future. I had to realize now that Selena, as the sole inheritor of the Island Trust, was going to be a rich woman. She told me that she was going to sell the house, that she could get a good price for it from some developers who would tear it down and build a condominium apartment building. I suppose inwardly I winced, but I had to acknowledge to myself that things change. Selena said she would be moving to New Orleans, probably before the island sale went through; however, everything was on track about the sale. Harry Hedrickson was handling the legal aspects of it for her. I wondered if she and Harry would marry now, but I didn't inquire.

As if reading my thoughts, she told me, rather coldly, "I think Harry will marry Mabel. It will help rehabilitate him in the community. In many ways they are well suited to each other."

I suppose I was only mildly surprised. As I thought about it, it did seem a very suitable match for the golden years of that pair.

Selena told me then that she had been to see Charles in Tallahassee. "It was just a few minutes," she explained. "We had to see and talk to each other through a screen. It was awful. He looks terrible, thinner than ever, and with haunted, sunken eyes. Oh, Colin, he just sat there and stared at me most of the time, and then finally, he said, 'Selena, I hate you.' And then, and I shouldn't tell you this, Colin, but he said, 'I hate Colin, too.' "

"Why, Selena? Why does he hate us so? Was it because we thwarted him last Saturday?"

"I think it was more than that. Charles and I never did get along very well, and as for you, he was always so jealous of you. It goes back to when we were children, playing children's games. He knew, well, that I liked you, and that bothered him. He always had to be first."

I couldn't think of anything to say. I was surprised though by what she had told me. As I have said here, I had always thought of Charles as a best friend, at least of those early years. One is so often surprised in human relationships.

Selena asked me if I would mind if she served the supper in here, on trays. I said that would be fine and that I would help her carry them. I had always liked the library better than the Randalls' overly gloomy dining room.

While we were eating, Selena said softly, "Colin, you've had such an awful time down here. I'm so sorry. Charles enticed you to come down here for his own selfish purposes."

We ate in silence for a while. Finally, I said, "Selena, you must have known that I cared for you very much, back in the old days."

She smiled rather wistfully and said, "Yes, I knew. Oh, Colin, you were so darling then. But, you know, you were always so, so perfect, so formal, so polite. You were Aunt Genevieve's good little boy. Maybe I resented that."

"Selena, I still care for you."

"Yes, and I still care for you, Colin, but our lives have grown so far apart."

"Selena, don't you suppose that our lives could be brought together again?"

She was quiet for a long while before she said, "No, our lives can't be brought together again. It's too late."

We finished our supper and talked of other, casual things. Finally, I got up to go, and she didn't stop me. We walked to the door together, to that door where we said good-bye so long ago in the past. I brushed her cheek with a light farewell kiss and stepped out onto the porch. She must have waited there for a last moment. Then I heard the door softly close behind me, but this time I didn't pause and look back.

As I walked down the street, which was dark now, I could smell the heavy fragrance of the magnolias, that evocative perfume of the southern night which brought back other nights of the past. The past, the past! It had vanished, as it does, from all but memory. I thought back to so very long ago, when there in the sandbox Selena had shared my romantic fantasies and had thrilled me with her words: "Oh, Colin, you make the bestest sand castles of anybody in the whole world!" That, I reflected, marked the high point of my courtship of Selena.

LAKE COUNTY PUBLIC LIBRARY
INDIANA